# THE MYSTERY
## OF THE
# CORNISH COAST

*Two private detectives are on a mission*

*Book #4 in the Quentin Cadbury Investigations*

## Christine McHaines

THE BOOK FOLKS

Published by The Book Folks

London, 2024

ISBN  978-1-80462-223-0

www.thebookfolks.com

THE MYSTERY ON THE CORNISH COAST is the fourth standalone cozy mystery novel in this series by Christine McHaines. Details about the other books in the series can be found at the back.

# Chapter One

December 2007

December had barely begun when Quentin got the call. The trill of his mobile phone disturbed the sleepy air and interrupted the dream that was playing out in his head. Forcing one reluctant eye open, he pressed the light on the bedside clock. 6 a.m. Nobody rang him at 6 a.m. – 6 a.m. didn't exist in Quentin's mind, especially on a Sunday. Groaning, he reached over to where the phone was on charge and picked it up just as it stopped ringing. Thinking it could be his mother calling from Australia, he switched on the bedside lamp and checked the missed call but the number was withheld. He slumped back on his pillow and tried to sleep, to recapture the dream, snippets of which came to him unbidden. Sun and sand and barbecues and beaches. And Wanda. Wonderful, bewitching Wanda. Where was she?

Turning over, he flung an arm into the space where she should be, encountering something warm and soft and smooth. A shrill cry jolted him out of his drowsiness as the black-and-white body beside him squirmed under the blow.

'Magpie! Sorry, boy.'

Sitting up, Quentin stroked the cat's silky fur. Magpie raised his tail, gave him a disdainful glare and jumped off the bed.

'No need to get shirty,' Quentin called after him. 'You know you're not allowed up here.'

The rhythmic patter of the cat's paws on the stairs was swallowed by a high-pitched ringing. Irritated, Quentin snatched at his mobile.

'Hello.'

Silence.

'Hello?' Quentin said again, wishing he'd switched it off overnight.

He was about to disconnect the call when a male voice said, 'Mr Cadbury.'

All thoughts of Magpie forgotten, Quentin froze. It couldn't be. Throwing off the duvet, he swung his long legs out of bed, stood up, opened the curtains and stared through the window, as if expecting to be able to penetrate the winter darkness and see the caller in the garden below.

'Yes, it's me, Mr Cadbury. I said you hadn't heard the last of me. I hope you've had a pleasant year, though I expect it seems a long time since your holiday. Nice place, isn't it, Australia?'

Quentin gulped. 'What do you want?' he choked out.

'You know what I want, Mr Cadbury. I want to kill you. Don't hang up. I said, I *want* to kill you, not I'm going to. Believe me, Mr Cadbury, if I really wanted you dead, you wouldn't be talking to me now.'

Quentin would have done anything not to be talking to this man, now or at any time. He should hang up, change his number. But he couldn't. Some perverse instinct made him want to hear what this man with the unmistakeable voice had to say – that, and the fact that he had pledged to report any such conversation to Detective Chief Inspector Philmore of the Metropolitan Police.

'I thought you were in prison,' Quentin ventured.

'Come now, Mr Cadbury, you surely must have worked out by now that prison wouldn't agree with me. A fastidious man like myself?'

Fastidious. The word ran round Quentin's head. And cultured. Since the first time he'd heard this man speak, he'd referred to him as Cultured Voice.

'No, Mr Cadbury, I'm not in prison. The Dutch authorities made the mistake of transferring me to more suitable accommodation.' There was a snigger, as though the caller was recalling his escape with repressed glee. 'It's surprising what you can achieve with friends on the outside.'

'So where are you?'

The snigger became a contemptuous laugh. 'Very droll, Mr Cadbury. Don't worry, you won't be able to trace this call. I never use the same phone twice – you know that from experience. How is the delectable Mrs Merrydrew, by the way?'

'None of your business,' Quentin snapped, anger replacing fear.

'All right, Mr Cadbury, enough of the niceties.' The change in the cultured voice was almost palpable. 'You've caused me a lot of trouble in the past and lost me a lot of colleagues and money. Now's your chance to make up for it.'

Quentin gasped. 'What the hell are you talking about?'

'It's quite simple, Mr Cadbury. You do a little job for me and I won't kill you. I think that's fair, don't you?'

Words failed Quentin. This man, this criminal, former big noise in an illegal organisation, was suggesting that he worked for him? After Quentin had helped break up the UK branch of the organisation and forced this man to go on the run?

'Wh-what?'

'You heard me, Mr Cadbury. I'll make it clearer. Either you do as I ask or you can start planning your funeral. Or perhaps Mrs Merrydrew would like to be detained as my guest again? Or both?'

'Don't come anywhere near her.' Quentin's voice trembled with rage. 'Don't you touch her.'

'I won't, Mr Cadbury, not if you cooperate. I'll give you time to think about my proposal. I'll call back tomorrow. Any sniff of the police – well, I don't need to tell you. Goodbye, Mr Cadbury.'

The line went dead. Quentin stumbled back and collapsed onto the bed, his mind numb.

'Looks like we've got trouble, boy,' he said as Magpie slunk back into the room and jumped onto his lap. 'What the hell am I going to do?'

## Chapter Two

'Quentin.'

The low, seductive tone of Wanda's voice brought Quentin out of his indecisive reverie. He had to tell her. They were business partners as well as lovers and she had a right to know that the threat against both their lives had been renewed.

He hadn't heard her come in. She only lived next door, but she still refused to move in with him – though they each had a key to the other's house and came and went as they needed; a situation Quentin had tried in vain to rectify.

'When did you go?' he asked. 'I didn't hear you get up.'

'I couldn't sleep so I went home, had a shower, fed Mozart and took him for an early walk. I've brought some things in for breakfast. It's nearly eight o'clock.'

Eight o'clock! Two hours, Quentin thought. Two hours I've been sitting here when I could have been doing something, something positive, something to...

'Quentin? What's wrong?' Wanda stood before him, her blonde hair still damp from the shower and her blue eyes searching his face.

Quentin could see the outline of her figure against the window, clad for winter in grey trousers and a turquoise high-necked jumper. She was as stunning as ever, despite her forty years. Normally, the sight of her in his bedroom on a Sunday morning would have aroused him, but today all he could think of was that phone call. *The* phone call, the one that, after a year of not hearing from his adversary, threatened their security.

Wanda plumped down on the bed beside him. 'Something's wrong. What is it?'

'I've had a phone call.'

'Not bad news? From Australia?'

'No. No one's died. Not yet.'

There was a pause before Wanda said, 'Not yet? Someone's ill. Your father. Not your mum?'

'No one's ill,' Quentin said, shaking his head. He turned to face her, still wondering whether to tell her.

Wanda, astute and alert to his agitation, guessed at the truth.

'Not him? It can't be, he was caught. Philmore said so.'

'Yes, he was caught, but he's escaped.'

'Escaped? How? Why hasn't Philmore told you?'

Quentin shrugged. 'Don't know. Perhaps he's only just got out. He said something about being transferred somewhere in the Netherlands. That's when he made the break. Bloody hell. Just when I thought we were safe.'

Silence fell between them and Quentin could almost hear cogs whirring in Wanda's brain.

'Have you rung Philmore?'

'No. He said no police.'

'What did he want?'

Quentin reached for his boxer shorts and climbed into them, retied the cord on his dressing gown and began pacing the room. There wasn't much space to pace in. The terraced houses in this part of Greenwich boasted two bedrooms over two rooms downstairs, unless, as in Quentin's case, the downstairs had been knocked through into one. Hitting his toe against the wardrobe, Quentin cursed.

'What did he want?' Wanda repeated.

Quentin hesitated.

Wanda stood up, caught his arm and stopped him in his stride. 'Whatever he wants, tell me. We're in this together. It was partly my fault you got tangled up with him in the first place. Tell me what he wants.'

Quentin fingered the heart-shaped mole by his right ear. He'd told her half of it. What was the point in withholding the rest? Anyway, he needed her support, her calmness.

'I don't know what he wants exactly, except he wants me to do a job for him. He didn't say what, only that if I don't do it—'

'He'll kill you,' she finished. 'OK. So when is he going to let you know what he wants you to do?'

'He's calling back tomorrow.'

It was Wanda's turn to pace. Seconds stretched into minutes, the only sound the light brushing of Wanda's feet on the carpet.

'All right,' she said eventually. 'Here's what we do. We ring Philmore and tell him what's happened and he'll arrange protection for us.'

'I'm not putting you in danger. He'll know if we get the police involved. You remember what he was like before. He knows everything. He knows we went to Australia.'

Wanda paled at that. 'Does he? Well, we're not obligated to Philmore, are we? You agreed to let him know if Cultured Voice, Whitelaw, or whatever his name is, contacts you, but he won't expect you to honour it if your life is on the line. You've already agreed to give evidence if you have to.'

Quentin grimaced at the memory of Philmore's telephone call some months earlier. Quentin's hopes of helping the DCI with another case had evaporated when, instead of asking for help, Philmore had warned that Quentin may have to appear in court. Things had been quiet since then.

'Still,' Wanda was saying, 'it's stupid to try tackling this alone. It's not like the other cases we've handled. It's life and death now. We must get help. You've got Philmore's private number, haven't you?'

'Yeah. I suppose you're right.'

'Of course I'm right. Have you still got that mobile, the one you used before?'

Quentin nodded, thinking of the pay-as-you-go mobile phone he'd bought to contact DCI Steve Philmore on their first case. A criminal gang had been routed with Quentin's help, but their leader, Whitelaw, had gotten away. With Whitelaw – or Cultured Voice, as Quentin called him – still on the loose, and after a threat that Cultured Voice would get even with him in the future, DCI Philmore had agreed to Quentin's suggestion that Quentin kept the phone and called him if he heard from the man again.

This arrangement was the reason Quentin had kept the same number for his everyday mobile phone. It was to be used as a trap, a means of communication between Quentin and the wanted man, if he ever carried out his threat to get even. Philmore had originally thought it would be foolhardy for Cultured Voice to do this – it would be far safer for him to keep his silence. But, as Quentin had pointed out, clever though he was, the man's plans had been thwarted by someone he viewed as a second-rate, interfering little nobody; a master criminal almost brought to ruin by a then twenty-four-year-old university dropout turned detective. It was a thorn in his side he couldn't ignore.

Shaking himself, Quentin went to the bedroom window. The weak December sun cast its rays across the garden, lightening the sky and giving a burnished glow to the terracotta pots that broke up the plainness of the patio slabs. He could see the gardens either side, pleasant spaces to sit but too small for lawns or big shrubs. Absently, he thought of his sister's and his parents' spacious houses and large gardens on the outskirts of Sydney and wondered if he should have stayed in Australia. Too late now, he thought. We're here, we've got a problem and we'll have to deal with it.

'All right,' he said, turning to Wanda. 'I'll try and get hold of Philmore, though he wouldn't be working on a Sunday unless there's something big going on.'

'It doesn't matter where he is or what he's doing,' Wanda told him. 'You're not making a social call, you're ringing him on police business. This man's committed crimes all over Europe and Philmore was chasing him for years. Our lives are in danger. Just ring him.'

Quentin padded downstairs and went to the bureau, a legacy from his late aunt, and scrabbled in a drawer for his second mobile.

'Out of battery,' he said. 'We'll have to wait till there's enough charge.'

'Well, we may as well have breakfast.' Wanda laid her hand on Quentin's arm. 'Don't worry, Quentin. We've – *you*'ve outwitted him before. You'll do it again.'

More by luck than judgement, Quentin wanted to say.

'Yes,' he said. 'Of course we will.'


# Chapter Three


As soon as breakfast was over, Quentin checked the phone and, leaving it plugged in, pressed the key to call the only number in the contact list. When the ring tone sounded, he held on for what seemed an age before ending the call.

'No answer,' he said as Wanda came into the room. 'Perhaps he's still asleep.'

Wanda looked peeved. 'Where's a copper when you need one! Try again later.'

They were just clearing the table when the mobile rang. Only one person knew the number of his second phone, so he knew immediately who it was.

'Quentin? It's Steve Philmore. Did you ring?'

'Hello, Steve. Yes, it's our friend – the one you said was in prison.'

'You've heard from him?' Philmore sounded incredulous. Then, as if recovering his composure, he went on, 'Sorry, Quentin, I only got back from holiday yesterday, so I've just found out about his escape.'

'Yes, I've heard from him. He rang this morning.'

'Well, that's a surprise, I must say. Looks like he's a man of his word. Lucky you are too. Thanks for ringing.'

Quentin felt a thrill when he heard this. A little less than three years ago he'd been a drifter, jobwise at least, with no particular purpose except to have a good time and to work as little as possible. Thanks to Wanda's influence, and a brush with a criminal gang which resulted in him working with the Metropolitan Police, he had gone on to set up his own detective agency with Wanda as a partner. More than this, DCI Philmore now listened to any information Quentin offered.

'So Whitelaw rang you?'

'Yes. Is he still using that name?'

'It's the one he uses in the UK. He gave the name Hoeker in the Netherlands. We don't know much about his background – he's covered his tracks pretty well. Can we get to the point? What did he say?'

'He wants me to do a job for him.'

Quentin could almost hear Philmore trying to make sense of this.

'A job? What sort of job?' Philmore asked.

'He didn't say. He'll let me know tomorrow.'

'Why does he think you'll do a job for him?'

'It's quite simple, really. If I don't do it, he'll kill me. Maybe Wanda too.'

There was a pause while Philmore digested this. 'I see. He's got some nerve, I'll say that for him. Ran a successful criminal gang for nearly twenty years, caught once but escaped, half of Europe's police force after him – the man's like a piece of elastic. Just when you think you've got him, he pings away and starts again.'

'Never mind that,' Quentin said irritably. 'What are we going to do?'

This time the pause was longer. Quentin heard Philmore clear his throat.

'You can't put yourself in such a dangerous position, Quentin. Who knows what he's planning? Refuse to do what he asks and disappear. We'll give you police protection.'

'I knew you'd say that, Steve, but I could pretend to go along with it and we might nab the bastard. I really need this guy off my back.'

'You and me both, but it's not that simple. I'd have to pass it up the line and I doubt the higher-ups would agree, and even if they do it's too dangerous.'

A mirthless laugh escaped Quentin. 'You know me, Steve, a sucker for a challenge. It's not me, it's…' He broke off and looked at Wanda.

As if reading his thoughts, Wanda screwed up a paper napkin and threw it at him. 'Don't make me an excuse. If you're in, so am I.'

Obviously hearing Wanda's words, a note of amusement laced Philmore's voice. 'How is Wanda?'

'She was fine till we heard from him,' Quentin said.

'Plucky lady, Wanda Merrydrew, but of course you don't want to put her in danger. I wouldn't either.'

Quentin's eyebrows lifted. Happily married DCI or not, Steve Philmore, like most red-blooded males, wasn't impervious to Wanda's charms.

'Look,' Quentin said testily, 'if we agree to this guy's demands, will you be there if things get nasty?'

'Haven't you heard anything I've been saying?' Exasperation sounded in Philmore's voice. 'Why don't we wait to see what he wants before we rush into anything? Call me when he rings again.'

'What the bloody hell's the good of that?' Quentin exploded. 'He'll want an answer straight away. He's not going to sit around for days and give me a chance to figure out how to get away from him. Disappearing's pointless, anyway. He's powerful enough to find me wherever I am.'

'Calm down and stop worrying. At least we know what he looks like now. The Dutch police have sent a photo. Whatever happens, you shouldn't get involved.'

'I'm already involved,' Quentin said. 'For all we know, he's just using this as a ploy to kill me.'

A sigh sounded in his ear. 'As you said, he's powerful. If he wanted to kill you, he'd have done it by now.'

Quentin had thought this a hundred times since the 6 a.m. phone call. Why didn't Cultured Voice just arrange for someone to get rid of him? It would be so easy. Sabotage his car, set light to his house, push him under a lorry. There was only one reason. Cultured Voice thought a simple execution was too good for him. He wanted to make use of him, for him to live in fear, to suffer before the final blow came.

'What the hell,' Quentin snapped, suddenly determined to get the better of the man who was threatening him. 'I'm sick of him and all he stands for. Whatever he wants me to do, I'll do it if it gives me a chance to nail him.'

'Very brave but not very wise,' Philmore said. 'I can't stop you doing what he says. Anything you do will be entirely your decision and your responsibility, but I'm telling you now, steer clear of the whole thing.'

'Like you said, you can't stop me. It's all right, Steve, I'll make it quite clear that anything that happens is down to me. Anyway, I've always fancied being undercover.'

'Quentin.' Philmore's tone became harder. 'This isn't a game. We have trained officers to go undercover.'

'Going all official on me now, are you? Listen, it was my idea to be used as bait. Admittedly when I suggested it, after that first case, he hadn't threatened to kill me, but it makes no difference. Either I go for it or I run, and I'm done with running. I ran halfway across the world and what good's it done me? I'll take my chances, but I'm not putting Wanda in harm's way. She can sit this one out.'

Even as he said this, he felt Wanda's hostile glare. He started as she rose, came towards him and wrestled the phone from his hand.

'Steve?' she said. 'Don't worry, we'll work it out. Quentin's just a bit tetchy after being woken up so early … Let's wait till he rings tomorrow, and we'll take it from there. Can you trace the call? … I know he doesn't stay on the line long and he uses a different phone each time. He must have a stash of them … All right, bye.'

'A bit tetchy?' Quentin quipped, rounding on her. 'Bloody hell, Wanda. Anyway, I meant what I said. It's me he wants to do the job, not you. You stay here and run the business. We are supposed to be a detective agency, you know.'

Wanda sighed. 'Let's see what he wants you to do before we make any rash decisions. Sit down and I'll get some more coffee.'

Despite his naturally optimistic temperament and tendency to see humour in most situations, Quentin was worried. Since meeting Wanda, he'd been accidentally thrown into two major cases, leading to her calling him the accidental detective. Both these cases had either directly or indirectly involved the man he knew as Cultured Voice. But their present dilemma was different. This time, if they took it on, it would be dangerous from the start.

Wanda returned bearing two cups – Spode, Quentin noticed, with saucers, another legacy from his late Aunt Josie which Wanda always used when she was there. Steam curled its way from the cup she handed him, and he sipped the hot coffee as he watched her sit opposite him. Her coolness and composure in almost any situation still amazed him, as did the fact that she stayed with him as a partner in more ways than one.

'I wish you were here to make coffee every morning,' he said, regretting the words as soon as they left his mouth. 'All right, don't look at me like that. I know what you're going to say.'

'Then why keep mentioning it?' Wanda leaned across and put her hand on his knee. 'It's for your own good, Quentin. Nearly fifteen years is a big difference.'

'It makes no difference to me.' Quentin fingered the mole by his ear and wondered how many times he'd said this.

Wanda shook her head. 'It will, one day. I thought we'd agreed. We stay as we are until it doesn't work anymore, or until you meet someone your own age.'

'I don't want–' Quentin stopped as Wanda held up her hand.

'Stop!' she said. 'Haven't we got enough to worry about? We should be making plans.'

Quentin sighed. 'How can we make plans when we don't know what he wants? This job could be in Timbuktu for all we know.'

Wanda's eyes, cornflower blue in the daylight, widened. 'I hope not. Then again, if he's wanted all over Europe, he'll have more sense than to operate in Britain again.'

A half-laugh escaped Quentin. 'He might not be in Britain, but he could oversee operations from anywhere. And let's be honest, we've both been a few feet from him but neither of us have seen his face. If it wasn't for that voice, I wouldn't have a chance of identifying him. Come to think of it, I should have asked Steve for a copy of the photo he got from the Dutch police.'

'Ask him next time you speak to him. Right, it's cold but it's a nice day. Let's get some fresh air. You could have a run in the park while I walk Mozart.'

Quentin nodded, thinking of Wanda's white West Highland terrier named after her favourite classical composer. He eyed the running machine that took up a corner of his lounge, which he used either when it was too wet to run outdoors or if he didn't have the time – or inclination – to go out. With his proximity to Greenwich Park however, he tried to get his exercise there whenever he could.

'I suppose you're right,' he said grudgingly. 'Moping round here won't do any good. Come on then. You go and get Mozart and I'll put my running gear on. When we come back, I'll have a shower and we'll go out for lunch.'

'Er…'

'What?' Quentin looked at Wanda, guessing his suggestion was about to be, if not rejected, then altered in some way.

'I'm supposed to be meeting Colin for lunch.'

Quentin groaned. Colin was an old friend of Wanda's who had known her late husband and had promised to "keep an eye out for her" after he died. He was also a rival for her affection, and despite Wanda's insistence that he was a valued friend only, Colin had made it perfectly clear that if Quentin was no longer on the scene he would readily take his place.

'That's all I need,' he snapped, 'him fawning over you and wanting to know what's going on.'

'He doesn't fawn over me,' Wanda protested. 'Anyway, we need to keep him onside. You never know when we'll need his help.'

That was true, Quentin realized. Although he hated the thought that Colin had known Wanda longer than he had, had a nice house in Wanstead, a steady income, was nearer her age and had proposed to her twice, he had to admit that Colin had occasionally proved useful. Over the last few years, his animosity towards the man had mellowed into grudging acceptance, though he wasn't sure the feeling was reciprocated.

'You can join us,' Wanda said soothingly. 'You need to keep busy. I'll go and get Mozart. He'll think it's his birthday, two walks in the same morning.' She stood and made for the door.

Magpie padded in and jumped onto Quentin's lap.

'What do you think then, eh, boy?' Quentin fondled the cat's furry ears. 'I don't know what'll happen to you if our friend turns really nasty. You might have to go and live with Colin.'

The idea of either Wanda or Magpie being with Colin strengthened his determination. Petty, in the grand scheme of things, but he couldn't help it. To date he hadn't gained much by his own efforts. His law degree still awaited completion, he'd never had a paid job for more than eight months, he'd lost his best friend to drugs and his family to Australia. The house he lived in was his mother's, inherited from her sister, Quentin's Aunt Josie. Wanda, Magpie and the detective agency were all he had. Damned if he'd let some criminal take them away from him, no matter how cultured his voice.

Lunch with Colin suddenly seemed inconsequential. 'What the hell,' he said to Magpie. 'Colin's the least of our troubles at the moment.'

He'd just changed into his running gear when his landline rang. The Sunday morning call from his mother.

'Hello, Quentin dear, how are you?'

'Fine, Mum, how about you and Dad?'

Until spending time with his parents in their Sydney home, relations between Quentin and his father had been strained. Quentin could only recall three occasions when his father had spoken to him by phone since emigrating three years before.

After the customary delay, his mother's voice came again. 'We're all good this end. It's pretty hot – they've got bushfires in some places, but we're all right here. How are things there, Quentin? Busy at work?'

'Not really, Mum. There is one case we might take on, though,' Quentin replied cautiously. 'It might involve me going away for a few days, so don't worry if you ring and I don't answer.'

He had no intention of telling her about the phone call and why he might be away from home, but he didn't want her to worry if she called and there was no answer. She had his mobile number but very rarely used it.

After the usual chat about Quentin's sister and her family, the conversation ran on until Wanda and Mozart appeared in the doorway.

'Better go, Mum, Wanda's waiting for me.'

'All right, dear. Give Wanda my love. Bye for now.'

'Bye, Mum. Love to all and we'll speak again soon.'

I hope, he thought. He replaced the receiver then followed Wanda through the front door.


# Chapter Four


Colin Ward, a middle-aged, slim man with a receding hairline and unremarkable features, looked a lot better when he smiled, which he did as soon as he saw Wanda. Quentin watched him greet her with a kiss and a hug that lasted longer than he thought necessary.

'Hello, love. Hello, Quentin.'

The smile, Quentin noticed, faded when Colin spoke to him.

'I thought Wanda and I were having a quiet lunch together,' Colin said when they were settled at the restaurant table. 'Are you just gatecrashing, Quentin, or is something up?'

'Why should something be up?' Quentin asked, immediately irritated.

'No reason.' Colin looked at him from behind his black-framed glasses. 'Except there is. I can tell.' He glanced at Wanda, who coloured slightly. 'And whatever it is, I want to know straight away this time. I'm fed up with being an afterthought, brought in because you're desperate for help and can't find anyone else. I'm not an employee, I'm a friend. At least I hope I am.'

Wanda gazed at him from under her long lashes. 'Of course you are, Colin,' she said, her husky voice low and seductive. 'And you always will be.'

Colin's expression softened, and Quentin marvelled at her persuasive abilities. The Lauren Bacall voice – named by Quentin's mother before he'd had any idea who Lauren Bacall was – formed part of her charm.

'We were going to tell you anyway, weren't we, Quentin?'

'Er, yes,' Quentin lied. They hadn't actually decided whether to mention the phone call to Colin.

A waiter approached and took their order. When he'd retreated, Wanda looked purposefully at Quentin and nodded. Reluctant to involve Colin but deciding that they needed all the help they could get, he said, 'It's our friend, the one who was in prison. He's escaped.'

The older man's jaw fell open. 'Escaped? He hasn't even come to trial yet.'

Quentin sighed. 'That's the problem. Apparently, they were transferring him somewhere in the Netherlands. That's when he made the break.'

Colin gave a low whistle. 'God, he's a slippery one. So you think he might come after you then, Quentin? I shouldn't worry too much. He'll have enough to do trying to stay free. He won't bother with you.'

As if noticing the look that passed between Wanda and Quentin, he went on, 'What? He hasn't – you haven't heard from him already?'

'He rang Quentin this morning,' Wanda explained. Quickly she told Colin the gist of the conversation, just finishing as their drinks arrived.

'My God,' Colin said when the waiter had moved away. 'He's got a nerve. I can't believe an internationally wanted criminal can escape and then be so brazen.'

'Nor can I,' Quentin said. 'But as he told me, it's surprising what you can do with friends on the outside.'

A silence descended between them. Looking baffled, Colin tapped his fingers on the table then cleaned his glasses with the bottom of his shirt. Wanda sipped her gin and tonic rather too quickly and Quentin stared into his whisky as if the answer to his problems lay at the bottom of the glass.

'Right,' Colin said eventually. 'So what are you going to do? You can come and stay with me if you're worried about one of his heavies turning up at your door. It might help until you decide what to do.'

'Thanks,' Quentin said, 'but I'll wait, at least until I know what he wants me to do.'

'Anyway,' Wanda muttered, 'Quentin's already decided to go along with it.'

'Have you?' Colin said. 'What, you want him to kill you up close and personal? All right, bad taste. You mean you want a chance to get him?'

'That, and the fact that if I don't do what he says, he'll kill me anyway.'

Colin pursed his lips and Quentin guessed what he was thinking – that Cultured Voice could kill him whether he did the job or not.

When their food arrived they munched their way through it in comparative silence, hardly noticing the background music or the hum and laughter of other diners. Sunday lunchtimes were always busy at the Cutty Sark, a pub and restaurant with a good menu on the bank of the Thames where Quentin had been many times.

'Right,' Colin said when they'd finished eating, 'what can I do?'

Quentin shrugged. 'We'll let you know when we hear from him again.'

'OK. Well, I'll say one thing for you, Quentin. Life's never dull with you around. Trouble seems to follow you everywhere. Don't you dare let any harm come to Wanda, or you'll have me to deal with.'

'Colin.' Wanda cast him a sideways look. 'You know very well Quentin wouldn't do that – but you also know I make my own decisions.'

A trace of bitterness sounded in Colin's voice when he answered.

'Well, if I don't know that then nobody does. All right, contact me as soon as you hear from him, let me know what he says and what Philmore says. I'd like to come back to yours for a bit, Wanda love, but Emma called and invited me over. I don't like to miss a chance to see her.'

'Of course you don't. How is Emma?'

'She's fine. I think she gets a bit lonely, what with Martin working long hours and playing football most weekends.'

Quentin remembered Colin's daughter as a pretty, dark-haired young woman whose wedding they'd missed while they were in Australia. Colin, long divorced and estranged from his errant wife, had obtained and kept custody of their daughter when Emma was thirteen. Despite Quentin's private belief that Colin's wife had probably left him because he was boring, he had to admit that Colin had done a good job of being a father. Having been made redundant after thirty years as a quantity surveyor and managing to secure a good severance deal and pension, Colin spent as much time as he could with Emma. Partly because he couldn't spend as much time as he'd like with Wanda, Quentin thought now. Not since I've been on the scene anyway.

The badinage between him and Colin, once quite acrimonious, had mellowed into light-heartedness, though Quentin had no doubt Colin would blame him if anything untoward happened to Wanda.

And if anything happened to Wanda, Quentin would blame himself.

\* \* \*

He was still thinking about the 6 a.m. phone call at seven o'clock that evening. When they'd left the pub, Colin had gone on to his daughter's and Wanda had gone home. After Quentin had fed Magpie, he sat brooding, wondering what he was going to say to his nemesis when he made demands in his cultured voice tomorrow. Quentin knew he wouldn't be able to sleep. He wished he'd managed to persuade Wanda to forego her quiet night and spend the evening with him. If only Wanda would...

His mobile rang, and he snatched it up, hoping it was Wanda yet knowing she always called on the landline when they were at home. He tensed when he saw the caller's number was withheld.

'Hello?' he said tentatively.

Nothing. In the few seconds' silence Quentin could feel the caller's presence; and he knew.

'Hello?' he said again.

Still nothing. Perhaps Cultured Voice was trying to unnerve him. As if he wasn't already unnerved.

He was about to hang up when the cultured voice spoke. 'Ah, you're there, Mr Cadbury. Good.'

'You said tomorrow.'

'So I did. But you should know being predictable doesn't pay. Unless you expect the unexpected, you get nowhere.'

'What do you want?'

A snigger sounded in his ear. 'How did I know you would say that? You're very predictable, Mr Cadbury.'

'Are you going to tell me why you called?' Quentin snapped, incensed. 'Because if not, I've got better things to do than listen to the ramblings of a crook.'

'Temper, temper. And I object to being called a crook. I prefer criminal mastermind.' The scathing tone became hard and businesslike. 'All right, here's what you're going to do.'

*Here's what you're going to do.* Despite his fear and decision to go along with this man's demands, Quentin's hackles rose. How dare he assume he would agree to anything he suggested?

'Are you listening, Mr Cadbury?'

'Go on,' Quentin said through gritted teeth.

'There's a package I'd like you to collect. Nothing obvious or unmanageable, just an ordinary package. Don't ask what it contains. Its contents aren't your business. And the recipient will know if it's been opened.'

'So I'm your courier now, am I?'

'Come now, Mr Cadbury, it's quite an easy task and you could make a holiday of it. Or perhaps you don't need a holiday? I shouldn't think you're overwhelmed with work in your little business. All you have to do is collect the package from wherever you're told and deliver it to another part of the country. What could be simpler?'

'If it's so simple why don't you do it yourself?' Quentin snapped.

There was a pause. Quentin could almost feel the other man's hostility. When Cultured Voice spoke again, his impatience was evident.

'Don't make me lose my temper, Mr Cadbury. Even a jumped-up little nobody like you knows why I can't do it myself. Now I've been very patient with you. You've caused me a lot of hassle and I'm offering you a chance to redeem yourself. Take it or leave it. It's no skin off my nose, but it could put yours severely out of joint. Do I make myself clear?'

'Crystal,' Quentin said miserably. 'Where is this package?'

'That's more like it. I knew you'd see reason.' Another pause. 'I think we've talked long enough. I'll call you back with the full details very soon. Be ready to travel at short notice. Goodbye, Mr Cadbury.'

Silence told Quentin the call was over. He banged his fist down towards the arm of his chair, missed and hit his knee. 'Bloody hell!' he yelled. 'Bloody, bloody–!'

He stopped abruptly, wondering whether to call Philmore, but decided against it. It would be better to call when he had details of where he had to go. Feeling the need to tell someone, he went next door to Wanda's. He used his key but called from the doorway, 'It's me, Wanda.'

Her answering 'OK' signalled him in. Wanda, dressed for a quiet evening in a blue satin dressing gown, looked up as he came in. She was curled up on her chaise longue with Mozart sprawled on her feet, a book in her hand and a gin and tonic on the low Georgian table beside her. Wanda's lounge, tastefully decorated and furnished with items from her late husband's antiques business, exuded a warm, pleasant ambience. A picture of Wanda with her late husband, Gerry, still sat on a walnut cabinet; Quentin had often sent a silent prayer of thanks to the man who had so conveniently died.

'What's up?' Wanda said, lowering her legs and pushing Mozart aside to make room for Quentin.

'He's called again.'

Wanda lay down her book. 'Has he? Already?'

'Yeah well, he can do what he likes, can't he?'

'Well come on, what did he say?'

'He wants me to deliver a package.'

Wanda chewed at her bottom lip, a habit which only showed itself if she was worried or thinking deeply.

'Right. Where from and to?'

Quentin shrugged. 'You know as much as I do. He said to be ready to travel at short notice.'

'Really? Shouldn't we be getting ready now then?'

'Well, I should hate to spoil your cosy evening,' Quentin said, glancing sideways at her. 'You don't seem at all worried.'

'Of course I'm worried!' Wanda glared at him. 'It's my way of trying not to think about it. If you take your mind off something, you can think more clearly when you come back to it.'

'I know. Sorry, but I can't do that just now. I wish he'd get on with it, that's all.'

'Quentin, you don't have to do anything. *We* don't have to do anything. We can disappear. Philmore will help us.'

Quentin shook his head. 'You don't want that any more than I do. No. We've got to nail this bastard once and for all.'

Wanda got up, went to the kitchen and returned with a large glass of whisky.

'Here,' she said softly, 'drink this. Then I know something that will take your mind off it for a bit.'

'Now?'

'Why not? We might be too busy tomorrow.'

Oh well, Quentin thought, she's probably right. He ran his gaze over Wanda. God, she was lovely. And sexy. And inviting him.

As if he could say no.

# Chapter Five

It was midnight when Quentin's mobile woke him. Throwing an arm over Wanda, he fumbled on the cabinet, picked up the phone and looked at the display. Number withheld. It couldn't be him again.

'Hello,' he said groggily.

'Sorry to wake you, Mr Cadbury.'

Jolted fully awake, Quentin hauled himself upright. Did the man never sleep?

'Well?' he said.

'Just some information for you, that's all. First thing tomorrow, hire a car.'

'What's wrong with my car?' he asked, thinking of his aging BMW in a lock-up garage a few streets away.

'I'm sure you can work that out for yourself, Mr Cadbury. You're not completely devoid of brains. Get a decent one, a fast one, but nothing too flashy or noticeable, if you get my drift.'

Quentin's mouth tightened. 'What then?'

'I'll ring you around nine-thirty and tell you where you're going. Got that?'

'Yes but–'

'Good. Till tomorrow then.'

The silence that echoed in Quentin's ear was worse than the measured tones of the cultured voice. Bloody hell, Quentin thought, the reality of what he'd let himself in for hitting him like a wrecking ball.

'What did he say?' Wanda, apparently having guessed who the caller was, pushed back her pillow and sat up.

'I've got to hire a car first thing and he'll let me know where I've got to go.'

'Right. He's really dragging it out, isn't he?'

Quentin swung his legs over the edge of the bed. 'Yeah. I'm going to get some things together. I don't want to be fiddling about in the morning.'

'So am I then,' Wanda said, throwing back the duvet. 'And don't say no. I'm coming.'

Knowing it was useless to argue, Quentin nodded and went home to pack a bag. He had no idea how long he'd be away. He might be told to collect and drop off the package anywhere. Well, it was December so he'd need warm things. He piled some winter clothes into the bag, added underwear and another pair of trainers, then some toiletries. That would do. Map? He'd buy a new one. He didn't totally trust satnavs.

Rummaging in a bedroom drawer he came across a compass, unused since his father had enrolled him for the Duke of Edinburgh's Award in the hope that he would follow him into the army, or at least "make a man" of him and enable him to get a "proper" job.

He took the compass and a pair of binoculars, as well as his Swiss army knife, which had proved useful several times. And the mobile he used to contact Philmore, along with the charger. After zipping up the bag, he took it downstairs. Magpie eyed it with suspicion, then mewed up at Quentin.

'Yes, I know. Sorry, boy, but I shouldn't be long. You'll be all right.'

Magpie arched his back and lifted his tail as though in disgust, then stalked away. Poor old thing, Quentin thought. He hates me being away.

Opening his bureau, his hand hovered over his passport. Cultured Voice had mentioned nothing about going abroad, but it was better to be prepared. He took it.

He was just wondering whether to go back to Wanda's or sleep in his own bed when she rang.

'I'm ready for the off tomorrow and I've set my alarm for six-thirty. I'll ring you then to make sure you're awake.'

Quentin didn't think he would sleep at all, but managed to drift off at about two o'clock in the morning. He'd set his own alarm but Wanda's call woke him before it went off. He tumbled out of bed, showered and made himself some tea and toast. After filling the automatic cat feeder, he dressed quickly and checked the time: 7.30 a.m. If Philmore wasn't up by now he'd be late for work. Taking his second mobile from his travel bag, he stood feeling the weight of it in his hand. He'd promised to ring the DCI as soon as he knew what his instructions from Cultured Voice were.

*No police, not even a sniff.* The words sounded in Quentin's head as he continued to gaze at the phone. Such a little gadget, but it may save his life. Or be his undoing. Or–

A key grating in the front door lock interrupted his thoughts. Wanda came in, complete with handbag, holdall, a carrier bag, blankets and Mozart. Quentin stared. Not only had he forgotten to bolt the front door last night, he'd forgotten about Mozart.

'We'll take him with us,' Wanda said, answering his unspoken question. 'He's no trouble and he's good in the car.'

'But we'll probably be away overnight. Can't Colin look after him?'

'Colin does it every time we go anywhere. I'm not asking him again. We promised to keep him in the loop and we might need his help. Don't worry about Mozart – we'll manage. At a push, he can sleep in the car – I've brought a couple of blankets.' Wanda lifted the arm over which two fleecy blankets were draped, then placed the blankets, carrier bag and holdall on a chair, her gaze dropping to the phone in Quentin's hand. 'Have you rung Philmore?'

'Not yet. I'm not sure–'

'I'll do it,' Wanda said. She tried to take the phone from him, but he swung it out of her reach. 'Do it, Quentin. We can't go into this alone. It's too dangerous.'

'It'll be more dangerous if he finds out we've got the police involved. He's an escaped prisoner. The idea of any police could tip him over the edge, turn him nasty.'

This earned him an incredulous look from Wanda.

'Turn him nasty! You're preaching to the converted, as you should well know. Or have you forgotten what I went through three years ago?'

'No, of course I haven't, and that's exactly the reason I don't want you involved, or risk involving Philmore.'

'Well, it's too late to think about that now. I'm already involved and so is Philmore. You don't think he'll let it go now you've told him that a criminal he's been after is up to his old tricks again? Anyway, he'll want to protect you – protect us. It's his job, protecting the public.'

Sighing, Quentin pressed the call button and raised the phone to his ear.

\* \* \*

Later, after Quentin had hired a car and completed the paperwork, he drove into a lay-by, where he sat waiting for the expected call. When it came, he answered with a curt 'Yes?'

'Have you done as I asked, Mr Cadbury?' the cultured voice demanded.

'I have.'

'And you're ready to travel?'

'I am.'

'Good. And you're alone?'

'Yes.' True enough. Wanda had taken Mozart for a walk along the road.

'Excellent. Set off now and drive towards Devon. I'll ring you this afternoon between two and three. If you're at Exeter before then, pull into the services and wait for my call. Understood?'

'Understood.'

'No questions?' There was a pause, as though the caller was suspicious of Quentin's monosyllabic answers.

'Plenty,' Quentin snapped. 'But none you're likely to answer.'

'Ah. That sounds more like the Quentin Cadbury I know.'

Quentin bridled. How dare this, this – criminal, say he knew him?

'You know nothing about me,' he said, swallowing his contempt.

'That's where you're wrong, Mr Cadbury. I know a lot more than you think. Now get going, and don't forget what I said.'

The line went dead and Quentin was left clutching the phone, his hand shaking slightly. His mind was crammed with his adversary's instructions: no police, come alone and… do as I say or I'll kill you.

# Chapter Six

The M25 was as busy as usual. Quentin cruised steadily in the hired Volvo, liking the feel of it and deciding that this model was definitely worth considering if he changed his own car. Wanda sat beside him, a newly purchased map on her lap, and Mozart lay on the back seat chewing on a rubber bone.

'When do you have to ring Philmore?' Wanda asked.

It was strange, Quentin reflected, that they usually referred to Steve Philmore as Philmore, but used his first name when they spoke to him.

'I told you. After we hear from Cultured Voice again.' He glanced in the rear-view mirror, trying to spot a car that Philmore might be in.

'We'll be with you all the way,' Philmore had promised when he'd rung him. 'Don't worry, we'll keep our distance. We'll be invisible.'

'You'd bloody well better be,' Quentin had replied, though he'd felt somewhat comforted by the thought of a police presence nearby. Not that they could stop a bullet. Or a knife. Or a sledgehammer.

'I must be crazy, getting into this,' he muttered under his breath.

'What was that?' Wanda asked.

'Nothing. Just thinking aloud.'

They passed Clacket Lane services in silence, Quentin remembering the part this service station had played in a previous case and knowing Wanda was thinking about it too. They carried on until they were approaching the junction with the M3. The traffic had slowed and a queue was forming ahead. An overhead gantry warned of delays due to an accident.

'We'll turn off here,' Quentin said. 'We don't want to get stuck in a jam for ages.'

'At least we haven't got to keep ringing Philmore to let him know which way we're going,' Wanda said as they turned onto the M3. 'What a brilliant idea, putting a tracker on this car.'

'Yes,' said Quentin.

He'd been surprised when Philmore's sergeant, DS Debbie Francis, met them near the car hire office with a technician who had swiftly and efficiently installed the tracker on the underside of the hired car. She'd also given him a copy of Cultured Voice's photo sent by the Dutch police, which he'd glanced at with the intention of studying it properly when he could.

He remembered DS Francis with mixed feelings. She made no secret of the fact that she thought him an ineffective, inept amateur, yet when he had helped catch a member of an international gang, she had praised him for his efforts.

Turning onto the A303, the traffic flowed reasonably well until they were coming up to Salisbury Plain. Then they crawled, passing the ancient obelisks of Stonehenge. Anxious to make up for lost time, Quentin put his foot down on the accelerator, praying they wouldn't get stuck behind a slow lorry or a farm vehicle. They didn't. The countryside flashed by until the road changed to the A30.

'I've just thought about what you said,' Wanda said suddenly, 'about him expecting you to be alone. Do you think we should separate at Exeter services? I mean, if someone's waiting there to give you the package…'

Quentin snorted. 'It won't be that straightforward, you can bet your life on that. He won't tell me where to make the pick-up until the last possible moment. Why would he risk me getting cold feet and running to the cops, telling them where I'm going? This way I might lead the cops to the general area, but the less I know the less I can give away.'

He stopped short of expressing a possibility he'd mentioned to Philmore previously – that the whole thing was an elaborate plan to get him where he could be killed and disposed of easily. A service station was too public for any such action.

'That makes sense,' Wanda said. 'So we don't need to worry about being seen together then, not at Exeter anyway.'

'I'm not sure,' Quentin said, shrugging. 'He's got eyes all over the place. The last time he arranged a rendezvous for me, he knew where I was every step of the way.'

'You mean he could be there somewhere, or have someone there, watching for us? Well then...' Wanda broke off, reached into her handbag and took out her sunglasses.

'I'll wear these,' she said holding them up. 'And I've got my snood. I'll put it over my head to hide my hair. If we get out, you go first and I'll go later. No one will be watching the car once you're out of it.'

'Cloak and dagger, eh? You shouldn't have come. I shouldn't have let you.' Quentin's remonstration was against himself rather than Wanda. He hadn't thought things through properly.

'It's a bit late for that now. You couldn't have stopped me coming. I could have followed you in my own car.'

'Yeah, right,' Quentin said sourly, thinking of Wanda's 1200cc Toyota. 'Like you'd have kept up with me.'

Wanda tossed her head impatiently. 'It's no good worrying about what we should have done. We're here now so we'll have to make the best of it. It's not far. We'll make it before two if we don't have any more hold-ups.'

Quentin grunted, too busy concentrating on the road to answer. He was surprised the call hadn't already come. Or perhaps it wouldn't come until after the appointed time. *Expect the unexpected.* If there was one thing Quentin had learned about Cultured Voice, it was that he wasn't predictable. Bloody hell, he thought, as he took the exit to Exeter services. He's got me dancing on a string like a puppet.

They reached the service station with time to spare. Quentin unfurled his long legs from the driver's seat, stretching his limbs gratefully. He pocketed both his mobiles, left the car and walked towards the service building. He reached the concourse and waited, making a show of reading the board advertising the facilities. After a few minutes, he turned to see Wanda walking Mozart towards the grass verge. True to her word, she was wearing sunglasses and had her black snood pulled over her head; not exactly a great disguise but perhaps making her less recognizable.

One of his mobiles vibrated against his hip and he scrambled to fish them out to see which one it was. His everyday mobile, so it must be Cultured Voice. He pressed the green button. 'Hello?' he said cautiously.

'Quentin? Heard any more?'

Quentin gasped in exasperation. 'Colin! What is it? I'm expecting a call.'

'From him? Didn't he ring this morning like he said he would?'

'Yes, and he rang last night.'

Colin's annoyance was evident. 'Why didn't you let me know?'

'It was midnight. I didn't think you'd appreciate having your beauty sleep disturbed.'

He heard the click of Colin's tongue. 'Don't be facetious. I said I wanted to be in at the start and you agreed. Where are you? You're not at home and neither is Wanda. You're not answering your landlines.'

'We're in Exeter.'

'Exeter! What the devil—'

'It's where we were told to go. There wasn't much point ringing you. We said we'd let you know if we needed help.'

'So much for keeping me in the loop. You're a pain in the arse sometimes, Quentin, and if anything happens to Wanda—'

'It won't. Philmore's on it. Look, I've got to go, Colin. I'm waiting for his call.'

'You bloody well let me know what's going on,' Colin bawled. 'Just you—'

Just you what, Quentin didn't hear. He cut the call off. Better to annoy Colin than Cultured Voice. Colin would rant and rave. Cultured Voice was capable of much more than that.

Wanda was still walking Mozart up and down the verge. Quentin hovered, wondering whether to stay where he could hear his phone ring or go into the service building. They hadn't eaten since breakfast and he guessed Wanda was as hungry as he was. Sod it, he thought, suddenly irritated. We have to eat. If I miss the call he'll have to ring back. He texted Wanda.

> *I'm going to get some lunch. You come in and get something but don't sit with me, just in case.*

He went inside, feeling slightly ridiculous. Philip Marlowe's got nothing on me, he thought drily.

After visiting the men's room, he joined the queue at the food counter, then found a table. The pie, chips, mushy peas and coffee weren't the best he had tasted, but they were hot and filling. He saw Wanda carrying a tray, her gaze sweeping the room for a free table. The snood had slipped, revealing her blonde hair, and she'd removed the sunglasses. If Cultured Voice was here, he'd have no trouble recognizing her, and if she was seen there was no point in pretending they weren't together. He beckoned her over to his table and she sat next to him.

'That was a wasted effort,' he said, indicating her snood.

'This thing keeps slipping, and I could hardly wear sunglasses indoors, could I?'

'Don't worry, I shouldn't think he'd risk showing himself here. He may not show himself at all.'

That thought depressed him. The reason he'd agreed to all this was to have a chance to nail the man, to drive the arrogance out of that cultured voice.

'You're probably right,' Wanda agreed. 'He'll get his minions to do the dirty work.'

Quentin glanced at Wanda's plate. The fish looked more batter than cod but she ate it uncomplainingly, then pushed the plate away.

'Let's have a look at him then, shall we?' she said.

Quentin drew out his wallet, extracted the photo DS Francis had given him and laid it on the table. Saying nothing, he stared at it, feeling the same sense of disappointment he'd felt when he'd first seen it. The face that looked out at him was ordinary in the extreme, no scars, no distinguishing marks, not even a freckle. He didn't know what he'd expected – a madness in the eyes perhaps, or a vicious snarl on the lips. The grey eyes looked cold, and the lips were set in a grim line.

Wanda looked at the picture and frowned.

'He looks like a million other men,' she said. 'How old is he?'

'Forty-five, Philmore reckons. That's according to the information from the Dutch police. They don't know for sure. They can't trace a birth certificate in the name he gave, and he hasn't got a criminal record prior to his arrest.'

'Well, he wouldn't have,' Wanda said. 'He's too careful. Still, he managed to get himself arrested, so he's made a least one mistake. He's clever enough to escape, though.'

Quentin nodded. 'Yeah. Come on, let's get back to the car.'

At Wanda's suggestion, they bought some bottled water, wraps and crisps in case they didn't have a chance to eat properly that evening, then left the restaurant.

It was nearly two-forty before Quentin's phone rang. He was in the gents washing his hands when he felt it vibrate against his side, though the ring tone was almost lost against the whirr of the dryers and running water. His hands still covered in soap, he pulled the mobile from his pocket, cursing as it slipped from his fingers, bounced off the edge of the sink and clattered to the tiled floor.

'Here you go,' a teenaged boy said, bending to retrieve it and handing it to Quentin. 'Hope it's not broken.'

Quentin muttered his thanks and looked at the screen. Intact, thanks to the flip-top lid. He pressed the green button just as the ringing stopped. A missed call, number withheld.

Wanda was already back at the car giving Mozart a drink and some food when he got there.

'What's up?' she asked, as if noticing his pained expression.

'Missed him,' he growled. 'Dropped the phone.'

Wanda rolled her eyes. 'Doing our Inspector Clouseau act again, are we?' she teased, gesturing Mozart back into the car. 'Don't look so worried. He'll get back to you.'

'I'm sure he will. Oh, there he is.'

Quentin turned away from Wanda and whipped out the phone, checked the display, then pressed the answer button.

'Yes?' he said.

'There you are, Mr Cadbury. For a moment I thought you'd deserted me.'

If only, Quentin thought grimly. 'I'm in Exeter services. Now what?'

'All in good time, Mr Cadbury. I trust you're suitably refreshed?'

Bloody hell, he can see us, Quentin thought. Panicked, he swept his gaze round the car park. Was he here, watching from a car or the services concourse?

'I don't like those services myself. I don't like any service stations, but they serve their purpose.'

No mention of Wanda, so he couldn't know she was here. Which meant he couldn't see them. And he'd said *those* services, not *these* services. He'd just assumed, rightly, that they would use the facilities. Quentin felt more assured of this at his adversary's next words.

'What car did you get, by the way?'

'A Volvo. Why?'

Cultured Voice ignored his question. 'What's the registration number?' he asked.

After Quentin had given the information, he continued, 'Right. So let's discuss the next part of your journey, shall we?'

'If we have to,' Quentin said tersely.

'Watch your tone, Mr Cadbury. You wouldn't want me to lose my temper, I can assure you.'

Quentin seethed inwardly. 'I'm listening.'

'Good. Take the A30 towards Penzance. Stay on until you get to a roundabout with Starbucks on the corner. An hour and a half, two hours max. Pull in there and wait for my call.'

'Starbucks? Where, exactly?'

'It's Cornwall, Mr Cadbury, not London. Keep on the A30 and even you can't miss it.'

Quentin groaned as the connection was cut. He stood muttering a string of expletives.

'What was that?' Wanda asked, evidently seeing him lower the phone as she came up beside him.

'Nothing,' he said. Apart from mild swear words, he tried not to use bad language in front of Wanda. He didn't know why – she was a woman of the world and must have heard enough of it. But she never used it herself and Quentin respected that.

'Well, come on, where to now?' she demanded.

'Starbucks, on the A30 somewhere near Penzance.'

'Right.' Wanda made a circular turn, shielding her eyes from the weak December sun. 'Do you think Philmore's here somewhere? I haven't seen him.'

'He might not have come himself,' Quentin pointed out. 'He might be controlling things from London. I hope he has though. He said he would.'

'Ring and find out,' Wanda said. 'Check the tracker's working and he knows where we are.'

'It'd bloody well better be working. Get in the car and I'll call him.'

'I'll drive for a bit,' Wanda said, sliding into the driver's seat. 'As I remember, the A30 is a straight road all the way through from here.'

Quentin had no memory of either the A30 or Cornwall. Apart from a year in Gibraltar, where his father had been stationed and which he'd been too young to remember, he'd spent most of his childhood holidays on the south coast near Littlehampton, where his grandparents had lived. He slid into the passenger seat and placed his mobile in the central well, keeping the pay-as-you-go phone in his hand. He brought up Philmore's number and pressed the key.

'Quentin? What's happening? Has he contacted you again?'

'Yep. No more info except where to go next. Starbucks, A30 near Penzance. He's taking us to the farthest end of the country.'

'Us? Wanda came with you then?'

'Yes,' Quentin admitted. 'Not my idea. Where are you?'

'Close enough,' came the reply.

Quentin imagined the detective chief inspector sitting in an unmarked police vehicle, his brown eyes staring through the windscreen, a patient look on his pleasant face and perhaps a few more grey hairs than when he'd last seen him.

'OK, we're following,' Philmore went on. 'I hope this is going to lead somewhere – we can't afford to be away from base for too long.'

'I hope so too, but I haven't got any option.'

'You did have before you started this, and you can pull out at any time.'

Quentin grunted. 'Bit late now. OK, I'll ring you if there's anything you need to know.'

'It's all right for Philmore,' he complained as he ended the call. 'At least he's getting paid for this. Probably claiming expenses too.'

'Now, now,' Wanda reproved. 'It was our decision to come, and we've got a lot to thank Philmore for. You might have been mincemeat three years ago but for him. Still, you did save a copper's life.'

Quentin grunted again. 'Better get going. With any luck we'll just make it before it gets dark.'

Easing the car from its parking place, Wanda drove out and took the slip road to the A30. The overhead gantry told them it was sixty minutes to Bodmin, and they carried on at a steady pace. Any hopes of getting to Starbucks in the daylight were thwarted when they came up behind a tailback of traffic just after they left Bodmin behind. Police cones and the wail of a siren heralded an accident, one that had closed off both carriageways.

'Bloody hell,' Quentin grumbled when they hadn't moved for 30 minutes. 'We'll never get there at this rate.'

'Could be worse,' Wanda said. 'We could be involved in that accident.'

'Tell that to our impatient friend. I'll have a look at the map and see if there's an alternative route.'

As he switched on the interior light, his mobile trilled. 'It's him,' he said, putting the phone to his ear. 'Hello?'

'Are you there yet, Mr Cadbury?'

'No. There's a hold-up, an accident. Serious, I should think.'

At that moment came the loud chugging of an engine overhead, and Quentin craned his neck to see a helicopter, red and white, rotors whirring above the hovering machine. "Cornwall Air Ambulance", he read on the side.

'It sounds noisy,' Cultured Voice observed drily. 'What's going on?'

'Helicopter, Air Ambulance.'

'I see. Well, I suppose that can't be helped. Unfortunately I think we'll have to miss this particular link in the chain now.'

Quentin waited until the cultured voice came again.

'All right, find somewhere to stay the night and wait for my call. Make sure your phone is charged. And no funny business, and I mean none. Remember that, Mr Cadbury.'

'Well?' asked Wanda when Quentin put the phone down.

'Whatever we had to do, it's too late,' Quentin said thoughtfully. 'Nothing else doing today. He said we'd have to miss that link in the chain, whatever that means.'

Wanda raised an eyebrow. 'You're probably right, he's giving you the runaround. He probably wants you to go on somewhere else again.'

'I bet he does,' Quentin said, thinking that Starbucks was another place that was too public for a killing. On the other hand, a busy place was ideal for a package to be handed over. That was never going to happen at Starbucks though, or Cultured Voice wouldn't have named it back in Exeter.

Wanda leaned back in her seat and rested her arms on the steering wheel. 'So what now?'

'He said to find somewhere to spend the night and wait till he rings.'

'Really? Well, at least we won't be driving all over Cornwall in the dark. Better let Philmore know.'

Quentin rang and repeated what they'd been told to do. He heard the frustration in the DCI's voice when he replied.

'All right, go with it. Ring when you hear again.'

'Oh, here we go,' Wanda said when the call ended. The traffic was moving, albeit slowly. Wanda turned the key in the ignition and the engine purred into life. They inched forward until they passed the spot where the accident had happened, falling silent as they saw the vehicles involved in the headlights – a van with the bonnet practically ripped off and two cars, one concertinaed beyond recognition and the second with the front pushed in.

'Oh, look at that!' Wanda said, shuddering as they passed the coned off area.

'Bloody hell!' Quentin breathed. 'If anyone's got out of that alive, it'll be a miracle.'

Which is what they needed now, he mused, his mind returning to their own situation. But perhaps their situation wasn't as bad as some. At least they were alive.

For now.

# Chapter Seven

'I think we've taken a wrong turn,' Quentin said as they made their way along an impossibly narrow lane hedged with wild vegetation.

As they had found to their cost when they'd had to back up after meeting an oncoming car, hedges often obscured a stone wall. Quentin guessed their last attempt at backing into a passing place had scratched the rear wing of the hired Volvo. Night was closing in and he didn't relish the idea of going much further in the dark. A few more turns through more narrow lanes, though, and they were back on the road where they'd seen the sign for a Travelodge.

'We've gone round in a circle,' Quentin moaned.

Following the signs, they found the Travelodge and were soon driving into the car park.

'Down, Mote,' Quentin said as Mozart placed a paw on the back of his seat. 'We can't take a dog into a hotel, by the way.'

'We can in these,' Wanda told him. 'I've done it before.'

'You said he could sleep in the car. You brought blankets.'

'I said at a push.'

'This *is* a push.'

'No, it isn't. A push is when there's no possibility of him sleeping inside. They do take dogs and Mozart's very good. He won't bark. Go in and see if they've got a room. Better still, we'll both go and take Mozart. They won't be able to resist him.'

Wanda was right. The woman on reception immediately made a fuss of Mozart.

'Hello, my lover,' she crooned in her thick Cornish accent. 'Have you come to stay with us or no?' She looked at Quentin and Wanda and smiled. 'Dear little dog,' she said.

A few minutes later, Quentin walked into a dog-friendly room on the ground floor. It was basic but large and clean, with a newly furbished en suite.

'Perfect,' he said, dropping the bags and plumping down on the king-sized bed. He stretched his cramped limbs, tempted to lie back on the duvet. How could he not be tired – disturbed at midnight, awake until two and up at six-thirty in the morning, then an interminable journey?

Rousing himself, he took off his shoes and coat and checked out the TV. Wanda arrived after walking Mozart round the car park, and sank into the bed next to Quentin.

After half an hour's relaxation and watching the local news, they freshened up and went for dinner in the restaurant attached to the hotel. It was warm and inviting and the food was good. When they'd eaten, they bought some drinks and carried them to their room. Wanda took

Mozart outside again, stopped at the car to pick up his water bowl and food, then settled him in the room before jumping in the shower.

'Do you think Philmore and Francis are here?' she asked when she'd finished. 'I suppose they must be if they're following our tracker.'

Quentin had been wondering that himself. 'Not necessarily. They can pick our trail up tomorrow. If they are here they'll keep a low profile.'

'I don't see why. Cultured Voice just told you to find somewhere to stay. He doesn't know where we are.'

'He's slacking then. He's usually got his finger on the button.'

'Even master criminals have to draw breath sometimes,' Wanda pointed out. 'And unexpected things happen to them too. Perhaps he's had to change his plans for some reason.'

Quentin grunted. 'Stringing things out, making me nervous, more like. Bastard.'

'Clever though,' Wanda said, throwing off the towel she was wrapped in and reaching for her nightie. Its flimsy material did nothing to hide the curves of her figure, supported by shoestring straps and falling in folds to her shapely thighs.

'Don't even think about it,' she said when Quentin tried to pull her towards him. 'We need to sleep. We don't know what's going to happen tomorrow. Anyway, I'm going to ring Colin.'

'Why?'

'Because he's my friend and I don't want to let him down, and because we may need his help.'

The tingle that had been mounting in Quentin was crushed like a grape under a sledgehammer.

'How can he possibly help from over two hundred miles away?'

'Because as much as he annoys you, he's got a knack of being useful wherever he is. Admit it.'

Quentin pursed his lips, remembering the times when Colin had actually helped him. They were outweighed by the number of times Colin had rung or turned up unexpectedly and either wreaked havoc or caused disharmony between him and Wanda.

'Call him then,' Quentin snapped. 'I'm having a shower.'

As he stood under the cascading water, the low murmur of Wanda's voice was obscured. He knew he was unfair to Colin but he couldn't help it. Perhaps they'd get on better if it wasn't for Wanda, or perhaps he was just directing his frustration at Colin today because he couldn't direct it to the man called Whitelaw, with his cultured voice and murderous intent – not directly, anyway.

'Yes, Colin's all right, thanks for asking,' Wanda said when Quentin had showered, shaved and got into bed.

'Bully for him.'

'Quentin.'

'Sorry,' Quentin mumbled. 'I'm just uptight, that's all.'

'You're not the only one,' Wanda reminded him. 'And don't take it out on Colin. He's only trying to help.'

'Is this really happening?' Quentin said, more to himself than Wanda. 'Are we really in a hotel room miles from home at the beck and call of a fugitive? I mean, you couldn't make it up, could you?'

Wanda climbed into bed. 'Well, we're here now, so we might as well get some rest while we can. Anyway, we know no one was watching us at Exeter. He wouldn't have asked what car you hired or the registration number otherwise.'

'Maybe.' Quentin sighed as Wanda put the light out. 'They know now, though, don't they?'

'Yes, well, they probably need to know for when you pick the package up. They'll want to be sure it's going to the right person. And we keep saying "they". What if he's working on his own? He hasn't been out of custody long.

It seems a bit soon for him to be back in the criminal ring already.'

'Don't be daft, Wanda. He had enough friends on the outside to help him escape, and whatever this package is, it's been brought here by someone, so other people must be involved. Still, that doesn't mean they're here now.'

'Anyway,' Wanda said, 'we don't know if Cultured Voice is even in the country. Philmore said they've checked and there's no record of him either leaving the Netherlands or arriving in England. He could be holed up somewhere abroad, issuing instructions by phone.'

'Possible,' Quentin conceded, 'but he'll have a false identity by now. He could have come in under any name, and he's pretty good at disguising himself.'

Wanda yawned. 'I'm too tired to think about it anymore tonight. Goodnight.'

'Night. I bet we can't sleep.'

After half an hour of seeing the pinprick of red light on the smoke alarm when he opened his eyes, and hearing the background hum that all these places seemed to emit, Wanda's deepened breathing told him she was asleep. Slipping an arm around her, he nestled into the curve of her body and managed to drift off.

* * *

It was one o'clock in the morning when he was jolted awake by something landing on top of him. He hit out in an automatic defensive action, only to encounter something soft and wet. The wetness nuzzled his neck and face.

'Mozart!' he moaned, attempting to push the dog off the bed. 'Mozart, what the hell are you doing?'

Wanda sat up and switched on the light. 'Down, boy,' she said, her voice thick with sleep.

'God, he gave me a shock,' Quentin said, trying to still his racing heart. 'What's he playing at?'

'He's in a strange place, that's all. He might want to go for a wee.'

'He doesn't normally go in the night, does he?'

'No, but this isn't normal for him, is it? We'd better take him out just in case.'

Swearing under his breath, Quentin got out of bed, put his shoes on and slipped into his coat. Then, not bothering to locate the dog's lead, he scooped up Mozart and set off along the dimly lit corridor.

Once outside, he let Mozart snuffle his way along, close to the wall of the building, cocking his leg as he went. The night was cold now, made colder by a brisk westerly wind. Wishing he'd worn his scarf, Quentin pulled up his collar and followed the dog, though he didn't relish the idea of having to call to Mozart right outside the hotel windows. He always felt silly calling Mozart in public anyway. People sometimes looked at him suspiciously, as though they expected to see the man himself appear in eighteenth-century clothes brandishing his latest music score.

In the dim light from the car park, Quentin strained his eyes to see the little dog, who had disappeared round the corner of the building. Quentin walked on, his mind on what may happen tomorrow and knowing that, whatever happened, he would be tired. He reached the corner and peered around it. It was darker here, but he could see the white, dog-shaped form sniffing at the adjacent bushes.

'Here, boy,' he called softly. Mozart came to him obediently, then trotted along by his side when he said, 'Heel!'

As they turned and rounded the corner again, a figure loomed a few yards in front of them, a dark shape facing away from them, hovering ominously beside a car. His car, Quentin saw, remembering the shape of the hired car. Taken by surprise, he stopped. Why would someone be lurking outside the hotel at one in the morning? Even if they'd just arrived, why would they be standing there by his car? Were they planning to steal it?

Another possibility leapt into his mind. Was someone standing guard to make sure he didn't escape in the night? Surely even Cultured Voice wouldn't go to those lengths. What would be the point? He knew Quentin wouldn't turn back now, if only because of the threat to Wanda. No. It was a local kid up to no good. The figure turned and bent down slightly.

I don't believe it, Quentin thought. He's breaking into my car.

Rational thought deserting him, he rushed forward and launched himself at the figure just as it straightened and turned towards him. Mozart, alarmed by Quentin's action, began to bark.

'Gotcha, you little thief,' Quentin croaked, grabbing the figure by both arms. 'Ouch!'

He recoiled as a foot kicked back forcefully and found his groin. Pain shot through him and he clutched at himself, hopping from one foot to the other.

'There's more where that came from.'

Quentin gasped as he recognized the voice over Mozart's frantic barking. A woman's voice. DS Debbie Francis.

'Bloody hell!' he cried out, unable to believe he'd practically assaulted a police officer. 'What the devil are you doing out here?'

'Quentin?' The detective sergeant's tone was incredulous. 'Why are you creeping about in the dark?'

'I'm not creeping about,' Quentin wheezed, still reeling from the kick he'd received. 'I had to bring the dog out.'

As if on cue, Mozart stopped barking and plonked himself at Quentin's feet.

'I thought you were stealing my car,' Quentin went on. 'I was going to make a citizen's arrest.'

'Were you now? I have every right to arrest you for assaulting a police officer.'

'For God's sake!' Quentin said. 'I was just trying to stop a car theft. Did you have to kick me so hard?'

'We're trained to defend ourselves. What do you expect when someone grabs you?'

'Fair point. Remind me not to get on the wrong side of you. I hope we're even now.'

'Yes, well,' Debbie Francis said, and Quentin knew she was recalling the time when he had deflected a blow from her. Mozart sniffed at her legs and she bent to stroke him.

'Why are you here anyway?' he asked.

Francis gave a hollow laugh. 'Police expenses don't run to posh hotels. This was the first one we found after you said there was nothing going on tonight.'

'I meant, why are you out here now?'

'My guilty secret,' she answered. 'I couldn't sleep so I came out for a smoke.'

A faint whiff of cigarette smoke emanated from her as she spoke, and Quentin could see the red of a stub still glowing on the ground.

'I'm trying to give up,' she admitted. 'I don't smoke on duty.'

'Why here though, by my car?'

'Is it yours? I didn't realize. I was just walking and leaned against it, that's all.'

The pain in his groin ebbing, Quentin said, 'I take it Philmore's here?'

'Yes, and he's pretty miffed. If this goes on too long he could be called back to London. Still, he really wants to get this guy. It would do his career a lot of good if he could nail him. Are you all right?'

'I'll live,' Quentin told her. 'But for goodness' sake, let's get some sleep before we have to go who knows where tomorrow or we'll be driving around like zombies.'

'All right.' Francis began walking towards the main door. 'What room are you in, by the way?'

'Eighteen,' Quentin said, falling into step beside her. 'You?'

She hesitated before answering. 'Ninety-five.'

'Right. Er, are we mentioning this little chat to Philmore?'

'Don't see why we should.'

'My thoughts exactly,' Quentin agreed.

He frowned as they walked along the rows of cars and his eyes fell on one nearer the hotel door. It was lighter here, and he felt a flush rise to his face as realization dawned. *This* was his car, the car he'd hired to come here. Similar shape, same colour as the one he'd thought was his, as far as he could see, but not the same make. God, he thought, the person I accused of stealing my car turns out to be a cop, and it wasn't even my car! What the hell else can happen tonight?

# Chapter Eight

It was eight o'clock when Quentin awoke the next morning. Wanda wasn't there and neither was Mozart, so he guessed they'd gone for a walk. He'd expected Cultured Voice to call early, but he hadn't heard his phone ring and he'd had no missed calls.

The door opened and Mozart trotted in, followed by Wanda.

'Morning,' Wanda said. 'Glad you've decided to honour us with your presence.'

'It's all right for you,' Quentin said, his voice scratchy from interrupted sleep. 'You're not the one who was out in the cold in the middle of the night.'

'No need to make a meal of it. I appreciate you taking Mozart out, that's why I didn't wake you this morning. Why were you so long anyway?'

'I met Debbie Francis having a smoke and we had a chat.' Quentin stopped short of telling her what had actually happened. He didn't want another Inspector Clouseau analogy.

'Cosy. I take it you haven't heard anything?'

Quentin shook his head. 'Nothing yet.'

Once again, Quentin felt like a dangling puppet waiting for his strings to be jerked into action. The idea that transporting a package was a ruse devised to lure him to his death was becoming stronger. This whole thing was an elaborate hoax, a charade, a trap. And he was walking right into it.

He jumped at the shrill of his mobile. Number withheld. He exchanged a look with Wanda and raised a finger to his mouth before pressing the answer button.

'Hello,' he said tentatively.

'Good morning, Mr Cadbury. I hope you're ready to continue your journey.'

'Do I have a choice?'

'Come now, Mr Cadbury, everyone has a choice. Luckily for you you've made the right one. A welcome change, if I may say so.'

'Where am I going?' Quentin asked, biting back the sarcastic reply that came to his mind. 'Starbucks?'

The snigger that was fast becoming familiar sounded in Quentin's ear. 'That would be most unwise, as I'm sure you'll appreciate. No, Mr Cadbury, I've arranged a new destination for you.'

'Really? And where would that be?'

'Bradford Bridge.'

Cogs turned furiously in Quentin's head. Bradford! Halfway up the country. So Cornwall was just a decoy.

'Did you hear me? I said Bradford Bridge.'

'I heard you,' Quentin said, wondering how many bridges there were in Bradford.

'It's on Bodmin Moor, near Colliford Lake. Quite a beauty spot, I believe. Rather isolated, but that won't worry an intrepid young man like you. Get to the bridge by eleven and wait for my call. And make sure you stick to the rules.'

The call ended abruptly.

'Well?' Wanda asked. 'Where are we going?'

'Some place called Bradford Bridge on Bodmin Moor. And he said to stick to the rules.'

'The rules? What, the "come alone and no police" rules, you mean?'

'Yep, that's it, I should think. He said this place is isolated, so he'll spot Philmore a mile off. You too.'

A determined look came over Wanda's face. 'You're not leaving me behind.'

'Well, I'm not taking you with me. It's too dangerous. You'd have nowhere to hide or run to if things got tricky.'

'Don't take me all the way then. Drop me somewhere nearby.'

'We'll check the map and I'll drop you in the nearest town, somewhere you can get lost in or get help if needed. Don't look like that. It's pointless risking him finding out you're with me, and if I get into trouble, Philmore will be nearby.'

'Not that near. You've already said he'll be spotted a mile off.'

'He'll be around somewhere. There are such things as binoculars and long-range cameras, you know. Anyway, if anything does happen to me you'll be free to raise the alarm.'

Wanda didn't look convinced. She sighed. 'I suppose you're right. You'd better ring Philmore. Better still, find out what room he's in and we'll go and see him.'

'Debbie's in ninety-five,' Quentin recalled. 'We'll start there.'

They made their way to room number ninety-five, Mozart trotting quietly beside them. Francis looked surprised when she opened the door. Despite her night-time walk around the car park, the detective sergeant looked alert and smart in a black trouser suit and a blue blouse. As if remembering her from the night before, Mozart scampered up to her.

'Morning, Debbie,' Wanda greeted.

'I'm not sure you should be here,' Francis said, looking up and down the corridor then ushering them inside.

'We've just come to tell you what's happening,' Quentin said.

'Wait,' Francis insisted. 'I'll call the chief.'

Two minutes later, Philmore came into the room.

He looked as Quentin remembered him – slim, brown-eyed and with more salt than pepper in his short hair. He wore casual trousers with a T-shirt and jacket.

'I've had a call,' Quentin said.

'You should have rung me,' Philmore replied, sounding agitated. 'So what does he want you to do?'

When Quentin had finished explaining where he had to go, Philmore turned to Francis.

'Get on to the local boys,' he said. 'Find out what you can about this place and get some back-up.'

'Armed back-up?' she asked.

Wanda gasped and Quentin felt a shiver run down his spine, but Philmore shook his head.

'No need, not now anyway. Get on it. We haven't got much time.'

DS Francis nodded, picked up her mobile phone, went into the bathroom and closed the door. The sound of her voice could be heard but not what she was saying.

'You don't think we need armed back-up?' Quentin asked Philmore, his anxiety rising.

'This man's on the run,' Philmore said. 'He won't be showing himself. And I think part of this is personal. Whitelaw's got a grudge against you, Quentin. He may be using you to transport something illegal, but if he is, it's part of a game. We know he's powerful. He can get people to carry out his orders, but I don't think he'll get some hitman to kill you. He'll want to do it himself, or at least be there when it's done.'

'So,' Quentin said slowly, 'you're saying I'm safe unless I meet him face to face?'

'Yes, unless something happens to make him change his mind, but I don't think it will. As I said, it's personal. That's what the police profiler thinks.'

'Steve,' Wanda said, putting on her most seductive voice, 'Quentin says I shouldn't go with him. Can I come with you?'

'Absolutely not.'

'What about in any other cars – you'll have local police cars with you?'

'Sorry, Wanda. For a start, you're too recognizable if you're seen.'

'But I've been in your car before when you were on a case.'

'That was different. You know it was. And Quentin's right. If they see you, it could blow the whole thing.'

'Steve… I can wear my snood and keep a low profile. Oh, all right.' Wanda gave up her cajoling and sighed.

Quentin grinned. Wanda's charm didn't fail very often, but he knew exactly why the DCI had refused her. He guessed Philmore had had a hard time convincing his superiors that Quentin could lead them to Cultured Voice. They definitely wouldn't have agreed to Wanda being involved.

'Anyway,' Philmore said, 'we're only interested in Whitelaw. We just have to hope that somewhere along the line one of his henchmen will lead us to him. If you've got to collect a package, someone's got to take it to the collection point.'

'You never know,' Wanda said. 'He might want to do something himself, if only to prove how clever he is. He was there the first time we had a run-in with him even if we didn't see him.'

'Yes, but it's different now,' Quentin pointed out. 'As Steve says, he's on the run, and he's too important to risk being caught when he can get someone else to do his dirty work. Anyway, there might not be a handover. I'll be surprised if I see anyone. I think I'll just have to pick something up from somewhere. Why would they expose themselves when there's no need?'

'Quite right,' Philmore said. 'Right, don't worry if you don't see us. It's highly unlikely our man will be there today. That's too simple for him. Still, better safe than sorry.'

When Quentin and Wanda were back in their own room, Wanda began collecting the items from the bedside cabinet. Her body language and rigid expression told Quentin she was still annoyed by Philmore's refusal to let her go with them.

'It makes sense, Wanda,' he said gently. 'He's only doing his job. He asked for this case especially and he's got to stay as close to the book as he can. He's already sticking his neck out for us.'

'For us? Doesn't the fact that the police have had this man within reach more than once, and let him slip through their fingers, count for anything? Don't fool yourself, Quentin. They need to catch him. Thanks to you, they know he's no longer incommunicado, and if they fail again they'll be the ones with egg on their faces.'

Wanda's cheeks were pink as she said this. Quentin was surprised. She had spoken vehemently, not in the usual calm, sophisticated way that defined her. Nevertheless, she was right. Cultured Voice had slipped through the net many times, at home and abroad.

'Right,' Wanda said, recovering her poise. 'We'd better get going. We don't know how long it'll take you to get to there.'

She reached for her bag and began packing things into it. Quentin followed suit and they were soon ready to leave.

'Let's get the map and see how far this place is,' Quentin suggested. 'If it's not far, we can grab some breakfast first.'

Bradford Bridge wasn't shown on their map. 'He mentioned Colliford Lake,' Quentin mused. 'So it must be near there. Doesn't look that far. Maybe forty-five minutes. Must be tiny though. It doesn't seem like the kind of place you can hide something in.'

'They're hardly likely to leave a package that might be worth thousands of pounds lying around on Bodmin Moor, are they?' Wanda countered. 'What will they say? Look under the third bush on the right?'

'No idea. Just have to wait and see. I might be sent on somewhere else, for all I know. Come on, we can get some rolls at least.'

They made for the restaurant, leaving Mozart in the car with a window slightly open, something Wanda insisted on even in winter. After tea and toast they told Philmore they were leaving and set off, taking the route along the A30 to Bodmin, where Quentin dropped Wanda and Mozart near the town centre. Quentin studied the map then carried on, keeping an eye out for any car he thought might be Philmore's. He didn't spot one. Stupid, he told himself. I didn't even think to ask what car they've got.

On the outskirts of the town, he saw two police vehicles in a lay-by, each occupied by two uniformed officers. One vehicle looked like a traffic car, but he couldn't be sure. There was nothing going on, no accident or anything that Quentin could see that warranted them being there. Perhaps they were Philmore's back-up waiting to be called, although by his estimation they were a fair way from Bradford Bridge. Or perhaps they were just lying in wait for speeding cars.

He followed the signs and eventually turned onto a side road. When the road narrowed and the landscape changed from cultivated fields to bracken and scrubby bushes, he knew he was on the moor. It looked desolate enough now, in the light of day, and he could imagine how lonely and forbidding it would feel on a dark, stormy night. Eventually he passed some cottages, one of which was named Bradford Lodge, so he knew he'd found the right place. There wasn't a bridge in sight, so he asked a woman by one of the cottages.

'Take the no-through road,' she said. 'It's not far.'

He did, and came to what seemed like an oasis on the moor. There was a river, widening out at one point and flanked by trees on either side. A small stone bridge traversed the water, beyond which the road wound further on. He parked the car before he got to the bridge and sat waiting. Another vehicle passed him, going straight over the bridge and out of sight. It was white, with two occupants, Quentin noticed, though from his angle he couldn't see them until they'd passed.

Cultured Voice had been right. This was quite a beauty spot, and probably popular with visitors in the summer. On a cold day like this though, Quentin didn't expect to see many people. The sky was overcast and the wind stung. No other cars went by, and Quentin wondered where Philmore and his promised police back-up were. As far as he could see, he was on his own.

## Chapter Nine

It was ten forty-five when the call came. 'You're there then, Mr Cadbury. Good.'

Quentin instinctively swivelled round to look for anyone watching him. There was no one. He waited, unease adding to his apprehension. There was something unsettling about knowing you were being watched by unknown eyes.

'How do you—' he began, but stopped. The vehicle that passed him. It must be them. He couldn't believe it would be Cultured Voice himself. Whoever it was, they must have reported in to him by phone.

'Never mind how I know. Get out of the car and walk to the bridge. Stand on the left-hand side until I call back.'

Quentin cursed as the line went dead. Should he ring Philmore or would he be seen with the phone near his ear? He thought of ducking down, calling Philmore before getting out, but decided against it. If Philmore was in position he should be able to see him on the bridge. And if he wasn't...

He reached for his scarf and wound it round his neck, then he got out and flinched as a gust of icy wind hit him. Shivering, he pulled the scarf up over his mouth and chin and walked slowly towards the bridge, glancing left and right as he went. There was no sign of anyone, no movement of bushes or shrubs. He got to the bridge and looked behind him. Nothing there either. By his own calculation he must have stood there for a least ten minutes, his hands starting to go blue with cold and his mind filling with impossible scenarios. He imagined someone springing out from behind, bundling him into a car and kidnapping him; or police descending on the unseen watcher by parachute, surrounding them or...

He jumped at the vibration of his mobile. 'Yes?' he answered, turning and scanning the area for movement.

'OK, Mr Cadbury, go back to your car, drive back the way you came and on to Colliford Lake. Avoid the park and the café by Bolventor. Take one of the unnamed tracks and wait there.'

'Why?'

But Quentin was talking to himself. Cultured Voice had gone.

Bugger it, Quentin thought as he stomped back to the car. He's got me running after him like a lapdog. As he sped away, he called Philmore.

'Where the hell were you?' he demanded. 'You couldn't have been there. I'd have seen you.'

'Never mind that, where are we headed now?' Philmore asked impatiently. 'Right,' he continued when Quentin told him. 'We're on your trail.'

'But they'll spot you,' Quentin pointed out.

'Got to go, Quentin.' Philmore rang off.

'Bloody hell,' Quentin groaned aloud. 'He's as bad as Cultured Voice.'

He drove on, eventually finding a track that led to the lake. He bumped over the stony ground, stopping as near to the water's edge as he could. The lake was big. Hills rose high on one side while the near side was flatter, with cultivated fields giving way to open scrubland closer to the water. The sky had grown darker, and grey clouds hung low over the hilltops, threatening rain.

Quentin got out and looked around. In the distance, he could see tiny figures, growing even smaller as they walked round the lake in the opposite direction. Otherwise, there was no one in view, and no other vehicles.

Back in the car, he noticed a tall van pulling up about a hundred yards away – cream-coloured, with orange and blue lettering and some sort of logo that he couldn't see from this distance. Was this it? Surely, they wouldn't park that far away if they were going to hand him something? Perhaps the profiler was wrong – they really were going to kill him and dump his body in the lake. But then why this elaborate goose chase? No, he thought, that didn't make sense.

Just then, he remembered the binoculars he'd brought with him, and went to the boot to get them. Noticing the bag with the water and wraps they'd bought yesterday, he took that too, then got back in the car. He raised the binoculars and focused on the van, praying he wouldn't see a face looking his way. "South West Lakes Trust", he read, feeling easier. He checked the driver's window but couldn't make out much through the steamed-up glass. Eventually a man emerged from the van, wearing a high-visibility raincoat and carrying a clipboard. He moved away into the scrubland.

Quentin switched on the engine and activated the heater. It helped warm him, though his feet still felt numb. While he waited, he tried to recall everything Cultured Voice had said to him so far, anything that might give him a clue as to where he was or what he intended to do. He dredged his memory but came up short. The man had been scathing but precise. He'd given nothing away.

It was another half an hour before the next call came. 'Where are you, Mr Cadbury?'

'At the lake like you said.'

'Good. Just sit there and wait.'

'Wait for what? How will anyone find me?'

'Don't worry, just wait.'

The call ended suddenly, but it had revealed one thing. The van that was parked a hundred yards away had nothing to do with Cultured Voice or he wouldn't have been asked where he was. He glanced in the rear-view mirror. The person with the clipboard was still walking around, looking at plants and turning over stones. Was it a genuine employee of the South West Lakes Trust or had Philmore somehow managed to get hold of the vehicle? If he had, it was a good cover. Except whoever was coming to find him might be put off by its proximity.

The mist on the van's windows had faded a little and he could see a second person in the passenger seat. He was certain about one thing – the person traipsing around the moor wasn't DCI Philmore or DS Francis. Someone else had that unenviable task. Turning in his seat to check no other vehicles were approaching, he reached for his mobile.

'Steve? Are you in a van at Colliford Lake? Can you see me?'

'Yes,' Philmore snapped. 'What's happening? We're freezing our balls off here.'

'You and me both. I've been told to wait. Mind you, if someone does turn up there might be nothing doing if they see you.'

'It shouldn't make any difference. We look like a perfectly legitimate organisation doing a perfectly legitimate job. They can still give you a package if they park on the other side of you. We wouldn't see.'

'All right, I suppose we'll just have to wait.'

Quentin pressed the off button and settled back in his seat. His stomach rumbled, and he reached over to the food he'd taken from the boot. After munching his way through a chicken wrap and a packet of crisps, he drank some water and felt better. Feeling cramped, he climbed out of the car and began walking round it. He saw the man with the clipboard return to the van and get in. The thrum of an engine made him turn to see a white vehicle on the distant road. When he was certain it hadn't turned down the track, he got back in the car.

A thin, drizzly mist was rolling in from the lake. Quentin rubbed his hands together, trying to warm them. Fifteen minutes later, his second mobile rang.

'Are you sure he said he was sending someone?' Philmore sounded agitated.

'Not exactly. He just said to sit here and wait. It could just be a wind-up. What shall I do if no one comes?'

Quentin pictured Philmore in the back of the van, desperate to get a lead on the man who was playing fast and loose with them. This was probably personal for Philmore too. Wanda was right. He'd been after this criminal for years, and Quentin guessed he didn't want another failed case on his hands.

'We'll give it bit longer,' Philmore said tetchily. 'Then we'll see.'

What there was to see, Quentin didn't know. They either stayed or left, as simple as that. He grimaced as the sky darkened further and the mizzle turned to heavy rain, thundering down on the roof like hailstones. Visibility on the moor was reduced and ripples spread over the lake as the rain hit the surface. Quentin wondered how people fared on the moor if they were caught unawares by a sudden squall. He could imagine being lost out here, wandering about with no transport and no map or compass; unseen rocks and plant roots, bogs, a hound baying…

The ring of his everyday phone broke his train of thought and he took the call.

'So, Mr Cadbury, have you enjoyed your time on Bodmin Moor? One should always explore the local area, don't you think?'

'What am I doing here?' Quentin demanded.

'Enjoying the peace and quiet and the scenery, I hope.'

'Look,' Quentin spluttered. 'What the hell is going on? I've been here for hours. I thought I was supposed to be picking up a package.'

'That will happen soon, Mr Cadbury, I promise. I just had to be sure you were following my instructions. I could hardly trust my valuable goods to you otherwise, could I?'

'You mean I've been sitting here all day for nothing? What a bloody waste of time!'

'Oh no, it hasn't been a waste of time, not from my point of view, I can assure you.'

'I'm not interested in your point of view,' Quentin snapped.

There was a pause during which Quentin could feel the caller's hostility.

'Well, you should be. You should be very interested if you want to carry on living. That's all for today. You can have the luxury of another night in a hotel or wherever you choose to stay. Don't leave the area and don't even think about going to the police. Believe me, Mr Cadbury, my arm is as long as the law's.'

As the line went silent, Quentin thumped his free fist down on the steering wheel, catching the horn and causing a loud elongated toot.

'Bugger it!' he muttered. Then, giving vent to his frustration, he shouted, 'Bugger it, bugger it, bugger it!'

His second mobile sounded and he snatched it up.

'Anything wrong, Quentin?' Philmore asked.

'Only that we've been played for fools. It's a no-show. He just wanted to make sure I was following his instructions, though how he knows whether I am or not beats me. Someone must have seen me somewhere along the line today. It must have been at Bradford Bridge. He knew I was there. Sending me here is his idea of fun. No one's been here or we'd have seen them.'

'So what have you got to do now?' Philmore sounded as exasperated as Quentin felt.

'Find somewhere to stay tonight and wait. He says I'll be picking up the package soon.'

Quentin heard Philmore asking Francis to tell the local boys to stand down before the call ended. He wondered if Philmore would come over and speak to him, or whether he should go to him, but the van was already pulling away.

Angry and frustrated, Quentin sat for a few moments, wondering why he'd ever agreed to this charade. The more he thought about it, the angrier he became. Eventually, he slammed the Volvo into gear, his mind still on Cultured Voice and the pointless mission he'd been sent on.

Straining his eyes through the relentless rain, Quentin drove slowly, yard by invisible yard. The windscreen wipers struggled to cope, and soon he couldn't see anything and was forced to stop. He tried to ring Wanda but he was out of signal. It amazed him how phone signals could fluctuate so much – a few feet could make all the difference, especially here in Cornwall.

Twenty minutes later the rain eased, and though visibility was still poor, Quentin could see he wasn't on the same track he'd come in on. He must have made a wrong turn. Sighing, he realized he was lost.

'Bloody hell,' he muttered, switching on the satnav and typing "Bodmin" as the name of the town. "Trouble finding satellites" was the only information it gave him. Suddenly he thought of the compass. Locating it, he watched the needle swing north. Did that help? He was sure he'd driven east when he'd left the lake, so if he drove west he should come back to the right path.

'Worth a try,' he said aloud, slipping the compass into his pocket. A relieved sigh escaped him as he came to a wider, well-worn track. 'Thank God,' he murmured. 'I didn't fancy spending the night here.'

"Please drive to highlighted route," a robotic voice told him as the satnav sprang into life.

Thanks a bunch, he thought sourly. Fat lot of good you are.

# Chapter Ten

Quentin found Wanda outside St Petroc's Church in Bodmin where he'd arranged to meet her. She bore his ranting about time-wasting in silence, until he ran out of steam and asked sheepishly, 'What sort of day did you have?'

'Not bad, considering I was left behind to twiddle my thumbs. Don't think I'm going to put up with that every time you have to go somewhere. Anyway, I went to the Shire Hall and did the Courtroom Experience, and learned how prisoners were treated in the old days. It's a pity Cultured Voice won't have that sort of treatment when he's caught.'

As if noticing Quentin's despondent expression, Wanda placed a hand on his knee. 'Cheer up. We'll find somewhere for dinner and we need somewhere to stay again.'

'We'll go back to where we stayed last night,' said Quentin.

'Or we could find a nice country pub,' Wanda suggested. 'Some do rooms as well.' She looked in the vanity mirror, angling it so that she could see the traffic behind them. 'You don't think we're being followed, do you?'

'No. Someone saw me at some point today, so it was right that you didn't come with me. I don't think they were there all day, though. I didn't see anyone at the lake, and Cultured Voice asked where I was. Mind you, when the rain came down, it was hard to see anything, so who knows?'

They found a pub and managed to get a room for the night. Mozart played his part, befriending the landlord's chocolate Labrador and winning the hearts of people in the bar. Wanda was delighted to find salmon on the menu, and after a hearty mixed grill, a red wine and two whiskies, Quentin relaxed a little. The open log fire cast flickering light on a huge Christmas tree, and he sat opposite Wanda thinking about what the next day would bring.

Wanda's voice brought him back to the present. 'I wonder where Steve and Debbie are. They could have come here with us.'

'I'm glad they didn't,' Quentin said. 'I can do without them tonight. Anyway, they know where we are from the tracker.'

The warmth from the fire made Quentin feel sleepy. Or perhaps it was the alcohol. He agreed readily when Wanda suggested an early night. She took Mozart outside while Quentin went upstairs to their room. The building was old but the bedroom was modern and the bed comfortable. Quentin was already drifting off to sleep when Wanda returned. Dreamily, he realized that under normal circumstances he would have enjoyed an early night with Wanda, but that beautiful thought was lost to sleep.

\* \* \*

A grey daylight was peeping in between the crack in the curtains when the persistent ringing of a phone awoke him the next morning.

'Heard anything?' Philmore rasped, as if he'd just woken up himself.

'No. I'd have called.'

'All right. Let me know the minute you do, in case I have to organise something in a hurry.'

Quentin yawned and let his head fall back on the pillow. Whatever else he was, Cultured Voice, alias Whitelaw, alias Hoeker, alias who knew what, obviously wasn't in a rush. It was ridiculous that he was dancing to the tune of a man whose real name he didn't know and whose face he had never seen in the flesh. The police mugshot didn't help much. As far as Quentin was concerned, all it proved was that his adversary was white and didn't have two heads.

Wanda stirred and gave him a sleepy smile. Desire flared but was instantly quelled. The possibility of being interrupted was off-putting; the possibility of being interrupted by Cultured Voice was more than off-putting. It drenched Quentin's desire like water on flames. He stretched and sat up, deciding to shower before Wanda had a chance to commandeer the bathroom. He was halfway across the room when he tripped over something and fell against the wall. Mozart yelped, making Wanda jerk upright.

'Sorry, Mote,' Quentin said, rubbing his elbow where it had hit the wall. 'Why did you have to sleep in the middle of the floor?'

'Don't blame Mozart,' Wanda said, jumping out of bed and pulling the curtains open. 'You should be looking where you're going.'

'It was dark!'

'That's no excuse. All right, Mozart, he didn't mean to hurt you.' Wanda scooped the dog up and thrust him into

Quentin's arms. Then she skipped into the bathroom, turning on the threshold and giving him a triumphant grin.

'She's done it again!' Quentin said to Mozart, who put his head on one side and yapped softly. He put the dog on the floor, then plumped down on the bed and sighed. 'Oh well, we should be used to it by now, eh, Mote?'

After breakfast, he and Wanda had just sat down in the pub lounge with their coffee when his phone rang. Number withheld.

'Yes?'

'Good morning, Mr Cadbury. I trust you slept well.' When Quentin just grunted, the cultured voice went on, 'I'll take that as a yes. OK, here's your itinerary for the day. As you're in Cornwall you may as well take advantage of one of its major attractions. Do you know the Eden Project?'

'I know *of* it,' Quentin said, picturing the images of the huge white biodomes he'd seen.

'A delightful place, I believe. Always busy, even in the winter, I'm told.'

Quentin waited, wondering why Cultured Voice was wasting time expounding the pleasures of somewhere he obviously hadn't been to.

'So, Mr Cadbury, here's what you'll do next. Drive to the Eden Project and stay with the car. I'll ring you at ten-thirty, and you'll tell me exactly where you are. Got it?'

'Yes, but—'

'No buts, Mr Cadbury. Just do it.'

Quentin shook his head as the call ended.

'Well?' Wanda said. 'Where to?'

'The Eden Project by ten-thirty.'

Wanda's raised an immaculate eyebrow. 'Good choice if it's for a handover,' she said. 'Big crowds. Who's going to notice anything going on there?'

She was right, but somehow Quentin still didn't think there would be a physical handover. As he'd said yesterday, he expected to collect the package from a dedicated hiding place.

'I'm coming,' Wanda continued in a tone that would brook no discussion. 'I know you're supposed to be alone, but we're a team. I can go to the Eden Project even if we don't stay together. It's huge.'

'Yeah, you're probably right. All right, come.'

'What, no argument, no "stay here and drink coffee"?'

Quentin shook his head. 'No. I'll call Philmore and tell him what's what.'

# Chapter Eleven

They found the Eden Project easily enough. As they drove through the entrance gates and along the approach road, Quentin expected to see the huge biodomes, but they weren't in sight.

'You can't see anything until you're inside,' Wanda said, guessing at his thoughts. 'It's in an old clay quarry. I read about it.'

The parking area was enormous and already filling up. It was separated into sections differentiated by the names of various fruits. There were still spaces in the Banana area.

'I'll drop you at the next one, Wanda, then come back and park here. You go on in. I'll wait till he's called then ring you.'

When he'd dropped Wanda and Mozart off, Quentin doubled back to the Banana area and nosed the Volvo into a space. Switching off the engine, he blew out his cheeks as nerves made his stomach churn. Was this where he'd collect the package or just another red herring? All he could see were people leaving their cars in droves – young and old, different nationalities, families, couples, children in pushchairs, someone in a wheelchair; a cross section of human life. What he didn't see was any indication of a police presence.

Yesterday's rain had stopped and the winter sun was warm through the windscreen. Within minutes, sweat beaded on his forehead and upper lip, adding to the moisture already making his palms damp. 'Come on,' he muttered as the hands on his watch slipped round to ten-thirty. He felt like a schoolboy waiting to be given a detention.

The call, number withheld, came on time.

'Where are you, Mr Cadbury?'

'At the Eden Project, in the Banana car park.'

'Banana. I hope you're not playing games with me.'

'I'm not in the mood for games,' Quentin replied. 'All the parking areas are named after fruits.'

'Really. How refreshing. All right, here's how you're going to spend your day. Leave your car but don't lock it. Then go and enjoy a day at the Eden Project. Make sure you go in and don't come out until at least four o'clock unless you hear from me before then. I don't want to hear that you're anywhere near the car. Got that?'

'Yes.'

'Good. Have a nice day, Mr Cadbury.'

The call was cut off.

Leave the car unlocked. That was a bit obvious wasn't it? They intended to put the package in the car while he wasn't there. That way he wouldn't see whoever left it there. No physical contact, no description he could pass on to the police. Risky though. What if the car was broken into or stolen? Unlikely, he decided. This wasn't an inner-city ghetto.

* * *

'Four o'clock?' Wanda echoed when he repeated what he'd been told. 'Does that mean he doesn't know when the package is being dropped off?'

'Your guess is as good as mine. Could be just to wind me up, keep me hanging about again.'

'Well, come and join me. Let Philmore know what he said, then it'll be up to him to mount surveillance on the car park.'

'All right,' Quentin said. He ended the call, reached for his second phone and rang Philmore, who answered immediately.

'What's going on?'

Quentin quickly repeated Cultured Voice's instructions.

'So our friend's still playing us for idiots.' Philmore's tone was one of irritation.

'Only me,' Quentin told him. 'He doesn't know you're here, or Wanda. At least, I don't think he does.'

There was a pause, as though Philmore was trying to think of the best course of action. 'OK,' he said eventually. 'Whereabouts in the car park are you?'

When Quentin had given the information, Philmore carried on. 'You go in like he said. I'll give the surveillance boys your description. I won't be far away and they'll let me know immediately if anyone goes near your car.'

'Let me know too,' Quentin said. Then, as another thought occurred to him, he rushed on, 'Hold on a minute. If you nab whoever delivers this package, our friend will be warned off, and I'll be mincemeat.'

'Don't worry, it's all in hand. Look, for all we know this car business might be a ruse. The package might be handed over inside.'

'That's a possibility I suppose,' Quentin conceded. 'All right, I'll waste another day faffing about looking at plants while a dangerous international criminal sends us on another wild goose chase. And what if someone does make contact while I'm in there? What protection will I have?'

'Don't worry, there will be someone behind you all the time. We've got back-up from the local force.'

Quentin began to think he'd been dropped onto the set of a spy film. He imagined turning round and spotting a figure darting behind a tree or a bush in an attempt not to be seen, or hiding behind a newspaper. Or perhaps a gangster film would be more appropriate. If Cultured Voice was after his blood, anything could happen. A lamb to the slaughter, he thought.

Deciding he had no option but to trust Philmore, Quentin pocketed his phones and Swiss army knife along with his wallet. As an afterthought, he also took the compass. *Expect the unexpected.* At the last minute, he grabbed the last packet of the crisps they'd bought at Exeter, and some dog treats and water for Mozart. Then, wearing his waterproof and scarf against the cold, he boarded a yellow shuttle bus.

On the concourse, he bought a ticket and entered the complex, where Wanda and Mozart were waiting for him. From this elevated position they could see the layout of the place – the way it was cleverly hidden in the dip of what had been a disused quarry, the gardens now planted with shrubs and grasses, the white biodomes dominating the scene like giant golf balls. Even in his apprehensive state, Quentin had to admire it. Someone had designed this very well.

'Oh!' Wanda breathed. 'Just look at this. It's wonderful.'

'It is. It's a long way down though.' Steep steps, already crowded with visitors, lay before them, winding through the middle of the landscaped slope. On one side, a zigzagging path meandered downhill to the attractions.

'Do you think we should stay together?' Wanda asked. 'I mean, if someone's here with a package, they'll report back to the boss, won't they?'

Quentin shrugged. 'Don't know. I suppose it would be safer to stay apart. We've both got our phones.'

Wanda sighed. 'I won't be able to go in anywhere with Mozart. Dogs are only allowed outside and it's not exactly hot today.'

'Well, we're not really here to see the place. Still, we might as well make the most of it. You go in,' Quentin offered, seeing her shiver. 'I'm not fussed about seeing things and you'll enjoy it more than me.'

Wanda grimaced. 'You mean it'll take my mind off the fact that someone might try to kill you?' she asked darkly. 'It's all right, you go first, then come and take Mozart over while I go in.'

'OK. I'll leave you the crisps in case you get peckish. I'll ring when I'm done to find out where you are.'

\* \* \*

The mood of the place was festive, and Quentin spent the next hour in the visitor centre, mingling with the children who rushed about excitedly. Impressive as it was, he couldn't concentrate enough to take in all the information. His mind kept straying to what may be happening in the car park and his eyes kept darting around to see if there was anyone watching him. At midday, he went back to relieve Wanda just as she was about to open the packet of crisps.

'I'll have those,' he offered, seeing her nose reddened with cold. 'You go up to the café, get some food and warm up.'

'I will,' she agreed readily.

Quentin sat on the bench and watched as she walked away, his heart contracting. It had been nearly three years, he reflected, and how his life had changed; from unemployed university dropout to private detective with a gorgeous partner. He only hoped things would stay that way. The thought of being without her filled him with dread.

He found a dog treat in his pocket for Mozart, who jumped up to get it, then sat looking up at him expectantly as he opened the crisps.

'All right,' Quentin said, dropping a couple in front of him. 'Don't tell your mistress.'

When Quentin had finished eating, he leaned his elbows on the wooden table, laced his fingers together and rested his chin on them, thinking again about the man who had brought him over two hundred miles from home. How does anyone have that much influence? he wondered. And this package – if it existed – what was in it? The man had dealt in all sorts of contraband, Quentin knew, but this time he feared it was something worse, something he dreaded the thought of handling. He'd seen enough of it. It had killed his best friend. He shuddered as he thought of Nathan, his promising young life cut short by cocaine. Drug running was as bad as murder in Quentin's book.

Wanda returned with a ham and cheese sandwich and coffee in a cardboard cup. 'Here,' she said, setting them in front of him. 'Stay with Mozart while I go and see the reindeer.'

'Reindeer?'

'Yes, they've got real reindeer here for Christmas. I won't be long.'

And she wasn't. Quentin had only just finished his sandwich when Wanda returned.

'They're lovely,' she told him. 'Very big. There's an ice-skating rink down there too. No good for me though. I can't even roller-skate let alone ice-skate.'

'I can. Mum used to take me and Shelagh when we were kids. I'll have a walk down and take a look.'

Detouring to see the reindeer on the way, he found four or five in an open enclosure, looking well fed and quite at home in their surroundings. Crowds of children stared wide-eyed at the creatures, no doubt imagining them hitched to Santa's sleigh.

Cameras and mobile phones were in evidence, and Quentin caught a rapid movement of an older boy in a baseball cap lowering a camera from his face, then darting behind a group of adults.

The action alerted Quentin and he stiffened. No, he decided after a few moments, it was just a kid taking pictures of some reindeer.

He left the reindeer and wandered down to the huge marquee-like structure that housed the ice rink. It was cold inside, and his breath hung in front of him like a cloud. Holding onto the barrier, he watched the skaters as they whizzed around, feeling sorry for the obvious first timers who held on tightly to other people or the penguin-shaped supports supplied for children.

Quentin felt a pang of nostalgia and had a sudden desire to be gliding on the ice himself. Well, why shouldn't he? Hadn't he been told to enjoy a day at the Eden Project? He glanced at his watch. It wasn't long since he'd left Wanda and he needn't skate for long – just enough to see if he still had the knack.

He hired some skates and ventured onto the ice, his long legs wobbling slightly. Within a few minutes, his confidence had grown. He sped around the rink, exhilarated by the blast of air that rushed past him and the feeling of freedom it gave him. After twenty minutes, he decided he'd had enough and, as he began to make his way off the ice, he spotted a boy in a baseball cap watching him from behind the barrier. He frowned, wondering if it was the same boy he'd seen earlier. He was so busy looking at him that he crashed into another skater, causing her to topple over, taking him with her.

'Sorry,' he gasped, struggling to his feet and helping her up. When she assured him she wasn't hurt, he looked to see if the boy was still there. He wasn't.

Deciding he was being paranoid, he collected his shoes and went to find Wanda.

He had almost reached the place where he'd left her when the ring of his second mobile made him stop. Philmore. Quentin's heart leapt. While he'd been skating something had happened – and he'd missed it.

He held the phone away from his ear as Philmore yelled, 'What the hell are you playing at, Quentin? Where do you think you're going?'

'What do you mean? I'm not going anywhere. I'm still in the Eden Project like we agreed.'

In the pause that followed, Quentin could hear Philmore's rapid breathing. 'Did you hear me, Steve? I said I'm still here.'

His eyes widened with disbelief when Philmore spoke again, his voice low now, as though he was speaking through clenched teeth. 'So if you're still there, who in the name of God is driving your car?'

## Chapter Twelve

'What's the hurry?' Wanda puffed as she tried to keep up with Quentin, Mozart trotting beside her. 'If the car's gone and Philmore's gone after it, what's the point of going to the car park?'

What indeed, Quentin thought, slowing his pace.

'Don't know,' he admitted. 'It's just – it doesn't make sense. Why would he make me come here, more or less spell out that something would be put inside the car, then take it?'

'Perhaps he didn't,' Wanda replied, almost tripping over Mozart's lead. 'It might be a car theft. After all, the car was unlocked.'

'Unlocked yes, but no keys. Whoever took it knew how to start it without keys.'

Quentin said nothing more until they reached the Banana section of the parking area. He didn't know why he felt the need to come here. It was as if he needed to see for himself that the Volvo wasn't there.

It wasn't. In its place was a white Honda Civic.

'Bloody hell!' he spluttered. 'Now what are we supposed to do?'

Wanda sighed. 'Well, I noticed a bus stop on the way in.'

'No bloody fear,' Quentin snapped. 'Philmore can get someone to pick us up.'

'Yes. That could take a while, though. Where are these local cops he told you about?'

The quip Quentin was about to make remained unspoken as his everyday mobile sang out its tune. He checked the screen. Number withheld. Slowly, he raised the phone to his ear. 'Yes?' he said cautiously.

'You can leave now if you wish, Mr Cadbury.'

'Where's my car?' Quentin spat. 'Why the hell have you taken my car?'

'Patience, Mr Cadbury. I take it you're back in the car park. Look in front of you. There should be a white Honda Civic, registration WK05 ABC.'

Startled, Quentin read the number plate of the Honda Civic that stood where the Volvo had been. 'What about it?' he asked, a premonition coming to him.

'That's the car you should be using from now on,' the cultured voice told him smoothly. 'The keys are under the mat on the driver's side. I hope you'll find it as comfortable as the Volvo.'

Quentin caught Wanda's eye and spread his free hand in bewilderment. 'Why do you need me to change cars, for goodness' sake?'

'Just a little insurance policy, that's all, in case you've inadvertently let the Volvo's registration number slip to anyone. We wouldn't want anybody to know where you are or what you're doing, would we?'

Quentin swore and drew an exasperated breath.

'Now, now, Mr Cadbury, no need for bad language. You'll find the package in the boot. It's your responsibility now, so be sure you know where it is at all times.'

'What? Aren't you going to tell me where to take it?'

'Not just yet. The recipient isn't available to collect it at the moment.'

'For God's sake!' Quentin choked out. What the hell did this man expect him to do? Just hang around for goodness knows how long with a suspicious parcel?

'I can hear you're frustrated, but you've only been in Cornwall a few days. There are plenty more nice places to visit. Anyway, I've got a little treat for you. Have you got a pen handy?'

Quentin mouthed "pen" to Wanda and she produced a pen and a notebook from her handbag.

'OK,' Quentin said, moving forward to lean on the car in front of them.

'PL31 2NR. I'd like you to go there tonight. Perhaps when you've seen that luxury you'll understand why I do what I do to maintain my lifestyle. Goodbye, Mr Cadbury, and don't forget, PL31 2NR.'

'What the—' Quentin stopped. He was talking to thin air again.

'They've swapped cars,' he told Wanda through stiff lips. 'The package is in this one.' He bounded forward, found the lever and opened the boot. Nestled in a corner was a brown cardboard parcel, oblong, about the size of a pint mug or glass. Quentin stared at it, unwilling to touch it.

'So this is it then,' Wanda said, coming up behind him. 'What do you think it is?'

Quentin didn't answer. He knew very well Wanda thought the same as him. She just didn't want to admit it.

'Leave it where it is,' she said, laying her hand on his arm. 'If we don't touch it, it won't have our fingerprints or DNA on it. If anything happens we can say it was planted there.'

'If anything happens? You mean if we're stopped by the drugs squad before we deliver it? That won't happen, will it? Philmore's got our backs. At least, he'd better have.'

'Yes, but it won't be so easy now, without the tracker. We'll have to keep in contact by phone.'

'What a bloody fiasco,' Quentin moaned. 'And look, they've left our map. How considerate of them.' He took out the map and slammed the boot shut. 'That bastard's sitting tight somewhere, laughing at us while we're running our backsides off.' He tried to imagine his adversary smiling in cruel satisfaction. All he could see was The Joker of Batman fame.

'We'll have to handle the package to deliver it,' he said bitterly. 'I've a good mind to throw it somewhere it won't be found or chuck the whole thing in and hand it over to Philmore.'

Wanda pursed her lips. 'There's nothing I'd like more, but that won't solve anything. This load of crooks will still be free and Cultured Voice will come after you with a vengeance. Me too, probably. Come on. It's no good thinking like this. Let's get in the car and call Philmore.'

Quentin found the keys under the driver's mat and slid in behind the wheel. While Wanda put Mozart in the back and settled herself in the passenger seat, Quentin rang Philmore.

'They've left another car here in place of the Volvo, a Honda Civic,' he explained. 'Why did you think it was me driving the Volvo?'

Philmore grunted. 'The surveillance guys had your description and said it looked like you. There were two of them in the Volvo but they didn't see the second until they were in the car and then not clearly; they couldn't see if it was a man or a woman, but they assumed it was Wanda.'

'Right,' Quentin said. 'Well, I've got the package but I've got to hold on to it until he tells me what to do with it.'

'Really? What the hell's he playing at now?'

Quentin felt Philmore's exasperation.

'Lord only knows,' Quentin replied. 'But he's given me the postcode for a place where he wants me to stay tonight. Maybe I've got to hand the package over there, or leave it in a room or something, though from what he said I'll be stuck with it for a while yet.'

'Why on earth would he bring you over two hundred miles to transport a package and risk leaving it with you?' Philmore said. 'It doesn't make sense.'

'No,' Quentin agreed. 'I thought I'd have to take it to another part of the country. That's the impression I got originally. Maybe he's testing me. What's going on with you?'

'A blooming farce, that's what. We're still following the runaways, but we don't want to spook them. We want to know where they go in case they lead us to Whitelaw, but we're not interested in small fry. If they lead us nowhere, we'll back off. I'm pretty sure they haven't spotted us yet.'

'Let's hope they don't or our friend will know you're on to him.' Regretting the words as soon as he'd said them, Quentin hurried on, hoping Philmore didn't think he was criticising his actions. 'What should I do now? Go where he told me to?'

'Yes. What's the registration number of this new vehicle?'

'Can't remember. Hold on a mo.' Quentin checked the number Wanda had written next to the postcode and relayed it. 'It's white,' he added. 'How are you going to back me up if you're following the runaways?'

'There'll be back-up – oh, got to go. Ring when you get there.'

Silence filled Quentin's ear.

'Well?' Wanda said as he lowered the phone.

Quentin shrugged. 'He hung up in a hurry. We've got to go on to this place like that moron said.'

That his tormentor was far from a moron, Quentin knew perfectly well. It wasn't only his voice that was cultured. From the crimes the man had been involved in previously, Quentin was sure his knowledge was extensive, that he'd dealt with the higher echelons of society as well as low-life thieves and ruffians.

'Not "our friend" anymore then?' Wanda jibed. 'All right, not funny. You do realize all our things are in that car, don't you?' she went on. 'All our clothes, Mozart's food?'

'That's the least of our worries,' Quentin said, typing the postcode Cultured Voice had given him into the satnav. 'We can buy clothes and dog food and we've got the important things with us.'

He thought of his two mobiles, his wallet, his Swiss army knife and the compass stuffed into his pockets. Wanda had also insisted that she kept his passport with her, and he knew she carried her purse, driving licence, house keys and mobile in her handbag at all times.

It took them less than half an hour to get to Bodmin from the Eden Project, passing through green fields shielded from the road by hedgerows, with white, chalk-like hills and tors rising above them.

'This is clay country,' Wanda told him. 'They make china from the clay they quarry here. It was a huge industry once.'

Quentin didn't answer. He wasn't in the mood for a geography lesson. He drove on, slowing as a tractor pulled out from a crossroads in front of them. The single carriageway didn't allow for overtaking, so they sat behind the slow-moving vehicle, Quentin tapping his fingers on the steering wheel impatiently. He supposed that if he was on holiday he would enjoy the slow pace of the country lanes, but he wasn't on holiday. If he didn't get this right, he may never be on holiday again.

'Not far now,' Wanda observed as they passed a road sign. 'Perhaps you should let me out just before we get there, in case I'm seen.'

'It's a hotel. He hasn't been at either of the other two hotels we've stayed at.'

'That's because he didn't know where you were. He knows this one.'

'I suppose there might be someone there watching,' he said. 'There was at Bradford Bridge. I won't book in yet, though. I'll just see where it is and then we'll go into town. We need new phone chargers.'

They carried on until they found the right location and drove up and down looking for a hotel. There wasn't one, not even a bed and breakfast. The building that dominated the road stood dark and forbidding, with high stone walls and a tall, sentinel turret. "Bodmin Jail", Quentin read on the gates, and then: "The Bodmin Jail Experience".

'Nice hotel,' Wanda quipped.

Seeing a couple approaching, Quentin wound down the window. 'Excuse me,' he called as they drew near. 'Is there a hotel in this road?'

The man shook his head. 'No, nothing in this road.'

The woman interrupted. 'They keep talking about making the jail into a boutique hotel, but who knows when they'll get round to it.'

The couple walked on and for a moment Quentin thought that he'd either misheard the cultured voice or that he'd been given the wrong postcode. He tried to recall what his adversary had said. *I'd like you to go there tonight. Perhaps when you've seen that luxury, you'll understand why I do what I do to maintain my lifestyle.* He hadn't actually mentioned a hotel. And he hadn't given the wrong postcode. Cultured Voice meant him to come here, to a jail, even if it was no longer in use. He wanted Quentin to realize that he wasn't just an ordinary criminal who'd been sent to prison, he was someone who prison hadn't been able to contain. And someone who used crime to make enough money and employ the right people to keep him out of jail.

Shaking his head in disbelief, Quentin imagined Cultured Voice laughing up his sleeve at this joke, at how Quentin would feel when he realized he'd been the butt of that joke.

He was jolted out of his musings when his phone rang. Number withheld. What did the man want now? To gloat over his ill-placed prank?

'Yes?' he said, deciding not to give Cultured Voice the courtesy of a proper greeting.

'Are you there yet, Mr Cadbury?'

'Yes,' Quentin said again.

'Good.' There was a hint of amusement in the cultured tones. 'Perhaps now you can understand a little of my side of things. Now, I'm trusting you to take care of my package. I should hate it to fall into the wrong hands. As I said, the recipient can't get to the appointed place just yet, so it's entirely in your hands, as indeed is your future. You do want a future, don't you, Mr Cadbury?'

'Of course I do! Why the hell else would I be running after you like a lackey?'

'Lackey. What an old-fashioned term.'

'Look,' Quentin interrupted, 'how long is this going on for?'

'As long as it takes. I'll try not to inconvenience you too much, but I hardly think another couple of days in Cornwall is a great hardship. Keep your phone charged and your petrol tank full. Don't stray too far from the Eden Project area. And look after my package.'


## Chapter Thirteen


'Baloney!' Quentin said to Wanda later.

After driving into the town he'd managed to get new phone chargers while Wanda was busy replacing the things they'd lost from the Volvo. Then they'd found the nearest pub. A pint of beer mellowed Quentin's mood.

'I don't believe a word of it,' he went on. 'The recipient's not available! He's having me on.'

Wanda looked at him coolly. 'What did Philmore say?'

Quentin recalled Philmore's stony reaction when he'd rung him.

'Not much. Not what he wanted to say, I'm sure, but what can he do? If he wants to nail this guy, he's got to stick with it. He's going to get another tracking device fitted to the new car.'

'Oh,' Wanda said, sounding relieved. 'That's something then. Did he say what happened when they chased the Volvo?'

'Yeah, nothing. They followed it to a caravan park near Truro. Two people, but not our friend so they called it a day.'

'I suppose this guy's got better things to do than steal cars himself,' Wanda said. 'Anyway, the police can check out the caravan owner, or who's been renting it, and search it later rather than give the game away now.'

'Yep, that's pretty much it. The local police are keeping them under surveillance.'

'Right. OK, so we'll be needing somewhere to stay again. I don't like this place much,' Wanda went on. 'Let's go back to where we were last night. They won't be full at this time of year and it was nice there.'

Her mobile rang and she retrieved it from her handbag. 'Colin,' she mouthed when she saw the number.

Not relishing a conversation with Colin, even an overheard one, Quentin stood up and went to the bar. He needed another drink and knew Wanda had drunk a glass of wine. Making a swift decision, he ordered a whisky for himself and a lime and soda for Wanda, hoping she wouldn't mind driving.

If Wanda minded, she didn't say so. She just took her lime and soda, her mobile still in her hand.

'How's Colin?' Quentin asked. 'Did you tell him what fun we're having? You can take him back a pasty. We'll have plenty of time to buy one. Or two. Or twenty-two.'

Wanda opened her mouth as if to speak, then closed it again.

'If we're going back to that pub, we should go now,' she said after several sips of her drink.

'The Travelodge is nearer,' Quentin said. 'That'll do. It'll be easier for Philmore to find as well. I don't suppose they'll bother with the new tracker till the morning. It doesn't look as though we'll be dashing off anywhere yet. Still...' He broke off, recalling Whitelaw's words. *Keep your phone charged and your petrol tank full.* Didn't that imply he could be sent somewhere far away at any time? *Expect the unexpected.*

'The Travelodge it is then,' Wanda said, a little too briskly.

Quentin guessed she didn't want to argue, and blessed her for it. He very rarely dismissed her suggestions, but tonight he just wanted to flop out on the nearest bed and sleep. He downed his Scotch and called to Mozart, who wriggled out from under the table and looked up expectantly.

Wanda swallowed the remains of her drink. 'Come on then.'

On the way, Quentin rang Philmore and told them where they were headed. When they got there, the receptionist remembered them, or rather she remembered Mozart.

'Hello again, my lover.' She grinned, leaning over the counter. 'I've got the perfect room for you.'

Animal appeal, Quentin thought. It opens more doors and strikes up more conversations than anything else.

'What about the package?' Wanda asked when they unpacked the car. 'We'd better not risk leaving it out here overnight.'

'No,' Quentin said. Reaching for one of the plastic carrier bags Wanda had got in town, he tipped the contents into another and kept hold of the empty bag. 'I'll use it like a glove,' he explained, 'then I won't have to touch it.'

'Good idea,' Wanda said. 'I always knew you had a brain somewhere.'

Ignoring her, Quentin collected the package. While Wanda took Mozart for a walk, Quentin went back to the hotel, holding the carrier bag as though he thought it might explode. Once inside, he stowed the package on a shelf, kicked off his shoes and collapsed onto the bed.

He must have dozed for a few minutes before he heard the low tones of Wanda's voice in the corridor. The door opened and she came in, her phone clutched in her hand.

'Who were you talking to?' he asked, his eyes half-closed.

'Oh, only Colin,' she said nonchalantly.

'Again? What did he want this time?'

'Nothing, really. You're tired. Go to sleep. We'll talk in the morning.'

She settled Mozart, undressed and slipped into bed beside Quentin, as though trying not to disturb him. Quentin turned, sighed, and snuggled up against her, realizing sleepily that this was the third night he'd missed an opportunity to make love to her.

Slightly refreshed after his doze, he whispered, 'I'm not that tired.'

'Well, I am,' she told him firmly, removing his hand from her breast.

Oh well, Quentin thought, there's always tomorrow. After all, we won't have anything else to do.

\* \* \*

He was awakened at seven forty-five in the morning by a phone call from DS Francis to say that they'd found the

Honda in the car park and that a new tracking device had been fitted.

'Good,' Wanda said, stretching her limbs and yawning. 'That's one thing we don't have to worry about then. Is it eleven o'clock they stop serving breakfast?'

'I think so,' Quentin said. 'So there's no hurry, is there?'

Wanda gazed at him from under her lashes. 'No,' she said huskily, then groaned as Mozart leapt up and placed his front paws on the bed and licked her hand.

'Down, boy,' Quentin said, expecting Wanda to say he needed to go out. When she didn't, he went on, 'You can hold on a bit longer, can't you, Mote?'

'He can,' Wanda said, 'if you ask him nicely.'

Quentin grinned and leaned over her. Her fair hair spilled out across the pillow and her naked shoulders showed white and creamy above the duvet.

'Pleeease,' he murmured not taking his eyes from her face, 'can you hold on a bit longer?'

'No,' she breathed, her eyes smoky with desire. 'Can you?'

\* \* \*

It was nearly nine o'clock when his second phone rang.

'Hello, Steve,' he said, rousing himself from the slumber he'd fallen into and realizing that Wanda was already in the shower.

'Christ, Quentin,' Philmore yelled. 'What the blazes are you doing now?'

Quentin blinked and sat up. 'Having a lie-in. Why?'

'Having a– both of you? You and Wanda?'

'Yes. What's going on, Steve?'

Silence, except for muffled background noises which told Quentin that Philmore definitely wasn't having a lie-in.

'I don't believe this!' Philmore ranted.

Quentin heard a feminine voice, though he couldn't make out what it said. He heard Philmore's when it came again though, and the reigned-in anger when he spoke.

'It's bloody well happened again. What's wrong with this idiot – is he stealing cars for his collection or what?'

Quentin jumped out of bed, ran to the window and stared into the car park. Wanda, emerging from the bathroom wrapped in a towel, stood still when she saw the phone at Quentin's ear.

'Steve.' Quentin gulped, blinked and pressed his face to the glass. 'Steve, our car's still here.'

Philmore's reply was so loud it hurt Quentin's ear. He put the phone on loudspeaker and held it away from his head.

'What do mean it's still there?'

'I mean it's still here. I'm looking at it now.'

Another silence. Then, 'A white Honda Civic, you said. That's what the tracker was attached to and that's what we're following.'

Quentin looked at Wanda, baffled. 'It can't be ours, Steve, because ours is still here. What's the registration number?'

'What? If you tell me we're following the wrong bloody car I'll slaughter you. Debbie, get closer.'

The background noises grew louder, and Quentin guessed Philmore had lowered the phone while they tried to catch up with the car they had so far been keeping a safe distance from.

'LW05 ABD,' Philmore said after a series of expletives. 'That's not the one you gave me yesterday, is it?'

An irrepressible smile tugged at Quentin's mouth and his lips twitched. 'No,' he said. 'Ours is WK05 ABC.'

'Of all the stupid, incompetent–'

Quentin didn't hear any more because the call was cut off. Philmore's last accusations weren't directed at him, he realized, but at the person who'd fitted the tracker. That would have been one of the local technicians, overseen,

Quentin surmised, by Debbie Francis. He cringed at the thought of the earbashing Francis was getting from Philmore, yet he couldn't stop himself laughing at the idea of Philmore in the unmarked police vehicle weaving in and out of the traffic to keep up with what he thought was Quentin's car.

'They've only fitted the tracker to the wrong car,' he told Wanda, chuckling. 'What are the chances of two cars, the same model and colour, being in the car park at the same time?' His grin widened. 'Now who's playing Inspector Clouseau?'

Wanda was sitting on the bed, an anxious look on her face.

'What? Come on, Wanda,' Quentin said, surprised at her reaction. 'You've got to admit it's funny. I mean, I suppose the registration numbers are similar, but at the end of the day the car they're chasing isn't ours.'

Wanda shook her head, took a deep breath and avoided his eyes.

'No,' she whispered. 'It's Colin's.'

## Chapter Fourteen

The grin on Quentin's face fell away like a mask from a Harlequin.

'Colin's! What the bloody hell is he doing here?' He rounded on Wanda, his mouth tightening. 'And how did he know where we were?'

Wanda didn't answer.

'So that's why he's been ringing you so much,' Quentin went on, 'to find out where we are. Why didn't you say so?'

'I didn't even know he was in the area until yesterday. He asked to be kept posted and I thought it was only fair to tell him. It couldn't do any harm, could it? How was I to know he'd drive all the way here? I had no idea where he was when he phoned. Anyway, when he called me last night, you know, when we were in the pub, he said he was in Launceston and wanted to know where we were.'

'So you told him!'

'Why wouldn't I? He's no threat to anything and we might need him. Look, I didn't tell you last night because you were in no mood to hear it and I didn't want any of your sarcastic remarks. I planned to tell you after breakfast, when you'd had a good night's sleep and felt better.'

'Did you tell him we'd be here last night?'

'Yes. I didn't know he was coming here though. I thought he'd be staying in Launceston.'

'So how can you be sure it's Colin's car?'

'The registration number.'

'Right,' Quentin said, mollified. 'So why are you looking so worried now? Scared me and Colin will be at each other's throats again?'

A wan smile touched Wanda's lips.

'Since when have I been scared of you or Colin? It's Philmore I'm worried about. What do you think he'll say when he finds out it's a friend of ours who's turned up out of the blue and led them a merry chase?'

Quentin groaned, imagining Philmore transferring his earbashing from his sergeant to him and Wanda.

'It's not our fault they fitted the tracker to the wrong car, is it?' Quentin spread his hands and began pacing the floor. 'And he can't blame Colin. It's not his fault we've got the same car as him. We didn't exactly choose the car ourselves.'

'No,' Wanda agreed, 'and Colin's car couldn't have been parked anywhere near ours or they would have noticed there were two of the same type of car and checked the number plate more carefully.'

'That's true. Well, it's not the end of the world. Everybody makes mistakes.'

A grimace flitted over Wanda's face.

'Philmore won't like it though. He won't want it reflecting on him. I'm guessing we'll be sworn to secrecy.'

She caught Quentin's eye and they both laughed.

'We needed some light relief,' she said, standing up. 'Can you take Mozart out while I get dressed? He must be bursting by now.'

\* \* \*

The earbashing from Philmore was much milder than Quentin had expected. At eleven o'clock, Philmore and DS Francis appeared at their door, followed by Colin a few minutes later. Philmore pushed his way into the room and sat on the dressing table chair while Francis remained standing, her eyes cast down and looking somewhat sheepish.

'Well now,' Philmore said after an uncomfortable silence. 'I think we've had enough of the theatricals. It's bad enough us having to stay out of sight as well as you, Wanda, and now you're here, Mr Ward. Can we expect anyone else to rally to your call, Quentin?'

'I didn't call them, Steve. They're only trying to help. It's just coincidence that Colin's car is the same as the one left for me, and getting the cars mixed up is an easy mistake to make.' Quentin glanced at Francis when he said this, feeling her discomfort.

'Yes, Steve,' Wanda purred, turning her cornflower gaze on him. 'If it's anyone's fault, it's mine. I insisted on coming with Quentin and I'm the one who told Colin where we were. I didn't think he would follow us, but it's only because he's worried about me.'

'Very noble of him,' Philmore grunted, 'but this is a police matter. Mr Ward, Colin, I must ask you not to get involved. It would only complicate things, and things are complicated enough.'

'Are they?' Quentin huffed, his earlier amusement replaced by irritation. 'Seems pretty straightforward to me. I just wait around till he tells me what to do, do it and then get the hell out. Or not.'

'It's not about you though, is it?' Francis said darkly. 'This bloke's an international criminal and he's got to be stopped.'

'Oh yes, I forgot. You need to make an arrest to cover up the fact that you've let him slip through your fingers – how many times is it now?'

'Quentin!' Wanda glared at him, then turned to Philmore. 'You'll have to forgive Quentin, Steve. I think the pressure's getting to him.'

Quentin was tempted to remind her that he was only voicing what she'd said a few days before, but resisted. Tensing, he waited for Philmore's rebuke.

'Sorry,' he said when it didn't come. 'It's all this waiting around.'

He sent an apologetic look to DS Francis.

'I didn't mean just you,' he explained. 'I meant the police force in general, abroad as well as in the UK.'

'Let's get back to the matter in hand,' Philmore said sharply. 'The guys who took the car from the Eden Project – they're father and son, apparently. We've got the names and the address they gave at the caravan park and we've checked them. Neither of them are on our database and the address doesn't exist. We won't bring them in. That would give the game away. If there's any chance of catching this bastard, we've got to take it. I'm not letting him go again.'

'What about the Volvo?' Quentin asked. 'It's still got the tracker on, hasn't it?'

Philmore nodded. 'Found abandoned, north of Truro somewhere. We'll keep it for a while – forensics might get something from it.'

'What about our bags?' Wanda asked.

'No trace of anything inside. Whatever was there, they took.'

'So they drove our car away,' Quentin said, puzzled, 'then dumped it? And took our bags? Why?'

'Probably because that's what they were told to do,' Francis said.

'All right,' Philmore continued. 'Let's get one thing straight. Do not – repeat, *not* – go anywhere without telling me. Got that?'

'We haven't,' Wanda protested.

'And you, Colin,' Philmore went on as if he hadn't heard her. 'Don't be seen anywhere near them. I really think you should stay somewhere else, or better still, go home and take Wanda with you.'

'I'd go if Wanda agreed to come with me,' Colin offered. 'But she won't.'

Wanda's generous mouth set in a stubborn line.

'I'm not deserting Quentin. And I am a detective, in case you've forgotten, Steve.'

Philmore exchanged glances with Francis as if to endorse his belief that all private detectives were amateurs who spent more time getting in the way of police investigations than anything else. Quentin half expected Francis to roll her eyes, but she held her composure.

'Steve's right, Wanda,' Quentin said gently. 'It's me he wants. If anything happened to you, I'd never forgive myself.'

'I haven't been in the way so far, have I?' Wanda demanded. 'I've kept out of sight.'

'All the same,' Philmore said.

'All right.' Wanda rose and walked to the window. 'If it's that big a deal, I won't go anywhere with Quentin, though we've already broken the rules, haven't we? I mean, we weren't supposed to involve the police, but here you are in the same room as us!'

Philmore flinched. 'Well,' he said. 'He may be clever but he can't see through walls, nor can anyone else he may have watching us. Look, Wanda, I know you can handle yourself, but it's not just you who'll be in danger if you're seen. It will make Quentin's position much more dangerous if he's found to be flouting instructions.'

'I realize that,' Wanda snapped. 'Why do you think I've been waiting around in cafés when he's been on his jaunts?'

Colin intervened. 'It's all right, Inspector.' Not having been as involved with Philmore as Quentin, Colin still referred to Philmore as Inspector. Erroneously, as it should have been Chief Inspector.

'We won't interfere. I'll keep Wanda company while Quentin is doing his bit.'

'Right,' Philmore said. 'Well, see you do. We've fitted the tracker to your car, Quentin – yes, the right one this time. I've organised for one of the dogs to have a sniff at the package, so we'll need you to bring it outside in about an hour to see if they can detect any drugs.'

Philmore stood up. 'Come on, Debbie. We'll wait for the dog handlers then it looks like we've got an afternoon off.'

# Chapter Fifteen

'It's a funny thing,' Colin said when Philmore and Francis had gone, 'but I get the distinct feeling Philmore wasn't pleased to see me.'

'Nothing funny about that,' Quentin said gloomily. 'Why are you here, Colin?'

'To help, if I can. There must be something I can do, even if it's only looking after Wanda.'

This earned him a glare from Wanda. 'I don't need looking after, thanks very much,' she said, rounding on him.

'I know you don't, love, but you know–'

Wanda lifted a warning hand. 'If you say you promised Gerry you'd look out for me, I'll scream!'

'Well, I did, but that's not the reason, not now,' Colin added with a meaningful look at Quentin. 'I just want to make sure you're all right, and you did say I could be in from the beginning this time. You should bring me up to speed on what's been happening.'

When Wanda relayed everything that had happened since arriving in Cornwall, Colin nodded.

'Right,' he said. 'So you think he's playing cat and mouse? And this package – sniffer dogs? Wouldn't it be easier for Philmore to look?'

'No,' Quentin said. 'We daren't risk tampering with it, not at this stage.'

'Why not?' Colin asked. 'I should think Philmore had the resources to be able to open the parcel and put it back together again without it being noticed, or X-ray it or something.'

'We're pretty sure it's drugs,' Quentin told him. 'I think so, and I think Philmore does too.'

'This Whitelaw's never been involved with drugs before, has he?' Colin asked.

Quentin shrugged. 'Not that we know of, but that doesn't mean anything. He's got fingers in lots of dirty pies.'

'OK. Well, I suppose there's nothing for it but to wait. Cheer up, Wanda. At least you won't be on your own when Quentin has to go off somewhere.'

Wanda gave him a weak grin. 'I know, Colin. Well, we've missed breakfast. Shall we go out somewhere for lunch?'

'Might as well,' Quentin said. 'There's bound to be somewhere close by.'

'Fowey's not far,' Colin said. 'There's a good pub right on the water. They serve lovely fish and chips.'

'So you're a tour guide now?' Quentin jibed.

'I was here last summer with Emma, if you must know,' Colin said. 'We came to Cornwall a lot when she was young too. Still, you don't have to take my word for it. You don't take it for anything else.'

'Shut up, both of you,' Wanda said, 'or I'll go and get the bus and you two can have a cosy tête-à-tête together.'

Quentin caught Colin's eye and grimaced. 'Sorry,' he said grudgingly. 'Truce, Colin?'

Colin grinned as he answered, 'Truce.'

'Honestly, you two,' Wanda said, linking each arm into one of theirs. 'Acting like a couple of schoolboys. You ought to be past that by now.'

* * *

After the police dog had done its job, it seemed the package could possibly contain drugs of some kind, though Philmore warned that this wasn't always accurate. It was enough to convince Quentin though, and he viewed it with more disdain than ever. Philmore also got the dog to check Quentin's Honda in case anything had been concealed before it had been left at the Eden Project, but it seemed that was clear.

When they were ready to go out for lunch, Quentin put the usual items in his pockets along with his phone chargers, and put the package into a holdall, borrowed from Colin, in case he was told to go somewhere while they were out.

'Is that likely?' Wanda asked. 'He said a couple of days, didn't he?'

'That doesn't mean it will be. He's not exactly predictable,' Quentin said; then he rang Philmore to let him know where they were going.

'You don't need to track me,' he told him. 'If I hear from our friend I'll ring straight away and you can pick up my trail from the signal.'

He pocketed the phone and turned to Wanda and Colin. 'We'll take separate cars, just in case,' he said. 'Let's go.'

* * *

Under normal circumstances Quentin would have enjoyed his visit to Fowey. Even in the December chill it was charming, with its narrow roads and ancient cottages with crooked windows. From the pub, they could see over the river, its myriad boats and ferries to the opposite bank giving the scene a nautical theme.

After what Quentin had to admit was a good fish and chip lunch, they strolled along the main streets. Quentin gripped the handles of the bag Colin had lent him as though he was afraid someone would mug him. Wanda examined the tiny shop windows loaded with Cornish curiosities. She bought a book in a shop dedicated to the author Daphne du Maurier, some dog treats for Mozart, and a cream tea to take back to the hotel.

'Come on,' Colin said, 'I'll take you on a pretty route back.'

In his own car, Quentin followed Colin and Wanda on a scenic tour, and relaxed enough to take in the countryside with its rolling hills, valleys and fields. What drew his attention most were the derelict tin mines, their cylindrical chimneys rising from the shells of the old engine houses and piercing the skyline like sentinels; an ever-present reminder of a long-ago trade – romantic in the daytime, but eerie by night, Quentin guessed.

He hadn't got far when his phone rang. A premonition coming to him, he pulled over to check the display. Number withheld. So much for a couple of days, he thought as he watched Colin and Wanda disappear around a bend.

'Yes?' he answered, apprehension rising.

'How are you doing, Mr Cadbury?'

'All right, I suppose.'

'Are you looking after my package?'

'Yes.'

'Have you got it with you?'

'Yes.'

'Excellent. And where are you exactly?'

'Not far from Fowey.'

'How convenient. Here's what you'll do next. Drive to Charlestown. Quite a picturesque place, I think, with those tall ships and the like. They do a lot of filming there, apparently, make TV programmes and so on. Do you watch much TV, Mr Cadbury?'

'Not really,' Quentin said, wondering what was coming and fighting the urge to tell his adversary to get on with it.

'You can learn a lot if you're selective in your viewing. Then again, there's nothing like the real thing, is there?'

Quentin shook his head, at a loss as to how to answer.

'So,' the cultured voice went on, 'your next task. You'll see the real thing in Charlestown. When you get there, go to the Shipwreck Museum and wait outside till you hear from me. Got that?'

'Yes.'

'Good. Thirty minutes, Mr Cadbury, and it'll pay you to remember what I've said.'

When the line went dead Quentin switched phones and called Philmore.

'Charlestown,' he blurted. 'Outside the Shipwreck Museum.'

'On the way,' came the response.

Quentin tried to ring Wanda and Colin but they must have been out of signal.

'Bloody hell,' he muttered, and punched out a text telling them where he was going.

When he was back on the main road, he drove the seven miles to Charlestown, following the signs. Finding a space on the roadside, he parked, picked up the holdall with the package and walked down towards the harbour.

The town was busy despite the cold of the December day, and Quentin mingled with the people going in the same direction. Even with the urgency of the situation on his mind, he couldn't help pausing to take in the sight of the two wooden ships moored side by side at their berths, their ancient gangplanks swaying precariously in the breeze and their tall masts piercing the skyline. For an instant, he imagined himself on one of them; an eighteenth-century mariner with over two hundred years between him and his present predicament.

The image vanished as he saw a signpost pointing to the Shipwreck Museum. Stomach churning, he turned towards it. The breeze stiffened, and he shuffled from foot to foot as he waited outside the museum, looking at his watch and counting the minutes.

A slight figure in a grey hoodie loitered at the far end of the building. As Quentin glimpsed it, the figure darted behind a group of people gathered by the ships. The boy from the ice rink? No baseball cap, so Quentin couldn't be sure.

Before he had time to think about it, the expected call came.

'Yes?'

'You're there then, Mr Cadbury. What do you think?'

Quentin grimaced. What was he supposed to say?

'It's very – evocative,' he said cautiously.

'I'm glad you think so. Are there many people about?'

'Quite a few, yes.'

'What else can you see?'

He's trying to find out if I'm really here, Quentin thought.

'Well, it's nearly Christmas, so there are lights and Christmas trees–'

'Very droll, Mr Cadbury. I'm sure there are lights and Christmas trees everywhere. You must be able to see more interesting things than that.'

'Well... there're the ships of course.'

There was a pause before the cultured voice came again.

'Really, I thought you were more observant. You're supposed to be a detective, aren't you? But you obviously don't know the real thing when you see it. I hope you're more observant when you're guarding my package. I'll be in touch.'

The call ended abruptly, leaving Quentin staring at his phone as though by some magic an explanation would appear on the blank screen. Snapping the lid shut, he turned and looked about him. He was meant to notice something, but what? And what did it have to do with the package?

With no further instructions, Quentin wondered what to do. Was he expected to search the place for something and report his findings the next time he spoke to Cultured Voice? Or was this a hoax to rattle him, or to make sure he was following orders?

Sliding the mobile into his pocket, he took out the second one and called Philmore.

'Nothing doing,' he said. 'He's just winding me up again. He keeps saying I should find the real thing, whatever that means.'

'Probably means something to him. So what have you got to do now?'

'He didn't say. He just said he'll be in touch.'

'Oh. If he wanted you to do anything else today he'd have said so, wouldn't he?'

'Yeah, he usually does, or he at least says when he'll call back.'

Philmore sighed. 'Another wasted journey for us then.'

'Looks like it,' Quentin said, echoing Philmore's sigh. 'I think I'll have a look round for an hour, see if I can spot what he's on about. If I don't hear anything else from him, I'll head back to the hotel.'

He rang off and started walking, studying the ships from all angles, passing over the bridge that joined one side of the berth to the other. He could see nothing relating to what Cultured Voice had said, so he went down to the sea wall and checked the stall selling shells, then looked over the wall to the beach. Nothing there either.

Checking his mobile to make sure he hadn't missed a call, he noticed a text from Wanda.

*We're here. I can see you – is it safe to ring?*

Quentin rang her himself. 'Where are you?' he asked, scanning the area.

'Over by the pub,' she replied. 'By the door.'

Quentin looked over at the pub opposite the ship berth. There was a throng of people milling about on the pavement. He searched for a blonde head but couldn't see one. Raising his gaze to the elevated terrace above, he saw a lone figure sitting at a table by the pub door. No blonde head, but definitely a female wearing sunglasses and a black snood.

'OK,' he said. 'Where's Colin?'

'I don't know. We split up.'

Quickly Quentin relayed what had happened since he'd been in Charlestown.

'The real thing?' Wanda queried. 'What's all that about?'

'Lord knows, but he said it three times.'

'Hmm. Well, I've got a good view from here. I haven't seen anyone tailing you or hanging about since I've been here, but keep away just in case. I'll stay here for a bit. Why don't you look around for another half an hour and if nothing happens, just go.'

Quentin made another circuit of the area, absorbing as much as he could. Ending up back outside the Shipwreck Museum, he looked at the building and the immediate vicinity, his gaze flickering over the windows and the advertising billboard for the adjacent café. Nothing remotely connected to his situation as far as he could see. Cultured Voice was talking in riddles.

He wondered if he should have gone inside the museum. No. Cultured Voice had asked what he could see, knowing he was outside.

He looked up to where he'd seen Wanda, but she wasn't there, so he texted her.

*Leaving now.*

He began the uphill walk to where he'd left the car. He'd just reached it when his phone pinged with a message. Wanda.

*How about this?*

Quentin stared at the photo she'd attached.

A gasp escaped him as he made sense of what he was seeing. An advert? Yes, an advert on the billboard he'd noticed. Pictures of fish and chips, burgers, apple pie, milkshake and, bigger than all these, a bottle. A bottle with a familiar red label. Coca-Cola, the label told him. And underneath, in bold black lettering: "The Real Thing".

Bloody hell! What was he supposed to make of that?

Before he had time to think, his mobile trilled.

'Are you still there, Mr Cadbury?' the cultured voice asked when he answered.

'I am.'

'And have your powers of observation increased?'

Quentin's thoughts raced. 'I believe they have.'

'So you know what the real thing is then?'

'Yes.'

There was a pause. Quentin waited for the question he was dreading.

'Excellent. And what do you make of it?'

Here goes, Quentin thought, praying he'd drawn the right conclusion.

'I presume it's a nod to the package I'm carrying.'

'Correct! Perhaps you'll make a good employee after all. That's all for now. Stay on your toes, Mr Cadbury.'

Numb with shock, Quentin wrenched open the car door and collapsed into the driver's seat. So it was true. He was walking around with at least half a kilo of cocaine on him.

\* \* \*

As soon as he drove the Honda into the hotel car park Quentin switched off the engine and sat staring through the windscreen. He felt wrung out. It seemed that Cultured Voice, not content with sending him on fruitless journeys, was playing mind games with him now. And how had he missed that advert for Coca-Cola? Coke, as it was often called; the real thing, like the popular song. He had looked directly at that billboard but not made the connection.

'Don't beat yourself up about it,' Wanda said when they were alone in their room. 'Not many people would have got it.'

'You did,' Quentin pointed out, wondering how he would have felt if he'd had to admit defeat to Cultured Voice. 'You saved the day.'

'Of course I did! I'm applying for *Mastermind* next series, didn't I tell you? Seriously, it's just a bit of lateral thinking. It's all the crosswords I do.'

'What I want to know,' Quentin said slowly, 'is how he even knew the Coca-Cola advert was there.'

Wanda raised an eyebrow. 'It wasn't part of the original picture.'

Mystified, Quentin watched her reach into her handbag. She drew out an object and passed it to him. It was some sort of light metal, shaped like a Coca-Cola bottle, with the tagline "The Real Thing" added at the bottom. On the underside was a magnet. The puzzle that had formed in Quentin's brain slipped into place like pieces of a jigsaw.

'The billboard must have been metal,' he mused. 'The boy I saw – he must have put it there. What sort of mind would think up a trick like that?'

'A clever one,' Wanda said. 'Anyway, it's done now. We can relax for the rest of the day.'

Quentin's jaw tightened. Relax. Another evening of waiting around, babysitting a package he wanted nothing to do with.

Nevertheless, the evening passed pleasantly enough, with Colin joining them in their room for their cream tea.

'I knew this would come in handy,' Quentin said, cutting the scones with his Swiss army knife.

'As needs must,' Wanda said, tearing the cream tea box into three to use as plates as Quentin began spreading cream on his scone.

'I can tell you haven't been to Cornwall before,' Colin said scathingly. 'It's jam first, then cream.'

Quentin paused momentarily, looking at Wanda for confirmation. 'Seriously? There's a wrong way to eat a scone?'

'That's right,' Wanda said over the hiss of the kettle. 'Cream first in Devon, jam first in Cornwall. You can't spread the jam once the cream is on,' she added, her face deadpan.

They sat around the room, munching and trying to forget that they were here on a mission and not on holiday.

'You've got cream on your glasses, Colin,' Wanda told him, handing him a tissue.

Colin removed his glasses and wiped away the cream, then polished them with the hem of his shirt, a habit he'd had ever since Quentin had known him. Quentin watched him, feeling a bubble of laughter rising inside. Colin looked slightly ridiculous sitting on the bed eating scones from a piece of cardboard, cream on his glasses and jam on his fingers. He looked at his own fingers and saw jam there too. Then he caught sight of the three of them in the dressing-table mirror, and the bubble burst as he began to laugh; high-pitched, infectious laughter that threatened to choke him. Within seconds Wanda and Colin had joined in, the three of them united in the moment. When he'd recovered, Quentin wiped his fingers and sipped his tea. Nervous tension, he realized, but he felt better for his outburst.

A phone rang, and he immediately tensed again, but relaxed a little when he realized it was his second mobile.

'Hello, Steve,' he said, after snatching it up.

'Heard anything more?' Philmore barked.

'No. I'd have told you if I had.'

Quentin heard Philmore's sigh and guessed he was impatient to be doing something positive.

'I'm hardly likely to go off without telling you, am I?' Quentin said. 'If I'm walking into a trap, I at least want you to know about it.'

'Are you sure you want to go through with this? I can get someone to take your place if you're having second thoughts.'

'How the hell would that work?' Quentin demanded. 'The man may not have seen me up close and personal but he has seen me from a distance. And he knows my voice. He's spoken to me often enough.'

'As long as you're sure. For goodness' sake, be careful. Whitelaw's dangerous.' Philmore sounded as though he was the one having second thoughts. He seemed more anxious now than he did when he'd first agreed to Quentin going along with Cultured Voice's demands.

'Look, Steve,' Quentin said. 'You couldn't have stopped me doing this. I'm the one he contacted and I'd be here with or without you. Just make sure you're there when I need you.'

'I'll do my best,' Philmore quipped, and rang off.

* * *

Quentin lay in bed that night wishing Cultured Voice would get on with whatever he was planning instead of sending him on pointless journeys. Why the hell isn't he? he thought sleepily. An answer came to him and he shot upright. 'He's not here,' he said into the darkness. 'He's not in the country.'

Wanda stirred. 'What are you talking about?'

'Cultured Voice. He's not here. That's why things are on hold.'

Wanda turned over. 'We said from the beginning he could still be abroad. Why have you thought of that now?'

101

'Because if he's not here and he's trying to control things from wherever he is, he has to rely on what his minions tell him.'

'And your point is?'

'Well,' Quentin said slowly, 'we know he's powerful and can pull strings, but he's not long out of custody. He may have planned this before he escaped, but he's got to be careful. He was caught and photographed, so for the first time, his face is known.'

'Exactly, that's why he's getting his minions to do things for him. How does that change anything?'

Thoughts whizzed in Quentin's head. 'I thought he was drawing things out just to ruffle me, but I think it's more than that. He's stringing things out to give himself time to get here.'

Wanda yawned. 'Well, if he's not here then he can't kill you, can he? So go to sleep.'

She rolled away from him. Quentin caught her arm. 'Come on, Wanda, this is important.'

Sighing, Wanda sat up. 'All right,' she said. 'Look, suppose he *wants* you running around with drugs. He might tip off the police and have you arrested, although Philmore could dig you out of that particular hole, but what if the drugs are stolen?'

'Stolen?'

'Yes, you know, from another gang or something. He could just as easily tip them off.'

Quentin took a moment to digest this. 'You mean… I'd be the target of another criminal gang? They'd do his job for him? Why would he go to all that trouble when he could hire a hitman?'

'Who knows how his mind works? Maybe he's bored and this is his idea of fun. My point is, nobody knows what he's planning, not the police and certainly not you or me. It's no good lying here trying to guess.'

Quentin gave a mirthless laugh. 'Well, you just did.'

Wanda felt for his hand and squeezed it. 'Only because you won't let me sleep. Right now, all we can do is wait to see what happens. We've got away from him before, and we'll do it again.'

'I wish I had your confidence,' Quentin muttered.

'Quentin!' Wanda put on her school-mistress voice. 'Snap out of it. You're brave and resourceful and we, *you*, are going to beat this man. Now lie down and go to sleep.'

'Yes, ma'am,' Quentin said. He lay down and closed his eyes, but how could he sleep after what Wanda had suggested?

# Chapter Sixteen

Quentin awoke from a dream in which a loud knocking filled the air. The knocking continued after he had opened his eyes. Wanda, he thought, realizing she wasn't in bed. He got up groggily and went to the door.

'Forgot the key,' Wanda said, coming in with Mozart at her heels. 'And I've seen Debbie Francis. She's just come back from the local nick. They've got photos of those two guys from the caravan park.'

'Good. Have we got a copy?'

'She's going to check with Steve, and if it's OK, we can take a picture on our phones.'

'It'd better be OK,' Quentin said testily. 'Those two could be sent to get me at any time. I've got a right to see the face of anyone who might try to kill me.'

He was about to go into the bathroom when his mobile rang. He sprang to where it sat on the wooden dressing table and grabbed at it, sending it skittering off the edge onto the floor. Number withheld, he saw when he'd dived to retrieve it.

'Yes?' he panted.

'You sound out of breath, Mr Cadbury. Perhaps you should do more exercise. Very beneficial, I believe.'

'You didn't ring to talk about my health. What do you want?'

'Patience, Mr Cadbury. That, I can tell you from personal experience, is definitely a virtue.'

'I suppose you'd know that with your track record,' Quentin ventured.

'Quite right, Mr Cadbury. You'll be pleased to know you're going on another little day trip. I think you'll enjoy it. All work and no play, as they say. I should think your life's quite dull under normal circumstances. I'm just trying to liven things up for you.'

The urge to press the off button was so strong, Quentin's fingers whitened with the effort of keeping them still. 'Are you going to tell me what you want or not?'

'Of course. I wouldn't waste my valuable time calling you otherwise. Where are you?'

'Not far from Eden,' Quentin said.

'Excellent. Make sure you're back there after your day out. St Michael's Mount, Mr Cadbury. Don't leave it too long or you'll miss the tide.'

Quentin was flummoxed. 'Am I taking the package with me?' he asked.

'Oh, yes. I've asked someone to meet you there, but if for any reason they don't make it, just enjoy the day. Goodbye, Mr Cadbury, and look after my package.'

The line went dead. 'Of all the…' Quentin muttered.

'Well?' Wanda demanded.

'St Michael's Mount. I've got to take the package. Someone might be meeting me or might not. I'm betting not. Too vague. He's playing games again.'

Wanda checked her watch. 'Nearly eight,' she said. 'The causeway's only passable at low tide. I'll go down to reception and use their internet to check when low tide is while you get dressed.'

'Good idea. I won't take long,' Quentin said as she left the room.

He'd just finished getting ready when Wanda returned.

'Low tide's at eleven today,' she told him. 'I grabbed a couple of croissants from the restaurant. Eat while I make you some tea.'

'Thanks.' Quentin bit into a stale croissant, then put the rest down and gulped his tea. 'I'll ring Philmore and let him know. I'll get him to send those photos to my phone. One of them may be whoever he's sending to meet me.'

Five minutes later, he was looking at a picture of the duo from the caravan park that the surveillance team had taken. Seen from a distance, one was a balding middle-aged man, the other no more than a teenager wearing a baseball cap. Quentin frowned. Was this the same youngster he'd seen at the ice rink? And the one he'd glimpsed yesterday?

'You go on, Quentin,' Philmore said. 'We'll catch you up.'

Ending the call, Quentin collected his things and turned to Wanda.

'Bye, Wanda.'

'Bye. Be careful, Quentin, and answer your phone when you see it's me or I'll worry.'

'I will if I can. Bye, Mozart. Look after your mistress.'

After kissing Wanda's cheek, he left before she had a chance to suggest going with him.

\* \* \*

Quentin had been driving for almost half an hour before he noticed Philmore's Audi in the rear-view mirror. It was reassuring to know he had support, even though he might not need it today. It was also reassuring to know Wanda was safe back at the hotel with Colin, although the thought of them spending the entire day together didn't sit well with him.

It was when he'd passed signs to Helston and Penzance that a screech of brakes and the crunch of metal from behind made him glance in the rear-view mirror. A flatbed lorry had jackknifed across both carriageways, its load of wooden A-frames spilling out onto the road. There were three cars between him and the lorry. Philmore's wasn't one of them. Pulling onto the hard shoulder, he rang Philmore's number and was relieved when he answered.

'Are you OK?' he said.

'Yes, but it looks like we'll be stuck here for a bit.'

'Well, it can't be helped. Catch me up when you can. I'll call if anything happens.'

He slipped back onto the road and drove on, quickly leaving the wail of sirens that filled the air behind.

As he turned at a sign to Marazion, a vista opened up before him, one he recognized from so many picture postcards. St Michael's Mount rose up from the sea, a castle-like building outlined against the morning sky and standing proud atop a rocky island in the bay ahead. Quentin was reminded momentarily of one of the few Shakespeare quotes he remembered from his school days: "This sceptred isle... set in a silver sea." The sea looked silver today, and the isle in front of him looked, if not sceptred, at least majestic. He imagined it at high tide, cut off from the mainland, its romantic turrets swathed in a ghostly mist.

He was jerked out of his thoughts when he whizzed past a signpost for the slipway car park. Muttering to himself, he found somewhere to turn round and drove back. When he got there, a thin column of figures was picking its way towards the island over the stony causeway, braving the walk in the sharp wind, now tinged with spots of rain. Drawing the zip on his jacket up to his neck and wishing he'd worn gloves, Quentin joined them, grateful for his rubber-soled trainers.

He reached the other side and turned to look back at the way he had come. Was the person who was supposed to be meeting him on the way or already here? He blew on his hands and retreated to the lee of the rocks where it was less windy. Should he climb the spiralling path up to the castle? Whoever he was meeting would have to pass the spot where he stood now, to get to and from the causeway, but he didn't fancy the idea of standing there in the cold for four hours or however long it was before the route to the mainland was impassable. The aroma of frying bacon and a sign to a café made up his mind.

From the café he called Wanda.

'It's freezing here,' he said. 'You're much better off where you are. What's Mozart barking at?' He frowned as background noises betrayed Wanda's whereabouts. 'You're not in the hotel, are you?'

'No,' Wanda admitted. 'Colin and I came after you and now we're stuck in traffic.'

'There was an accident, so it's probably the tailback from that,' Quentin told her. 'Philmore was held up too. You might as well go back. You can't do anything, and I don't think anything's going to happen anyway. Philmore won't be happy if you turn up. Don't worry about me, Wanda. I've got to ring Philmore now. I'll call later, OK?'

'OK. Bye, Quentin.'

Knowing that Wanda cared enough to follow him in case she could help warmed Quentin's heart as much as the bacon butty and coffee had warmed his body. It was pointless for her and Colin to be coming after him, though he had to admit, he'd feel easier if Philmore was nearby. He took out his second phone and rang him.

'Hello, Steve,' he said.

'Are you there yet, Quentin?'

'Yeah. Nothing doing so far. What's going on with you?'

Philmore's exasperated huff told Quentin he wasn't happy. 'They made space enough for us to get through after they saw our ID but we must have picked up a screw or something from the wreckage. Debbie's at a garage getting a new tyre. I've commandeered another car but I've still got a way to go.'

'Bad luck,' Quentin said, feeling the DCI's frustration. 'Any casualties?'

'No fatalities, but a few taken to hospital.'

'Well, don't rush, we don't want another accident. I don't think you'll miss anything.'

'You're probably right,' Philmore agreed. 'I don't think our friend would put himself anywhere he couldn't get away from in a hurry. Still, I've arranged local back-up. I've given them your description and car reg, and told them to give you any help needed. The surveillance team at the caravan park have been in touch. The guys who stole your Volvo are on the move and they were following, but somehow they've managed to lose them. They may be coming your way, so keep an eye out.'

'OK, Steve, thanks.'

The call ended and Quentin put the phone away and hoisted the bag with the package further onto his shoulder. He was afraid to let go of it. Images of someone coming from nowhere and making off with it swam before his eyes and he gripped the strap tighter. Stupid. If that happened, it would be a random mugging. The man Quentin knew as Cultured Voice would have a safer plan than that. Although, Quentin reasoned, how could he control the way his workers operated when he wasn't there to oversee them?

Bored, he started the ascent up to the castle. His long legs carried him quickly. He found a bench on the terrace at the top and sat down to catch his breath. Warm from the exertion and with the bag safely beside him, he watched people as they either reached the end of their climb or emerged from the castle and began their descent. He checked his phone for the photo of the two who'd taken the Volvo, but saw no one resembling either of them. Perhaps they were just inconsequential cogs in a much bigger wheel. Perhaps their usefulness was over.

He was so wrapped up in his thoughts, he didn't see the figure until it sat down next to him. Alarmed, he grabbed the bag and held it protectively on his lap. He swivelled round, surprised to see a boyish face enveloped in a grey hood with the drawstring tightly laced under the chin. Something stirred in his memory. The boy from the caravan, the one in the photograph? The one he'd seen at the ice rink and maybe yesterday? Huge brown eyes looked at him, and well-formed lips smiled, revealing teeth like pearls.

'Cold up here, isn't it?'

The voice, high-pitched and with a soft Cornish burr, shattered Quentin's perception of what he was seeing.

'Yes,' he said. 'Freezing.'

'Gluttons for punishment, aren't we, coming up here in the depths of winter? Must want our heads seen to.'

In a swift movement, the hood was pushed back and a cascade of dark hair tumbled free, instantly transforming the face in front of him.

'Yes,' Quentin said again, wondering how he could have mistaken such a pretty girl for a boy. He judged her to be about seventeen, with wide brown eyes and the creamy, unlined complexion of youth.

'You here on your own?' she asked.

'Uh-huh.'

The girl laughed. 'Don't say much, do you? I bet your girlfriend has to speak for both of you. Or maybe you can't get a word in when she's around.'

'How do you know I've got a girlfriend?'

She studied him for a moment. 'No, no girls for you. Boys neither. I'd say you were the older woman type.'

Quentin was dumbfounded. Surely that couldn't be just a lucky guess?

'Don't tell me,' the girl went on. 'Blonde, blue eyes, sophisticated, right? Dangles you on a string, I'll bet.'

Quentin gasped. Suspicion rose in him, and he gripped the holdall tighter. 'What do you want?' he said, his voice brittle.

The stranger looked offended.

'Nothing,' she said. 'Just making conversation.'

Confused, Quentin stared at her. She was the picture of innocence but he didn't trust her. Was this who he was supposed to meet? She'd described Wanda to a T. Except he wasn't dangling on Wanda's string. Was he? One thing was certain – he'd never met this girl before. Anything she knew about him could only have come from one source.

'Look,' he said. 'Whatever you want, just tell me.'

'Well,' she said with an impish grin, 'I'd like to know why your lady friend has abandoned you to the elements when you could be tucked up in the warm together.'

'That's none of your business,' he snapped. 'Nice try, but no thanks.' He stood up abruptly and began walking away, his cheeks burning.

As he reached the top of the path, he swung round, expecting to see her following or still sat there looking annoyed at his sudden departure. As it was, he saw neither because she wasn't there. She'd disappeared as quickly as she'd arrived.

# Chapter Seventeen

Quentin waited near the causeway for over an hour, hoping to see the mysterious girl leaving, but there was no sign of her. He knew he'd have to get across the causeway in the next few minutes or he'd have to wait for the infrequent boat.

Suddenly a latecomer ran past him and started across the causeway. Quentin stared after the hooded figure, momentarily rooted to the ground.

'Better hurry, mate,' a man in fisherman's gear called to him. 'You'll be getting wet else.'

Quentin got wet before he was a quarter of the way to the mainland. He hurried after the hooded figure, but she was smaller and more nimble than him. His running experience counted for nothing when he couldn't see where he was placing his feet. By the time he was almost there, he was wading through knee-deep water. He tried to run the last few yards, slipping and falling onto his outstretched arms, the bag hanging off his shoulder and swaying dangerously close to the water. He picked himself up and made it to the beach just as the figure in the grey hoodie turned and looked straight at him. The girl smiled; then she turned and was gone before he knew what was happening. Seconds later, he caught sight of her in the passenger seat of a white van, a Citroën Berlingo, as it drove past him at speed towards the exit. She lifted her arm in a wave, obscuring the view of the driver. Quentin stared after the van, trying to see the number plate, but it was covered in dirt.

'Bloody hell!' Quentin mumbled. He had no idea what was going on and he made no attempt to give chase. By the time he got to his car, the van would be long gone. One thing was certain – what had happened wasn't a casual conversation with a stranger. She'd been trying to get him to talk about Wanda. Why? Had she seen her at the Eden Project? And if she'd been sent to meet him, why hadn't she taken the package?

He tramped over the beach, water squelching in his shoes and jeans clinging to his legs. When he got to the car, he opened the bag and was relieved to see the package was still dry. He switched on the engine, turned the heater up and rang Philmore.

'What happened to you?' Quentin demanded.

'I got held up. Why? Has something happened?'

'You could say that. I think those two from the caravan were here. They just took off in a white Citroën Berlingo, and if it was them, then the younger one isn't a boy, it's a girl.'

Quentin relayed the events as they'd unfolded on the island.

'Why didn't you ring me or the Penzance police before you left?' Philmore asked. 'I told you I'd arranged back-up from the local force. We could have followed them.'

'Sorry, I was too concerned with where she'd gone and getting back before the causeway was impassable.'

Philmore sighed, and Quentin waited for a tirade that didn't come.

'Well, the names given at the caravan park were Jack and Sam Hughes,' Philmore said. 'I guess they could be short for Jacqueline or Samantha, but like I said, they're not on our database. We're checking the surveillance photos against our mug shots, but that'll take time. It doesn't look as though they'll be leading us to our man, not today anyway.'

'Well, I don't know about you, Steve, but I'm wet, tired and fed up. I'm heading back to the hotel,' Quentin said, and hung up.

* * *

Quentin sat in the hotel bar with Wanda and Colin. Nursing his second whisky, he was feeling better after a hot shower and a change of clothes.

'What I can't understand,' he said between sips, 'is why he sent the girl, why he sent anyone, if they weren't going to pick up the package. It doesn't make sense.'

'Perhaps he's trying to find out if I'm with you,' Wanda said.

'Or remind you what's at stake if you don't play by the rules and do everything on your own,' Colin put in.

'At this rate, the wretched package is never going to get delivered,' Quentin growled.

'You've only had it two days,' Wanda pointed out.

'Two days too long,' Quentin answered.

'He said it would be soon, didn't he?' Colin eyed Quentin as though he was enjoying this whole thing.

Well, he would be, Quentin thought, spending time alone with Wanda while I'm chasing my tail all over Cornwall. And if he sits any closer, he'll be in her lap.

'I don't think his idea of soon is the same as mine,' he said, pushing his jealous thoughts away. 'I'm going to turn in. Coming, Wanda?'

The look Wanda gave him told him she recognized the jealousy in him. 'When I've finished my drink, Quentin.'

She twirled the glass around in her fingers, making no effort to drink from it. Her way of telling him he had no need to be jealous of Colin. And that she would come to bed when she was good and ready.

# Chapter Eighteen

The piercing notes of a phone woke Quentin. He stumbled blindly from the bed to the dressing table where his mobiles were on charge, stubbing his toe on the bedframe in the dark. Guided by the ring tone, he snatched a phone and threw it down again when he realized he'd picked up the wrong one. He grabbed the other and stared at the display. Number withheld.

'Yes,' he mumbled.

'Did I wake you, Mr Cadbury? What a pity.'

Quentin waited, putting a finger to his lips as Wanda sat up and switched the bedside light on.

'You're obviously not a fan of early mornings, Mr Cadbury. Personally I find six o'clock the perfect time to rise. I hope you enjoyed your little trip yesterday.'

'What do you want?' Quentin hissed.

'What do you think I want? I want you to deliver my package, of course.'

About time, Quentin thought. 'When?'

'Now.'

'Now?' Quentin shook his head and tried to blink the sleep from his eyes.

'No time like the present, and it's nice and quiet at this time of the morning. Of course it depends on where you are. Where are you, Mr Cadbury?'

'Why? Where am I going?'

'Answer my question, Mr Cadbury. Where are you?'

Quentin tried to think through the haze of sleep. Where was he?

'Still close to Eden,' he said.

'That'll do nicely, and the timing will be perfect. Is my package still safe?'

'Yes.'

'All right, here's what you'll do. Drive to St Austell Leisure Centre – they open at six. Get a locker and put the package inside. Make a note of the locker number and don't get it wrong. Then leave. I'll ring at seven-thirty to get the locker number. Don't pull any stunts. Someone will be there soon afterwards, so if the package isn't there, I'll know. Will it be there, Mr Cadbury?'

'Yes,' Quentin said, reaching for his clothes.

'Until seven-thirty then, Mr Cadbury.'

Quentin snatched up his second phone and called Philmore.

'We're on! St Austell Leisure Centre,' he blurted, putting the phone on loudspeaker so Wanda could hear while he got dressed. 'I've got to put the package in a locker. Someone will pick it up soon after. I've got to be in and out by seven-thirty so I'm heading out the door now.'

Not waiting for an answer, he grabbed the bag, his phones and keys and rushed out to the car.

* * *

He got to the leisure centre at 6.55 a.m. and was surprised to see about a dozen cars already in the car park. He made his way to the building and approached the reception desk.

'You can sign up for temporary membership to use the gym,' the girl behind the counter told him. 'You can go and have a look round and one of our coaches will have a chat to you.'

'Thanks,' Quentin said, putting on a winning smile.

'Just follow the signs,' the girl said, turning pink under his gaze.

Quentin scrutinized the overhead signs and made for the male changing room, pushed the door open, then hesitated. Suppose the person collecting the package was a woman? What if it was the girl he'd seen yesterday? He could hardly go into the women's, but there was a family room, so perhaps he should leave the package there. He decided to stick with the male changing room and went in.

He selected a locker, opened it and slung the package inside. Good riddance, he thought sourly as he did so. He pushed in a coin, then locked it, pocketed the key and walked back to the entrance.

His eyes widened when, instead of the young receptionist who'd greeted him, he saw DS Debbie Francis in a sweatshirt emblazoned with the centre's logo. Her face was pale without her usual make-up and her brown hair was scraped back into a ponytail as if she hadn't had time to brush it. When she saw Quentin, she shook her head as though to tell him not to stop, then nodded towards a woman in a leotard at the coffee machine in the otherwise deserted foyer.

Bloody hell, the power of the police, Quentin thought. That was quick work. Now she'd be able to see exactly who was coming and going.

As if to justify his rapid exit, he walked past reception brandishing his phone. 'No signal,' he called so that the woman at the coffee machine could hear, and walked out.

When he got to the car, he sat holding his phone, waiting for it to ring, once more feeling that he was spending his life waiting to be told what to do. He didn't for one minute believe that his job was done. Cultured Voice, he was sure, had more in mind for him.

The call came at seven twenty-eight.

'Have you delivered my package, Mr Cadbury?'

'Yes,' Quentin said, tight-lipped.

'Good. And what's the locker number?'

Fingering the key, Quentin glanced at the wristband. 'Twenty-seven.'

'Good,' said the cultured voice again. 'And where are you now?'

'In my car at the leisure centre.'

'I thought,' came the icy retort, 'that I'd made it quite plain that you were to leave as soon as you'd done what I asked.'

'You did, but… won't you need the key?' Quentin held his breath, wondering how his adversary would react to this show of innocence.

The answer came in a throaty laugh. 'You think I need a key to open a locker?' The laugh gave way to iciness again. 'You must be very naïve if you believe that, Mr Cadbury. Leave immediately and go back to wherever you were this morning. Stay there until you hear from me.'

'Why? I've delivered your package–'

'I don't know that yet, do I? Leave now.'

Silence told Quentin the call was over. He looked about to see if there was anyone who could be watching him. A couple of girls toting sports bags were walking towards the leisure building, but otherwise the place was still quiet and

Quentin couldn't see anybody looking in his direction. Keeping his hands below the dashboard level, he switched phones, brought up Philmore's number and repeated Cultured Voice's instructions in a text.

"OK," Philmore replied. "Better do as he says. We don't want to blow the whole thing."

Quentin left the car park reluctantly, wishing he could stay and see who collected the package. He drove a few yards before pulling into a space at the roadside, from where he could just see the leisure centre entrance. Switching off the engine, he kept his eyes on the mirrors. He didn't know what he hoped to gain, but he couldn't go back to the hotel yet.

Within forty-five minutes, a steady stream of traffic had built up. Vehicle after vehicle passed him, including a white van, possibly a Citroën Berlingo. Was this the same van the girl had got into at St Michael's Mount? A dark blue Audi followed in its wake, passing Quentin before he realized it was Philmore and Francis. He started the engine, indicating to pull out and cursing when a bus crawled past him and blocked his path. The Audi and the van were soon out of sight.

When he reached the end of the road he was unsure which way to turn. Frustration filling him, he pulled into a lay-by and called Wanda.

'Good move,' she said when he told her about Francis being at the leisure centre. 'Bet she's got a good description of whoever picked the package up. If they're following them then they'll know their registration number as well.'

Quentin shook his head at this. He hadn't had time to notice the number plate on the van that had passed him today, but the rear number plate on the van he'd seen yesterday had been covered by mud and dirt. If that's the one Philmore was following, it would be hard to read.

'Are you coming back now?' Wanda was saying.

'Not yet. You go and have breakfast. I won't be long. See you later.'

His gaze fell on the real reason he didn't want to go back to the hotel for breakfast: McDonald's. He wasn't overly fond of fast food, and he knew Wanda abhorred it, but just occasionally he succumbed to a habit he'd acquired in his student days.

A few minutes later, he was perched on a stool at a counter by the window, savouring the saltiness of sausage meat and the crispness of hash browns. Gazing idly through the window, he tried not to hope that this would soon be over. He couldn't have been brought here just to transport a package to a place only a few miles from where it had started out. A master criminal wouldn't trouble himself with such a triviality unless he had a more sinister motive in mind.

When he was back in the car, he sat brooding over what his nemesis intended for him next. Was the man even in the country? Was he running things from abroad? Or was he somewhere in between?

Bloody hell, he thought savagely, bringing his fist down on the steering wheel. The man's a bloody illusionist. Now you see me, now you don't.

Sighing, he turned on the ignition and drove back to the hotel.

## Chapter Nineteen

Wanda and Colin were not in their rooms when Quentin got back, so he took the opportunity to call his parents. He never told them about stressful situations, but he found his mother's soothing voice calming. After ten minutes of trivial chat, he felt better.

As he put the phone down, there was a knock at the door and he frowned. It couldn't be Wanda. She would use her key. Opening the door a crack, he peered through and saw Philmore.

'Well?' he asked, pulling the door fully open. 'How did it go?'

'No good,' Philmore said gloomily. 'Debbie got a good look at the bloke who collected the package, and she's sure it's the one from the caravan site. We tried to follow him but we lost him in all that traffic. We've got someone watching the caravan but it's not the outcome we hoped for. We're still no nearer to nailing Whitelaw.'

Still finding it hard to think of Cultured Voice as Whitelaw, Quentin said, 'I'm waiting for a call. He was going to check I'd delivered the package and get back to me.'

'And he still doesn't know where you are?'

'Don't think so. I haven't told him, though he obviously knows I'm somewhere in this area.'

Philmore looked puzzled. 'What the hell's he playing at, I wonder. I suppose there's nothing for it but to wait. If it goes on much longer… Right, let me know as soon as you hear anything.'

The DCI had just got up to leave when Quentin had another call. Seeing the number was withheld, Quentin nodded to Philmore and pressed the loudspeaker button as he answered.

'Yes?'

The cultured voice rang out into the room. 'Well done, Mr Cadbury. It seems you've completed the first part of your mission successfully.'

'*First* part?'

'Well now, a simple task like that isn't exactly a true test of your capabilities, is it? There is something else I need you to do before you go back to your little detective agency.'

'That's not what we agreed,' Quentin said, not relishing the idea of more days of uncertainty. 'I've done what you asked.'

'So you have, but have a little patience, Mr Cadbury. Aren't you enjoying your holiday?'

'It's hardly a holiday. What do you want? More games, I suppose. Another one of your ploys to give me the runaround, like stealing my car?'

There was a pause, as though the person on the other end of the line was deciding what to say. His voice hardened when he spoke.

'I'm giving you the runaround because you blatantly disobeyed my orders. I'm reliably informed that there were two bags in your car. The second bag evidently belonged to a woman. There was dog food as well. I'm disappointed in you, Mr Cadbury. I thought you'd know that when I say come alone, I mean come alone.'

Quentin froze. He knew Wanda was with him. Well, of course he did. How stupid he'd been leaving the bags in the car. What would he say if he knew Philmore was there as well?

Not waiting for a reply, Cultured Voice went on, 'We'll discuss that another time. Just remember this – if anything happens to Mrs Merrydrew, it'll be your fault. You have a few days before your next mission, so you'll have time for some more sightseeing. Where are you staying, by the way?'

The question threw Quentin.

'Why do you need to know?'

'Come now, Mr Cadbury, I can't have you skipping off before you've finished your next task, can I? Just tell me the name of the hotel or wherever you're staying. And believe me, if you lie, I'll soon find out.'

Quentin looked at a Philmore questioningly. The DCI shrugged, then nodded. Reluctantly, Quentin gave their location.

A mocking laugh rang out. 'A Travelodge? A beautiful woman of the world like Mrs Merrydrew, and a Travelodge is the best you can do? Really, Mr Cadbury, you have so much to learn.'

The call ended. Silence filled Quentin's ear and rage filled his heart. Or was it anguish? Did he really not deserve Wanda? Face burning, he avoided Philmore's gaze.

'Sarcastic bastard, isn't he?' Philmore said. Then, as if noticing Quentin's discomfort, he went on, 'Well, at least we've got another chance to nail him. More waiting around, though. The super won't be happy.'

'I'm not happy either,' Quentin muttered. 'Now he knows Wanda's here and where we are.'

'I shouldn't worry. He's not stupid enough to turn up here. He'll probably get one of his gang to ring reception and check that you're booked in. Anyway, we're here for you.'

'Yeah. It's good to have you on board, Steve.'

A brief look of understanding passed between them. Then Philmore was gone, leaving Quentin just as frustrated and apprehensive as before.

\* \* \*

With her presence having been discovered, Wanda saw no reason not to be seen with Quentin unless he was on one of Cultured Voice's errands.

'Well then,' she said that afternoon, 'if he's said you've got to wait again, there's no need to be moping around here all day and night, especially on a Saturday. I was looking at the brochures in reception and the Christmas lights are on in Mousehole. They're spectacular, apparently. It's over an hour's drive but what else have we got to do?'

'Might as well,' Quentin said gloomily, still concerned about giving their location away.

'Good. Cheer up, Quentin. We'll feel better if we go out and take our minds off things. I'll ring Colin. We'll take two cars just in case.'

Quentin resisted the urge to suggest they went on their own, knowing it was sensible for Colin to join them and to take a separate vehicle. *Expect the unexpected.*

When he told Philmore what they were doing, he tried to dissuade them.

'But we're not on one of his missions,' Quentin said, 'and he didn't say anything about staying where we are, so I think we'll be all right.'

'That's what you thought when you went to Fowey, and he sent you to Charlestown,' Philmore reminded him. 'We couldn't get to Mousehole very quickly. We'll come, so at least we'll be close if we're needed, and I'll put the local force on alert.'

It was dark by the time Quentin and Wanda got there, but they caught the charm of the village immediately. The ancient narrow streets sported cafés, boutiques and art galleries as well as fishermen's cottages, and they wished they'd come earlier to explore the history of the place in daylight.

After meeting up with Colin and finding somewhere to eat, they joined the throng walking down to the harbour. The journey had been worth it. The display was indeed spectacular. The place was aglow with thousands of different-coloured lights, their reflections shining up from the water. In the harbour itself, myriad boats were also illuminated, a rainbow of colours soaring into the night sky and revealing the dark outline of St Clement's Isle, which lay just outside the harbour.

Colin and Wanda edged further along, trying to get a better view, while Quentin, his eye level above most of the people around him, stayed where he was.

'Quite a show,' he heard Colin say as he passed. 'Emma would love this.'

The mention of Colin's daughter made Quentin think of the girl on St Michael's Mount. He wasn't sure why – probably the dark hair and eyes and elfin features. As if by thought transference, he caught sight of a slight, hooded figure in front of a crowd just opposite, staring at him. As soon as his gaze fell on it, the figure darted behind the front line of people.

'Bloody hell, she's stalking me,' he murmured, convinced it was the girl from yesterday. He surged forward, intent on catching her up and challenging her. Elbowing his way through the spectators, he tried to get sight of her.

'Sorry,' he said when he knocked a man's arm and hot coffee spilled from his polystyrene cup.

Using his height to full advantage, he gazed over heads and glimpsed the figure disappearing round a corner. He pushed free of the crowd and sprinted after her, dodging people still walking towards the harbour. A knot of teenagers, standing in the middle of the narrow street, didn't yield as he approached, and by the time he'd run round them there was no sign of the hooded figure. Admitting defeat, he rang Philmore.

'Young woman, grey hoodie,' Philmore repeated. 'OK, we'll keep an eye out, but if it's the one from the caravan we won't pick her up. I'm still hoping she'll lead us to Whitelaw.'

Quentin rang off and went back to the harbour.

'Where did you disappear to?' Wanda asked when he found her and Colin.

'She was here, the girl from St Michael's Mount.'

Wanda's eyes widened. 'Really? Are you sure?'

'Pretty sure. I mean, as soon as I spotted her, she ran. Why would she if she was just here to see the lights?'

Wanda considered this. 'You think she followed us here? Why?'

'It's Quentin's magnetic personality,' Colin quipped. 'She can't help herself.'

'Now, Colin, this isn't the time for petty digs,' Wanda said quickly, as if sensing that Quentin was about to make a cutting reply. 'You called a truce, remember? And if it was her, then she was here for a reason, probably on orders from you-know-who, so it's nothing to joke about.'

Suitably chastened, Colin said, 'All right, all right, I get the message. Just trying to lighten the mood, that's all.'

'I think she was at the ice rink too, and Charlestown,' Quentin said, grateful that Wanda had stood up for him and deciding to stay with the matter in hand. 'What's confusing me is why she was there and why she's here. I mean on St Michael's Mount she spoke to me, so why run away now?'

'Maybe she's being paid to keep tabs on us,' Wanda suggested.

'Hold on a minute,' Colin interrupted. 'Is that her over there?'

Quentin followed his gaze to a figure in a hoodie on the end of a line of people by the jetty. It was lost, as a swathe of people moved in front of it, then reappeared as the swathe moved on.

'Can't tell from here,' Quentin said. If it wasn't for the myriad lights the person wouldn't have been visible at all, he realized. 'I'll get closer.'

He made his way towards the jetty, Wanda and Colin jostling through the crowd behind him. When he got nearer, the hooded figure cut in front of the line of people and walked quickly to the first road ahead.

'Stay here,' Quentin told Colin. 'We can't all go after her.'

Quentin increased his pace, and Wanda hurried to keep up with him.

'Perhaps you shouldn't go after her,' she panted. 'We don't want Cultured Voice to know you've spotted her.'

'She spoke to me as bold as brass at St Michael's Mount,' Quentin countered. 'He can hardly blame me for spotting her now.'

They kept on, the crowds dwindling to almost nothing the further they got from the harbour. When they reached a corner, the person they were tailing stopped in their stride. Quentin stopped too, causing Wanda to career into his back when she came up behind him. Afraid the person would whirl round and spot them, the pursuers leapt behind an old telephone kiosk.

Their quarry carried on. Quentin and Wanda followed, trying to keep pace without it seeming obvious. The front doors of the cottages lining the street were set back from the pavement, and Quentin and Wanda dodged into these recesses whenever it looked as though their quarry might turn and notice them. It was darker here, and the figure ahead of them was just an outline.

They had nearly reached the car park at the top of the village before the figure stopped again, pulled out a mobile phone and looked at it as though checking for the time or a message. Suddenly the figure turned sideways, prompting Quentin to pull Wanda into the shadow of a row of bushes skirting the car park.

'She's waiting for someone,' Quentin whispered.

For a transient moment, he imagined Cultured Voice materializing out of the gloom like ectoplasm. Just then, someone emerged from an adjacent road and made a beeline for the figure.

'Quick,' Quentin said, thrusting his phone at Wanda. 'Ring Philmore.'

He edged away from the bushes and crept nearer. Then he halted. The person approaching their quarry – a man, Quentin could see now – suddenly veered sideways, walked straight past the slight figure and carried on towards Quentin. Quentin drew an exasperated breath as recognition dawned. Colin!

At that moment, the hooded figure swung round, pushed the hood back and spoke into the mobile phone. In the light from a car park lamp post Quentin could immediately see the difference between the face he'd glimpsed earlier and the one he was looking at now. This was a boy, possibly mid-teens. There was no doubt as the person's voice reached Quentin's ears, the words indiscernible but the deep tone unmistakably male.

Quentin stepped forward and met Colin as he approached.

'It's a boy,' Colin said at once.

'I can see that,' Quentin snapped. 'How come you got here so quickly?'

'Same way as you. I left the Zimmer frame at home today. Thought you might need an extra hand.'

Wanda, having rung Philmore and seeing Quentin and Colin together, came to join them.

'It's not her, is it?' she said, nodding towards the boy. 'Or you wouldn't be standing here like this.'

The boy looked up as he lowered his phone. As though uncomfortable at three people staring at him, he moved further along the car park fence.

'Let's go, or we'll be accused of loitering with intent,' Wanda said. 'I'll call Philmore back and tell him it's a false alarm.'

'More like a case of mistaken identity,' Colin quipped as they started back towards the harbour.

'Well, I'm sorry,' Quentin huffed, 'but I didn't get a proper look at him, and in that grey hoodie–'

'It looked pale blue to me,' Colin interrupted, 'but who's counting?'

'Shut up, Colin,' Wanda said, sharing Quentin's disappointment.

'I'm sure it was her I saw earlier though,' Quentin said, 'but she's probably long gone by now.'

'I don't know if she is or not,' Wanda answered. 'And right now, I don't care. We've come to see the lights and I'm going enjoy them for a bit longer.'

'The lights are fantastic but it's cold and it's an hour's drive back,' Quentin pointed out. It wasn't the cold or the drive that unsettled him. It was the thought of being watched wherever he went, and the frustration of a fruitless chase.

'You stay a bit and come back with Colin,' he said. 'I'm going to make a move.'

Before either of them could protest, he turned and strode away from them, retracing his steps to where he'd left his car. So much for taking our minds off things, he thought when he reached the Honda.

The man who had blighted his life had ruined a perfectly nice evening. Again.

# Chapter Twenty

'We'll go out for the day,' Wanda said over breakfast the next morning. 'It'll be better than sitting about doing nothing.'

'Count me out,' Colin said. 'I could do with a day sitting about doing nothing.'

Quentin and Wanda hadn't got further than Redruth when, in the rear-view mirror, Quentin noticed a white vehicle.

'Oh-oh,' he groaned.

Wanda shot him a look. 'What is it?'

'Behind us – a white van, maybe a Citroën Berlingo. Looks like the one that girl went off in from St Michael's Mount.'

Wanda glanced in the wing mirror. 'Does it? How can you tell? They all look the same.'

'Don't turn round,' Quentin warned, checking the rear-view mirror again. 'Two people, I think.'

Wanda pulled a face. 'Could be anyone. What, you think they're following us?'

'Don't know, but I'm not having them on our tail all day. I'm fed up with her turning up all over the place.'

Wanda stared into the wing mirror. 'All I can see is the front wing. Are you sure you're not just being paranoid?'

'Don't know that either, but we'll soon find out.'

Spotting a brown sign ahead, Quentin steered the car into the nearside lane. He veered off into a side road without indicating, wheels squealing as the car spun before straightening up and losing speed.

'Thanks for the warning,' Wanda complained, putting her hand up to her neck. 'That's a good way to get whiplash.'

'Sorry. Didn't see the sign till the last minute. You OK?'

'I'll live. Anyway, they didn't follow us. Where are we?'

Quentin slowed as they came to a signpost. 'Wheal Peevor,' he read aloud.

'I read about that,' Wanda told him. 'It's one of the most complete tin mines in Cornwall. Let's have a look. We've got plenty of time.'

'All right,' Quentin grunted, not relishing the thought of looking at old ruins.

He drove forward, took a turn onto a muddy track, and there was the mine, bigger than any he'd come across; three separate stone buildings, partial walls enclosing the remains of a once thriving trade, including the engine houses and the adjoining chimney stacks. There was a roughly laid out parking area, and Quentin pulled into it.

'You don't have to come if you don't want to,' Wanda said. 'I'll just have a quick look.' Immediately she got out and walked towards the buildings, stopping at the first information post. Then she carried on, negotiating the bumpy terrain up the slight incline until she was behind the first ruin and out of sight. Mozart barked, jumping up at the window as if in protest at being left behind.

'It's all right, Mote, I'm with you.' Quentin switched off the engine and stayed where he was, gazing at the imposing remains.

Testament to Britain's industrial past notwithstanding, he couldn't hack history today. The place was deserted, the sky grey and the mine dark and forbidding in the dull December light. The purr of a car's engine disturbed the quiet as a white van nosed its way along the muddy track towards the parking area. A Citroën Berlingo.

Stiffening, Quentin waited until it was closer, then leaned forward to get a better view. He could see the driver was a man. His passenger's face was obscured but Quentin knew it was the girl from St Michael's Mount. He could feel it. 'Bugger it,' he muttered. 'They must have doubled back.'

As though the driver had noticed him, the Citroën didn't swing into the parking area. It stopped and made a clumsy three-point turn as if to drive back the other way. Instead of leaving, though, the Citroën stayed, the engine idling. Now Quentin could see the passenger, and he gasped. It *was* the girl from St Michael's Mount.

The passenger door opened, and the girl got out. Looking over at him she smiled and waved, for all the world as though he was a long-lost friend, then started towards him.

'Sam!' he heard the driver call.

Ignoring him, the girl called Sam carried on. Quentin wound down the window as she approached. He recognized the same grey hoodie and leggings she'd worn before, though today the hood was down.

'Hello,' she said when she was near enough. 'On your own again? What have you done with your girlfriend now?'

Just then, Wanda appeared at the top of the path leading to the mine, picking her way carefully over the uneven ground. She stopped when she saw the white van and the girl, as if uncertain what to do. Sam followed Quentin's gaze, and seeing Wanda she suddenly whirled and ran back to the Citroën. She wrenched open the rear nearside door, reached in and snatched something from the seat. A camera, Quentin saw. She stepped away from the van as if to get a better view, and pulled the camera from its case as she turned towards Wanda.

'Oh no you don't,' Quentin murmured, rage burning in him.

In a flash he was out of the car, darting towards where the girl stood. He covered the thirty or so feet between them before Sam knew what was happening. He was almost on her when she saw him and tried to get back into the van. The camera strap dangled from her fingers and Quentin managed to grasp it as she fought to get the van door open. Giving an almighty tug, Quentin pulled the camera from her weakened grip, raising it by the strap just before it hit the ground.

Quentin grinned in triumph. 'Gotcha!'

'Give it back,' yelled Sam, lurching forward and trying to the wrestle the camera from him. 'Dad!'

The driver's door opened and for a split second, Quentin hesitated. He could get back to his car and be away quickly, but Wanda couldn't. Making up his mind, he ran up the track towards the ruins, turning when he reached Wanda. Sam and her father were coming after him.

'Get out of sight,' he panted. 'I'll outrun them.' He grabbed Wanda's arm and hauled her back up the incline to the nearest building. 'Hide,' he commanded.

As she disappeared, he looked back to see his two pursuers halfway up the path. He swivelled round and took off again, the strap round his neck and the camera bouncing against his chest. He ran until he reached the last building, ducked inside it and waited. The girl came past, evidently quicker on her feet than her father, whose gasps Quentin could hear from along the track.

'Give it up, Sam,' the man called. 'S'not worth it. We've done our bit.'

'He's got my camera!' Sam's tone was defiant. 'That cost me six hundred quid! Why should I let him take it?'

The man's voice was closer when he gasped out his reply. Though the girl sounded Cornish, her father had a definite Cockney accent. 'This wasn't in the deal. Swop the motors and plant the goods, that was my job. Yours was to take photos and you have.'

'He wants a picture of the woman now.'

'Well, he can whistle for it.'

'But we'll get paid extra if I get it.'

The man had caught up with her. Quentin could hear him breathing loudly on the other side of the wall. 'It's too late now, we're done here. We don't need extra. There'll be other jobs.'

'Not without my camera there won't. He's here somewhere, so is she,' Sam snapped.

Plucky kid, Quentin thought. Shame she's working for Cultured Voice.

He stood stock-still, afraid that any sound might alert the pair. There was a lull in the conversation, and what sounded like people walking away. They've moved on, Quentin thought, slumping against the wall in relief. Mistake. He heard a movement behind him and whirled round to see both the girl and her father coming towards him. They must have crept around the wall and found the gaping hole at the back.

The man pushed his daughter behind him and stepped forward. Jack, Quentin remembered from what Philmore had told him about the two in the caravan. This must be them. Jack and Sam – Samantha – Hughes.

'I'll take that,' Jack said, holding out his hand.

Quentin eyed him warily. Jack was about the same height as him but with a definite paunch and a hard but pasty look.

Bloody hell, Quentin thought, recalling that this man had been mistaken for him at the Eden Project. What sort of description had Philmore given to the cops on surveillance? Surely he didn't look anything like this bloke? No, Jack was much older than him, and judging by the way he'd panted after his run up the path, nowhere near as fit. In a fair fight, Quentin could beat him.

'I don't think so,' Quentin said, ignoring Jack's outstretched hand.

'Give it to me, you thief,' Sam shouted. She bounced up to him, her dark ponytail swinging.

Thief! Quentin almost laughed. 'If I'm a thief, what does that make you?'

'Shut up!' Jack glared at him, his voice hardening. 'Give it back or you'll be sorry.'

'Take it if you want it so badly,' Quentin taunted, holding the camera above his head.

Another mistake. Jack's fist slammed into his midriff and he doubled over, bringing the camera down but maintaining his grip. Jack raised his arm for another punch but dropped it suddenly, his face contorting.

'Argh! Get off me, you little mutt!' He staggered back, shaking one leg furiously as he fought to free himself from Mozart's sharp teeth.

Sam tried to pull Mozart away and the little dog released his hold on Jack, wriggled out of Sam's grasp and went for her ankle, his teeth catching her leggings and clinging on. Quentin was about to take his chance and run, but as he tried to get to the opening, Jack recovered and lunged at him, bringing him crashing to his knees. Jack kicked at his thigh then raised an arm as if to land a blow but stopped when a voice floated through the air.

'I wouldn't do that if I were you.'

# Chapter Twenty-one

Quentin's assailant stepped back and turned, as did his daughter. Straightening up, Quentin looked towards his rescuer. Wanda was framed in the gaping hole, the gun in her hand pointing to where the pair stood blinking in surprise.

'I know how to use this,' she said calmly. 'I trained as a police markswoman.'

Relief swamped Quentin, along with a surge of admiration for Wanda. She'd come up trumps again. Struggling to his feet, he side-stepped the girl and her father and went to stand next to Wanda, his arms across his bruised midriff.

'Get him off me!' Sam yelled, trying to separate her leg from Mozart's jaws.

'Here, Mozart,' Wanda called.

The dog pulled back from the girl's ankle, the material of the leggings ripping as he did so. Mozart obediently trotted over and stood by his mistress's feet.

'There might be some photos on here the police would be very interested to see,' Quentin said, holding up the camera with one hand. 'Perhaps you'll think twice before you decide to work for a bastard like Cult– Whitelaw again.'

'Never heard of anyone called Whitelaw,' Jack growled, eyeing the gun with a look of disbelief and Mozart with equal distaste.

'Now why doesn't that surprise me,' Quentin said. 'You've probably never seen or heard him and you probably never will, but he's the one behind this whole operation.'

'Did you know we'd be dealing with people with guns, Dad?' Sam asked, doubt clouding her face.

'Nah, course I didn't! I wouldn't have taken the job else. You think I'd put you in danger?'

Sam shook her head.

'So who gave you your orders?' Quentin asked, hoping to get at least one name to take to Philmore.

Jack shrugged. 'The bloke who hired us.'

'I think what my friend really wants is a name.' Wanda's tone was cool, unruffled.

'Called himself Dave. That's all I know.'

Quentin's hopes slid away. How many Daves were there in the world? He knew he was grasping at straws but he had to ask. 'How did he speak? Accent, posh, what?'

'Didn't notice anything special about his voice.'

Not Cultured Voice then. An intermediary.

'How come you knew where we were?' Quentin asked.

'None of your bleedin' business,' Jack snarled, as though he'd forgotten he was directly in the line of fire. His expression changed when Wanda shifted slightly and his gaze fell on the gun.

'Not very bright, are you?' Sam put in. 'I would have thought you could have worked that out for yourself.'

Her hostile glare pierced Quentin like an arrow as he tried to fathom the answer. 'So,' he said slowly, 'you were told where we were and sent to get a photo of my partner.'

'And,' Wanda cut in, 'you already knew what car we were driving from when you delivered it to the Eden Project. Make a habit of stealing cars, do you?'

Sam looked sullen. 'Give me my camera.'

'No chance.' Quentin waved the camera as though to emphasize this point. 'So you were told to get a photo of my partner.' He indicated towards Wanda. 'What about me? Or have you already got one of me? Is that why you've been following me around?'

Without answering, Sam moved as though to jump forward.

'Stop!' Wanda brandished the gun as Jack caught hold of his daughter's arm. 'We're going now. Don't move from here until you hear our car driving away. Unless you'd rather we call the police now and wait till they get here?'

When there was no answer, she went on, 'I didn't think so.' She turned to Quentin. 'Come on.'

'Just one more thing,' Quentin said. He raised the camera and photographed father and daughter. 'Nice meeting you,' he said sourly, still recovering from Jack's punch and his ungainly fall.

'I was right about her though, wasn't I?' Sam threw at him as he turned to leave. 'She is dangling you on a string.'

Ignoring this but with cheeks burning, Quentin stepped towards Wanda. He waited until she'd backed out into the open and whispered, 'Go in front of me, just in case they come after us.'

'Stay, Mozart,' Wanda commanded.

Mozart stood barring their adversaries' exit while she and Quentin scrambled down the track, Quentin's progress hindered by the pain in his bruised midriff. Halfway down, Wanda called Mozart and he bounded to join them. When they reached the end of the track, Quentin paused and took shots of the Citroën, front and back. How much help it would be, he didn't know – the number plates were still obscured with dirt, but maybe the police could enhance them. As they got to their car, they saw Jack and Sam at the top of the track.

'Damn,' Quentin moaned, dropping into the driver's seat, 'we should have taken their car keys. Then we could have called Philmore and had them picked up.'

'It doesn't matter,' Wanda said. 'We've got photos and they're small fry. Let's get going. Are you all right to drive?'

'Yeah. It'll take my mind off the pain. If it gets too bad you can take over.'

He felt a beat of victory as they drove back to the main road. At least they had outwitted one element of Cultured

Voice's plan. And the photos on the camera might be useful.

* * *

'I didn't know you'd brought that toy gun,' Quentin said after they'd reached the main road. Sam's parting words still rankled and he hoped Wanda wouldn't mention them. 'How come?'

'Well, it's been useful before so I packed it just in case. Lucky they didn't see me creeping up on them.'

'But how come you've still got it? Wasn't it in the bag we lost in the Volvo?'

'Originally yes, but since we've been in Cornwall I've had it in my handbag.'

'You've been gadding around Cornwall with a gun in your handbag? Bloody hell, you're like Mary Poppins. What else have you got in there?'

'Nothing much, but a girl's got to be prepared. While those two were going after you, I ran back to the car for it. Got to you just in time by the looks of things.'

'So why didn't you offer it to me when I went off on my jaunts?'

'You've got Philmore covering your back. And if it looks like you're armed it could get you into more trouble, so best to use it sparingly. And imagine being searched and found with a replica instead of the real deal. Cultured Voice would have a field day with that.'

Quentin nodded. The gun was deceptively realistic, and had served its purpose on several occasions.

'Better ring Philmore,' Quentin said. 'Tell him what happened. Don't mention the gun though. I know it's not real but I'm not sure it's legal to threaten anyone with a weapon, even a fake one.'

'Well, anyway,' Wanda said thoughtfully, 'if those two are the sort our friend is hiring to do his dirty work then he's slipping. Not exactly discreet, are they? Still, I suppose if you're banged up abroad someone else has to do your hiring for you. The girl's got a lot to learn, but then she's very young. Everyone makes mistakes. We're all only human after all.'

Human. In spite of the photo he had seen, Quentin wouldn't have been surprised if the elusive man they were chasing had sprouted horns and a forked tail. He shook his head and wondered if he'd ever get the chance to find out.

## Chapter Twenty-two

Not wanting to go back to the hotel just yet, they found a restaurant on the outskirts of Truro. Wanda bought a local newspaper and after their meal, she did the crossword while Quentin scanned the news. He looked up and caught Wanda's eye as they heard another customer ordering a drink.

'I'll have a Coke please.'

Memories of Charlestown came flooding back. Bloody hell, he thought. Every time I hear that or see the advert, it'll remind me of him.

'Come on,' he said, standing up. 'Let's get the bill.'

Back at the car, Wanda was giving Mozart a drink when Quentin's phone rang. Number withheld.

'Him again,' he muttered. A few days, Cultured Voice had said, but if he'd been told what had happened at Wheal Peevor that morning... Bracing himself, Quentin pressed the answer button.

'Yes?' he said, looking up and seeing but not registering the three imposing spires of Truro Cathedral.

'Sorry to intrude on your day of leisure, Mr Cadbury, but I thought you might be bored, so I'm going to brighten up your afternoon. Are you alone?'

Quentin hesitated.

'I'll take that as a no. The persistent Mrs Merrydrew, I assume. At least, I hope it is, and that there's no one else there with you. Is anyone else there, Mr Cadbury?'

'No,' Quentin said, alarmed. 'No, of course not.'

Sweat beaded on his forehead at the thought that his nemesis had somehow found out about Philmore.

'Good, because I've planned a little visit, something you and Mrs Merrydrew will both enjoy.'

'Look, I've done what you asked—'

'Really, Mr Cadbury, I've already explained that such a simple task is not enough. You demonstrated your powers of observation in Charlestown, but I've got one final test for you before I know that you'll suit my purpose. Surely you want to make the most of your holiday? Cornwall is full of delightful places.'

'I can find delightful places by myself,' Quentin blurted.

'Just as well, because that's what you're going to do. I hope you like puzzles. You need to find this location and get some proof that you've been there. Do you have a map?'

'Yes,' Quentin said, wondering what was coming.

'Excellent. There are hundreds of coves and beaches in Cornwall. The one you're going to has a name that's rather jolly. As it's getting late, I'll give you a clue. You'll find it where the compass always points. Did you get that?'

'Yes, but—'

'It isn't a request, Mr Cadbury. It's an offer I advise you not to refuse. I'll call you later to see how you got on.'

The call was abruptly cut off.

'Well?' asked Wanda.

'This is getting ridiculous,' Quentin complained. 'I've got to find a beach or a cove with a jolly name. It's another goose chase.'

Wanda shrugged. 'Probably. All the same, better do as he says.'

Quentin sighed. 'Yeah. Apparently it's where the compass always points, so presumably it's on the north coast.'

Immediately Wanda reached onto the back seat for the map. She found the pages for Cornwall and spread it out on her lap.

'I'll start at Bude and work down,' she said, running her finger under the coastline. 'Some of these places are tiny. We could do with a magnifying glass. Why couldn't he have given you the postcode like he did for Bodmin Jail?'

After they'd both scanned the map several times, it was Wanda who spotted a pale blue name against a small inlet.

'Porth Joke,' she read aloud. 'Could that be it?'

'Sounds jolly enough,' he said, taking the map and looking where Wanda pointed. 'Sending me there would appeal to his weird sense of humour. Better get going.'

Wanda put Porth Joke into the satnav but it wasn't found. Between the map and the road signs, she navigated their way to Crantock, the nearest village to Porth Joke on the map. They could see no signs to where they were going so they asked somebody.

'You mean Polly Joke,' the woman they asked said with a knowing smile. 'Its real name is Porth Joke, but the locals have been calling it Polly Joke for years. Keep on the West Pentire Road and you'll come to it.'

They carried on, coming to a halt when they couldn't drive any further. There was no vehicular access to the cove.

'Bloody hell!' Quentin said in disbelief when he read the signpost. 'Polly Joke Beach.'

'This is like when he sent you to Charlestown and Colliford Lake,' Wanda said. 'Nothing's actually going to happen.'

'No, but he wants proof that I've been here. I'll take a photo of the signpost. That should do.'

'Good idea,' Wanda said, 'but he may want more than that. Better have a look on the beach just in case. Anyway, we're here, and he knows I'm with you, so we might as well give Mozart a run.'

'I suppose you're right. Come on then, Mozart.'

When they'd a taken a photo of the signpost on Quentin's phone and attached Mozart's lead, they began walking down the path to the cove. It was quite a way. Before it was in sight, Mozart was straining against his lead and sniffing the air as if he could smell the sea.

A mist was descending and it felt colder. When they got to the beach it was deserted. Rocks of all different shapes and sizes rose up from the sand like miniature mountains, black against a yellow canvas.

Off the lead, Mozart bounded away. The cove was deep but narrow, so the whole of it was in view. While Mozart ran about, occasionally stopping to sniff at his surroundings, Quentin walked around looking for something else to prove that he'd been here. There was nothing except rocks, sand and a few strings of seaweed. Deciding that the actual task he'd been set was simply solving the riddle of the "jolly beach" and then finding it, he joined Wanda and perched on a low rock. They sat for a while, listening to the sound of the waves breaking on the shore. Before long though, the mist had thickened, and minutes later they could hardly see where the sand ended and the water began.

'Let's go before we can't see our way back,' Wanda said. 'Here, Mozart.'

The little dog, usually so obedient, didn't appear. She called again, louder this time. Still no response. Wanda started to walk along the beach, calling for Mozart as she went. Quentin followed. The mist was fast becoming a dense fog and the clifftops that towered above the cove were practically obscured.

'Mozart!' he called, then cursed as his foot hit a low rock.

'I can't find him.' Wanda sounded anxious when Quentin almost bumped into her.

'He can't have gone far,' he assured her.

At that moment they heard a faint bark.

'Mozart!' shouted Wanda.

An answering bark wafted through the fog. Wanda and Quentin turned to follow the sound. After several more shouts and barks, they found themselves in a shallow cave. Quentin took out his phone and switched on the torch. Its brightness lightened the fog that had seeped in, and they found Mozart on a ledge, his collar caught on something protruding from the rock. An iron hook, Quentin saw, perhaps for tethering a boat.

Wanda freed the collar and Mozart leapt into her arms.

'Let's get out of here,' Quentin urged. He was secretly wondering how high the tide came up, and how long that would be. He imagined being marooned in the cave, their exit cut off by the water.

Wanda attached Mozart's lead and they edged their way out. Back on the beach, the fog seemed denser than ever. Quentin was disorientated. Should they turn left or right? Right, he decided. They walked arm in arm, peering ahead for any dips in the sand or unseen rocks.

Suddenly, a shape loomed in front of them. Not rock-shaped, more... more human. Quentin stopped, tugging on Wanda's arm so that she stopped too.

Quentin's heart flipped as the shape moved. Bloody hell, he thought. Cultured Voice has sent someone to spy on me after all. Someone or some*thing*...

The shape would have looked human, but the head was decidedly inhuman. It was swollen at the top and there was some sort of antenna sticking out of it.

Quentin gasped and stepped back, treading on Mozart's paw and making him yelp. The shape moved towards them, as if drawn by the sound. Instinctively Quentin raised his fists, knowing it was useless to try to run in the fog. He stood mesmerised, his heart hammering and his mouth dry. He felt Wanda's hand on his back and wished she hadn't come. Colin was right. He'd put Wanda in danger and he would never forgive himself.

The shape drew nearer, moving awkwardly. Then the outline of a hand appeared and the contours of the head changed. Wanda pushed past him and approached it.

'Wanda!' he cried in panic.

Ignoring him, she stopped in front of the shape. The fog muffled her voice when she spoke.

'Hello,' she said. 'Not a good day for snorkelling, is it? Are you all right?'

'Yes, thanks,' a female voice replied. 'I must admit I was scared out there for a minute. Stupid of me, going out on my own today.'

Joining Wanda, Quentin could make out the snorkel tube and the wide goggles pushed on top of the woman's head. She wore a winter wetsuit and flippers.

'I know how quickly the weather can change here,' the woman went on, 'but it was fine when I started. I know this part of the coast reasonably well and I'm used to staying in the water for a long time, but when the fog came down, I lost my sense of direction and went out too far. I was lucky not to be caught in a riptide. I'm supposed to be at Crantock.'

Although she was obviously experienced in snorkelling, Quentin was amazed that the woman was so calm after what could have become a tragedy. He also felt somewhat foolish, failing to recognize her for what she was, especially as he'd snorkelled in Australia only the year before.

'We can give you a lift to Crantock,' he offered, recovering his composure.

'Thanks. I'd appreciate that.'

It took them forty-five minutes to navigate their way off the beach and crawl the one and a half miles through the fog to Crantock. By the time they'd dropped off their passenger and were heading back to the hotel, the fog had lifted and darkness was setting in.

'It's like we've passed through a portal,' Wanda said. 'Foggy on one side, clear on the other.'

'Yes,' Quentin said absently. He wished there really was a portal, one they could step through and leave this debacle behind for ever.

# Chapter Twenty-three

'Good job with the camera yesterday,' Philmore told Quentin as they sat in a corner of the hotel lobby the next morning. 'We'll be getting the pictures downloaded and see if they tell us anything. We're not picking those two up yet, just in case they lead us to Mr Big. You never know.'

'I don't think they'll get anywhere near him,' Quentin speculated. 'I–'

He broke off when his mobile rang. He looked at Philmore after he saw the number was withheld. Lifting the phone to his ear, he said, 'Yes?'

'Good morning, Mr Cadbury. Did you find the place with the jolly name?'

'Yes.'

'And what was it called?'

'Polly Joke.'

'Very good. And how do I know you actually went there?'

'I took a photo of the signpost.'

'Very enterprising. For obvious reasons, I'll have to take your word for it. Now here's another place you'll enjoy. Penzance, though I'm given to understand the pirates no longer frequent that town.'

Thanks to Wanda's love of opera and all classical music, the reference to *The Pirates of Penzance* wasn't lost on

Quentin. He ignored it, nevertheless. 'Penzance? Where in Penzance?'

'It doesn't matter, anywhere will do. Be there by twelve-thirty.'

Quentin checked his watch. Could he get to Penzance in two hours?

'Did you hear me?'

'Yep, I heard you.'

'Good. Twelve-thirty, Mr Cadbury.'

'He's gone,' Quentin told Philmore. 'Penzance.'

'So I gathered,' Philmore said, 'but you won't be staying there or he would have been more specific. Looks like we're on another road to nowhere. I'll go and get Debbie. Ring when you're ready to leave.'

Quentin went back to his room, collected his things and threw them into his bag. He was just about to ring Wanda when she and Colin returned from their late breakfast. Quickly he explained about the call.

'I don't know if I'll be back today,' he said. 'You two can stay here. Or not,' he added, seeing the impatient toss of Wanda's head.

'If you think I've come all this way and waited all this time to keep missing out on things, you can think again,' Wanda said hotly. 'I can't sit here wondering what you're doing all day.'

'OK, OK. Just stay out of sight or Philmore won't be happy. Bye, Wanda.'

He stooped and planted a kissed on her cheek.

'See you then, Quentin,' Colin said brusquely. 'Don't do anything I wouldn't do.'

Ignoring him, Quentin strode out of the room and went out to his car, frowning when the key fob didn't unlock the door. He realized his mistake when he stepped back – this was Colin's Honda. Shaking his head, he found his own and glanced back at the hotel, wishing Wanda was with him but glad she would have company while he wasn't here.

He made it to Penzance with thirty minutes to spare. He drove along the seafront, found a parking space and walked along the promenade, passing the deserted Jubilee Pool lido. He carried on until he found a shop and bought a hot pasty, a coffee and a bottle of water. He managed to drink half the coffee before his mobile rang. Number withheld.

'So you're in Penzance, I assume, Mr Cadbury.'

'Uh-huh,' Quentin replied, swallowing a mouthful of coffee.

'Good. We'll make a good employee of you yet. Just a few more steps before I'm sure you can be trusted.'

Enraged by his adversary's audacity, Quentin gasped.

'You sound surprised, Mr Cadbury. You shouldn't dismiss my offer out of hand, you know. In fact, being a detective would be the perfect cover. After all there are bent policemen, so why not bent private detectives?'

'I'm not bent,' Quentin said through gritted teeth. 'And I don't intend to be, so forget it.'

'Really? What a pity, for you anyway. You'd make a lot more money than you do as a detective. You haven't exactly had an illustrious career, have you? No career in fact, till I came on the scene. I thought you'd jump at the chance.'

'Well, you thought wrong. Are you going to tell me what you want me to do?'

There was pause before the cultured voice came again. 'What would *you* like to do, Mr Cadbury? Right now, if you had the choice?'

'Go home and never hear from you again,' Quentin snapped.

'Oh dear. And here I was thinking we'd struck up a rapport. Never mind. You'll come round sooner or later. In my experience, people will do almost anything for money.'

'Can we get to the point?'

'Yes, as you're so impatient. Drive to a place called Porthcurno. It's quite near that wonderful open-air theatre, I believe. Shame there are no performances at this time of year. Park somewhere there and wait until I call you. Shall we say one-fifteen?'

'I don't know, shall we?' Quentin quipped, tired of Whitelaw's delaying tactics.

'A few more remarks like that and I'll be replacing my offer of work for something more unpleasant. One-fifteen.'

The line went dead. Cultured Voice's self-assurance penetrated Quentin's skin, upset his sense of balance. Breathing heavily, he muttered a string of profanities. What annoyed him most was that the man seemed to know so much about him. One thing he didn't know was apparent – precisely where Quentin was at this moment, and that Philmore was on his trail. As he strode back to his car, he called Philmore.

'Steve, it's Porthcurno, then wait again. I think he's playing silly devils now. All this is just to wind me up, I'm sure. You could be wasting your time. We both could.'

'Maybe,' Philmore agreed, 'but I'm not backing off now. He could be luring you into a trap and I don't want anything happening to you, even if you are a pain in the backside.'

'Thanks. I love you too. Where are you?'

'Close enough. Better get going.'

Quentin was beginning to think he preferred waiting around in hotels to driving around all day without knowing his ultimate destination. Resignedly, he set off.

It didn't take long to get there. Porthcurno was a pretty village with no vehicular access to the beach, so he parked at the Museum of Global Communications, which, he recalled from a TV documentary, was dedicated to the growth of communications since the first undersea telegraph cable had been laid here. There were only a few other vehicles here, and he spotted Philmore and Francis's

146

Audi pulling into a space at the far end. He sat waiting, his hand clamped over his mobile. When it vibrated against his palm, he raised it to his ear.

'Right, Mr Cadbury.' Despite the cultured tones, Whitelaw's voice was clipped and stony. 'There's a track signposting the coastal path. Find it, drive down there until you can't go any further, park the car and start walking. There shouldn't be many people about at this time of year, but if there are, don't stop or talk to anyone. Make sure you're alone. If there's another car anywhere near you, I'll know. Cars aren't allowed down that track but you're quite good at flouting the rules. Keep your phone with you. Don't bring anything else. Got that?'

'Yes but—'

'Twenty minutes.'

'Twenty minutes,' Quentin repeated into the silence as the call ended. He snatched up his other mobile and repeated the instructions to Philmore.

'Don't get close,' he finished. 'This feels different. I think he'll have eyes on me now. I've only got twenty minutes so I need to go.'

Replacing the phone, he exited the car park and found the track, cursing as he saw the sign to the coastal path too late and had to find a place to turn round and go back. When he got to the turn-off, he noticed the sign saying the road was unsuitable for vehicles and swung into it, bumping along the dirt track and hoping he wouldn't meet any walkers. The December day was cold and windy, the sky the colour of steel, but he knew some intrepid walkers were not put off by the weather. Luck was with him though, and there was nobody in sight.

After a few hundred yards, the track widened enough to park a car on one side; possibly for emergency vehicles, Quentin guessed, knowing the nearby cliffs could be dangerous. Beyond that point, the track became impassable for all but pedestrians. Placing his mobile in his pocket, his hand hovered over his second phone. *Bring your phone, don't bring anything else.* As far as he knew, his adversary didn't know he had a second phone. Quentin was willing to forego his Swiss army knife in case he was searched, but the second phone was his only direct contact with Philmore. Deciding to risk it, he placed it in the opposite pocket, then climbed out from the car. A gust of wind blew cold around him as his mobile rang and he fished it out, straining to hear the cultured voice when it spoke.

'Walk down the track, Mr Cadbury, for about a hundred and fifty yards. You should see a gate on the left-hand side. Climb over it and follow the hedge round the field to the right. When you get to the end, you'll be at the cliff edge. I'm reliably informed that it's quite an easy climb down from there. If there's anyone following you they'll be seen, so make sure there isn't. I don't think you want to be responsible for anyone being hurt, do you? Be on the beach in fifteen minutes.'

Silence followed this one-sided conversation. Climb down a cliff? In this wind? Quentin had rarely climbed more than an extended ladder. Oh well, he thought as he started walking, there's a first time for everything.

He found the gate, scrambled over it and began walking along by the hedge. He was well hidden here and needed to call Philmore before he got to the cliff edge. He gazed around him. No one could possibly see him here. Surely it would be safe to ring Philmore?

He felt for his second mobile. As his hand closed around it he remembered Bradford Bridge. Cultured Voice had known he was there. Someone had seen him somehow. Desperate to let Philmore know where he was, he made a pretence of stumbling, and while he was on his knees, he quickly took the phone out, brought up Philmore's number and pressed the call button.

'Don't talk but keep listening,' he said when it connected. 'I think I'm being watched. I'll keep the phone on in my pocket in case you can hear. I'm supposed to be on the beach in fifteen minutes.'

Not daring to take any more time, he slipped the phone back into his pocket. He didn't know how long the airway would stay open or when the signal would die, but it was worth a try.

He got to his feet and carried on walking. The further he was from the path, the more isolated he felt. It was pretty desolate here, he realized, especially in winter. The only sound was the crashing of waves on the shore, growing louder with each step he took. The field came to an abrupt end, and he stopped as it fell away. He would have fallen away too if he hadn't been prepared. Cautiously, he peered over the edge to the beach, some fifty or sixty feet below. It was hardly a beach at all; no sand as there had been yesterday, just a strip of shingle. He stared down the cliff in dismay. Cultured Voice must think he was a mountaineer! It wasn't sheer though, and he could see places where he could put his hands and feet. Setting his mouth in a grim line, he screwed up his courage, turned round and began his descent.

Thankful for his sturdy trainers, he felt for each foothold as he went, sweat forming all over him despite the cold. Several times the wind threatened to throw him off balance, but he clung on. It seemed an age before he reached the bottom. He couldn't feel his hands and saw that his nails were torn and blood oozed from a cut on his finger. I must be mad, he thought as he jumped onto the shingle.

The cove was tiny, hemmed in by encircling cliffs. The place was deserted except for a boat tethered to a small rock, water licking around it. An empty boat. Bloody hell, he thought, blowing on his hands, next I'll be getting a call telling me to row off somewhere. He drew a long breath. His only experience of rowing consisted of an hour in a pleasure boat on a lake as a boy.

He began walking along the stretch of beach towards the boat; a dinghy, he could see now, with an outboard engine. The mouth of a cave yawned to his left and he thought how ideal this place would have been for smugglers. Passing the cave, he caught a movement from the periphery of his vision. He started to whirl round. Too late. He gasped as something flung itself around his neck and squeezed.

## Chapter Twenty-four

Catching hold of the arm that threatened to strangle him, Quentin tried in vain to wriggle away from its vice-like grip.

'Come quietly, if you know what's good for you,' a gruff voice said into his ear. 'Someone wants a little chat with you and he won't like it if you make a fuss.'

The arm dropped away from Quentin's neck and both his arms were caught from behind. A huge hand held them fast while another wrapped what felt like string around Quentin's wrists.

'Move,' the voice commanded, pushing Quentin towards the dinghy, untethering it then shoving it further into the water. 'Get in.'

Quentin felt his arms almost being wrenched from their sockets. Water lapped round his ankles, filling his shoes and soaking his feet as he was shunted towards the dinghy. He wondered how he was expected to get in with his hands tied and the boat bobbing about. He clumsily raised his right leg and brought it down on the edge of the dinghy, causing it to tip. He tried again with the same result.

'Go on!' instructed his captor, and as if tiring of Quentin's awkward attempts, he pushed hard against his back. Quentin fell forward, tumbling into the boat with a thud. Pain seared though him when his nose connected with the fibreglass and blood oozed down into his mouth. When he struggled to his knees he felt the boat sway as the other man climbed aboard, and saw him readying himself to sit on the bench seat near the outboard motor just a few feet away. For a wild moment Quentin thought of headbutting him, knocking him off balance and using the chance to jump out and make a run for it. But he was too late. His opponent planted his rock-solid frame on the seat, his meaty hands already reaching for the starter.

The engine spluttered into life and the little craft pulled away from the beach. Any thoughts of tackling his assailant faded as Quentin watched the shore grow distant. It was no good jumping now. He couldn't swim or climb the cliff with his hands bound. He remained on his knees, feeling the swell of the waves as they chugged further out. His nose throbbed and blood continued to trickle from it. This is the end, he thought. He's going to tie rocks to my feet and throw me over the side. He tried to draw a deep breath to calm himself, but the blood in his nose ran down the back of his throat and made him cough. What really calmed him was what this thug had said – *someone wants a little chat with you.* If someone wanted to talk to him then he was safe, for the moment at least. And there were no rocks in the boat. Not even stones.

Convinced that the person who wanted to talk to him was the man behind this whole thing, the knot that had formed in his stomach grew tighter. He didn't know what he expected, what he should feel; fear, yes, but also a tingle of excitement to realize that he was going to come face to face with the man he knew as Cultured Voice at last. But this man didn't want to see him for fun. He wasn't going to offer him tea and cake or engage in conversation about the weather. Quentin had thwarted him, and he knew, with undeniable certainty, that Cultured Voice was not the forgiving sort. He had sworn revenge, and Quentin had a feeling he was about to find out what form that revenge would take.

'Where are we going?' he croaked, looking at the man opposite.

The answer came in a growl. 'You'll know soon enough.'

It wasn't just his hands that were meaty, Quentin saw. He was meaty all over; his neck rolled over the top of his sweater and his fingers were like sausages. But those fingers weren't soft like sausages. They were hard, solid, like the thick arms and broad torso. All ideas of headbutting fled from Quentin's mind. He'd probably break his neck against those muscles. For a few random moments he wished he'd taken up boxing or weightlifting instead of running. Then the reality of what was happening struck home and all he could think of was how he could get out of this situation, how he could outwit the man who was waiting for him and escape. No ideas came to him, and he wondered if they were heading for another lonely cove or whether he was being taken out to sea, perhaps to a bigger boat.

The answer came when the cove slipped out of view and they rounded the headland. There, lying at anchor, was a yacht. Quentin's heart flipped. Instinctively, he knew that's where they were bound. Cultured Voice may never have set foot in England since his escape from the Netherlands.

The yacht loomed larger as the dinghy ploughed through the waves, glistening white in the winter sun that slid out from behind the grey clouds, rocking back and forth with the swell. Quentin felt slightly nauseous and his stomach churned. "*The Blue Albatross*", he read on the side of the yacht. As far as he knew, albatrosses weren't blue, but right now he wouldn't have cared if they were green with red spots as long as he didn't have to go aboard.

Something moved on the deck, a male figure, Quentin thought. He swallowed, his pulse quickening. Was that him? The sickness he felt now wasn't entirely due to the motion of the boat, he realized. Bloody hell, what an idiot he'd been to take this on. He should have refused to go along with it, asked for police protection.

The dinghy was turning, ready to come alongside the yacht. Then Meaty Man was throwing a rope to someone who came forward to catch it and secure it to a stanchion on deck. When the dinghy had been made fast, Meaty Man jerked his head towards the yacht's ladder. Quentin tried to get up from his kneeling position, stumbled and sank back again. Meaty Man kicked at his thigh and Quentin forced himself upright. How the hell do they think I can get up a ladder with my hands tied behind my back? he thought savagely. As if by thought transition, an instantly recognizable voice came from above.

'It's all right, Jim, you can untie him now. I'm sure our guest doesn't fancy a long swim back to shore. The water's pretty cold.'

Quentin didn't fancy the swim but he would have done anything to avoid getting on the yacht. He had a premonition that once he was on, the only way off would be as a dead man. But then if he risked the water he'd probably die from hypothermia before he got back to shore, and it was unlikely he'd outswim the dinghy or a gunshot. The possibility that the man on the yacht was armed was becoming more of a probability with each tortuous second.

The meaty Jim reached into his pocket and brought out a knife. It reminded Quentin of the flick knives he'd seen in some of the old films his mother used to watch. He stood as still as he could on the swaying dinghy, not wanting the knife to miss its target and cut him. He knew the edge was acutely keen when it sliced through his bonds like butter. He felt Jim's hand on his back immediately, pushing him towards the ladder. Reluctantly, he gripped the rungs and slowly hauled himself up.

The first thing he saw when his head was level with the deck was a pair of feet in beige deck shoes, and then legs clad in white trousers. He caught a whiff of something he couldn't place, something other than the brine of the sea. Cigarette smoke? Catching hold of the railings either side of the ladder head, he heaved himself onto the yacht.

'Welcome aboard, Mr Cadbury. Good to meet you in the flesh at last.'

The man who had spoken stood casually by the companionway, a slim cigar between his fingers. A beige jacket over a white open-necked shirt and a beige and cream cravat completed his apparel. The man himself was of slight build, middle height, thin-lipped and dark-haired. Unremarkable in every way. Except for his eyes, steely grey behind gold-rimmed glasses; eyes that bored into Quentin, betraying the politeness of the greeting his cultured voice had given.

A man in jeans and an anorak hovered by the railings a little further along, then nodded as the man with the cigar spoke.

'It's all right, Pete, I don't think Mr Cadbury is going to give us any trouble.'

Quentin turned as his meaty captor came aboard. Except he wasn't his captor now, Cultured Voice was. And he scared Quentin far more.

The man called Jim looked at Cultured Voice as though for instruction. 'Shall I frisk him boss?'

'No need, Jim. You stay here with Pete. Mr Cadbury isn't the gun-carrying type.'

Instantly Quentin thought of the imitation gun Wanda had used at the tin mine. Clearly this hadn't yet been reported to the man in front of him.

'This is only a friendly meeting,' Cultured Voice went on. 'Mr Cadbury and I are going to have a cosy chat in the cabin. I'm sure he'd like to be warm and comfortable. Wouldn't you, Mr Cadbury? It's a little windy out here.'

A little windy was an understatement, Quentin decided as a gust blew through his hair and found its way between the edges of his clothes. But then Cultured Voice understated everything, even death threats.

'Why have you brought me here?' he ventured, dabbing at his bloodied nose with his hand.

'Patience, Mr Cadbury. Come now, let's get below and we can talk.'

'I've got nothing to say to you.'

'But I've got something to say to you that I think you'll find quite interesting.' Lifting a beige arm, Cultured Voice drew on his cigar then threw the butt over the side.

Quentin watched it swirl in the wind, then bob in the water like a cork until it was swept away on a wave. At that moment Quentin would have liked to have been that cork, or anything that would take him away from his present situation.

He glanced back to the man who had arranged this meeting and his eyes widened. His captor had pulled a pair of thin white latex gloves from his jacket pocket. Bloody hell, Quentin thought, this is it. He's going to kill me, and he's making sure he won't leave any trace of himself behind. The man eased the gloves over his hands, but not before Quentin noticed a wide gold signet ring on the third finger of his right hand. It made an oval lump in the glove.

Cultured Voice gestured towards the cabin door. Quentin didn't move. The man called Pete took a step nearer. Three against one…

'After you, Mr Cadbury,' Cultured Voice said.

Quentin gave a sideways glance towards the two heavies, ruled out an attempt at escape and walked towards the cabin. He stumbled down the hatchway and immediately looked around for something he could use as a weapon. He noticed nothing suitable before his captor was there beside him, a sardonic smile on his face.

'Do sit down, Mr Cadbury.'

Quentin took the seat indicated, a velvet-covered bench seat running the length of the cabin. Cultured Voice sat on a free-standing chair, positioning an oblong table between them. A strategic move, Quentin realized. There was no way he could get out of the cabin in a hurry. He stared across at the man who had threatened his life, his mind in turmoil. What on earth was going to happen now?

# Chapter Twenty-five

'Very nice, isn't it, this yacht?' Cultured Voice said. 'On the small side as yachts go, but quite sumptuous.'

Quentin couldn't disagree with that. His gaze flickered around, taking in the polished wood, the gold door handles and porthole surrounds, the richness of the furnishings.

'Yours, is it? I suppose you can afford it with your ill-gotten gains.'

'Unfortunately not mine. It belongs to a good friend. It's at my disposal for as long as I need it.'

Quentin shook his head in disbelief. 'Why are we here?' he demanded. 'I've delivered your precious package. What more do you want?'

Cultured Voice looked at him steadily, his expression unchanging. 'Oh, a lot more, Mr Cadbury, a lot more. For a start, you can look behind that cushion next to you.'

For a long moment Quentin didn't move. More games, he thought. Realizing he had no choice but to play along, he grasped the cushion and pulled it forward. Behind it was an oblong package, brown cardboard, like the one that had been left in the Honda.

'What is it?' he asked, not touching it.

'What does it look like?'

'Look, Whitelaw, or whatever you're calling yourself these days—'

An unpleasant snigger broke from his adversary's lips. 'Whitelaw! I haven't used that for some time, but never mind. It will do for now. *Mr* Whitelaw, that is.'

Mister my arse, Quentin thought, thinking there were lots of names he could give this man, none of them pleasant.

'Look,' he said again, 'you asked me to do a job for you and I've done it. I'm not delivering any more packages.'

'It's not another package, it's the same one.'

'What?' Quentin was stunned. He'd driven all over Cornwall to deliver this parcel and it ends up here?

'Open it. Well go on, Mr Cadbury, it's perfectly harmless.'

'Harmless!' Quentin spluttered. 'People die from this stuff, and you call it harmless?'

'I can assure you this package is quite harmless. Useful, in certain circumstances.'

Quentin snatched up the box and banged it down on the table. He attacked the tape, breaking another nail as he clawed at it. If it contained what he thought it contained, he'd have a hard job stopping himself from ramming it down the other man's throat. His captor watched, looking faintly amused. When Quentin was finally able to remove the tape, he slipped a finger under the flap and levered off the lid. He peered into it, unwilling to handle the contents. Eyes widening, he stared into the box in confusion.

'What the...' he began.

He reached into the box and drew out the round, soft, white object that fitted snugly inside. Several tightly packed pebbles dropped out from the space in its centre.

'A toilet roll!' Quentin spluttered. 'I've driven halfway round Cornwall to deliver a toilet roll!' He threw the roll across the cabin in disgust. 'Your idea of a joke, I suppose. Well, I'm not laughing.'

'Oh come now, Mr Cadbury, I thought your sense of humour was broader.'

Quentin pushed at the table and stood up. 'I've had enough of this. I was stupid enough to agree to your terms when I should have told you to drop dead.'

The other man's expression changed. 'I can assure you, I'm not planning to do that any time soon. I suggest you sit down. Or have you forgotten my two friends spoiling for a fight up on deck?'

In the heat of the moment Quentin had forgotten. Now he sat back down, rage bubbling up inside him. It sat quietly smouldering, like a volcano threatening to erupt. Saying nothing, he waited for the cultured tones to come again. When they did, his rage increased.

'Quentin. What an old-fashioned name for someone so young. Still, if you're going to work for me, we needn't carry on being so formal. Can I call you Quentin?'

'No you bloody well can't.'

Cultured Voice leaned back in his chair. 'As you wish. All right, Mr Cadbury, let's get down to business. Seeing as you've successfully delivered one package, you can deliver more.'

Quentin was thrown. Delivered a package successfully? A toilet roll that ended up with the person who'd dispatched it? And why the pebbles? To give it weight, mislead the bearer, he realized now.

'No bloody way. I'm not taking anything anywhere.'

'But you already have, Mr Cadbury. Quite unwittingly, but you have.'

Quentin pursed his lips and fingered the mole by his ear. What on earth was this bastard on about now? The man was talking in riddles again.

'What do you mean?'

A smirk crossed the older man's face, fleeting, but Quentin saw it. 'Are you going to tell me or not?'

'Not exactly a patient man, are you? The goods I wanted transported have reached their destination safely, thanks to your cooperation.'

'Really. And how did I have anything to do with that?'

'It's quite simple. They were hidden in your bag, the one you left in the car when you went on your little jaunt to the Eden Project.'

Quentin stared blankly cross the table.

'Think about it. Or perhaps it's too subtle for you to understand.'

Quentin's mind raced.

'So,' he said slowly, 'when they took the car, they put something in my bag, and then what? Took the bag with the stuff in and delivered it somewhere else?'

'Exactly so. I'm glad you've got a brain under that thick skull of yours. Although I'm not sure you can work out why we did it that way. Surely you didn't really think I'd entrust my goods to a jumped-up little nobody like you, not on the first mission anyway. I had to be sure you'd do what I asked.'

Beating back his anger, Quentin said nothing.

'So,' the cultured voice went on, 'can you guess why we did things the way we did?'

The urge to wipe the smug expression from this man's face was becoming stronger. Resisting, Quentin said, 'Because if whoever was transporting the bag was caught with it, they could say it wasn't theirs, that they'd been asked to take the bag and didn't know what was in it. Or better still, if they were cornered, get rid of the bag altogether, then the bag would be found, traced to me, and I'd be charged with drug smuggling. Very neat, but I don't think the police would swallow that.'

'No? Oh, your friend in the police force. Still, it would be very inconvenient, wouldn't it, having to explain it all? Even a DCI in the Metropolitan Police can't work miracles overnight. Such a nuisance. Which brings me to another point.'

The cultured tones had an edge to them when they continued. 'You were specifically instructed to come alone. You didn't. Of course, we both know how stubborn Mrs Merrydrew can be, and how tiresome that infernal dog of hers is, but I still blame you. Not only should you have been strong enough to persuade her not to come, you shouldn't have told her anything about it in the first place.

It makes one wonder who else you told. The person who took your car says he thought someone was following him, though he could have been mistaken. What do you think, Mr Cadbury? Was he mistaken?'

Quentin scrabbled for an answer. Bad enough Cultured Voice knew about Wanda. If he thought the police were involved it would reduce Quentin's chances of getting out of this alive to zero. Or was he still playing games? Had he known that Philmore was in on things all along? Was that the real reason he'd played the toilet roll trick? His ego would get a double boost if he thought he'd outwitted Quentin *and* the police at the same time.

'Well, Mr Cadbury?'

'How the hell do I know if anyone was following him? I was stuck in a car park without a car, or at least without the one I went there with.' Desperately trying to steer the conversation away from the possibility of Philmore being involved, Quentin rushed on. 'And why all the running around before Eden? Starbucks, Bradford Bridge, the lake?'

'I don't see that it's any of your business, but I don't suppose it will hurt to tell you now. It's nothing sinister. I wanted to make sure you were actually here, in Cornwall, not sitting in some nice safe place and stringing me along. I've never really had a good look at you. I wanted a photo, but you couldn't get to Starbucks before dark and your scarf was hiding your face at Bradford Bridge so my photographer couldn't get a good shot.'

'And the lake?'

'Oh, that was just to check your obedience, Mr Cadbury.'

Reaching into his inside jacket pocket, Cultured Voice continued, 'Luckily my photographer had better luck at the Eden Project.' He drew out a photo and laid it on the table.

Quentin gasped, then gulped as he stared at it. There he was at the ice rink, sprawled on the ice, seemingly looking straight up into the lens.

'Not a particularly flattering likeness, but my photographer's quite an artist. She managed to isolate the face and enhance it.' He laid down a second picture, head and shoulders, with Quentin's face as clear as day.

'I believe you've met Samantha,' Cultured Voice drawled, answering Quentin's silent question. 'Very talented and quite useful, but unfortunately I'll have to dispense with her services if she doesn't stop doing things her way instead of mine. At St Michael's Mount she was supposed to get you to admit that Mrs Merrydrew was with you without making you suspicious. That's what happens when you send a girl to do a woman's job. I'm sure Mrs Merrydrew could do better.'

'What was the point of sending anyone if you knew—'

Cultured Voice's eyebrows lifted above the gold-rimmed glasses. 'If I already knew Mrs Merrydrew was with you? No point really, except I wanted to keep you entertained, alleviate your boredom. And I have to test all my operatives. Samantha hasn't carried out any jobs that didn't involve photography. I think she'll be sticking to photography. She's good at that, don't you agree?'

He obviously had no idea about the incident at the tin mine or that Sam no longer had her camera. Quentin didn't enlighten him. He didn't want to inflame his present situation.

'So,' Cultured Voice was saying, 'now my colleagues know who they're looking for, if I ask them to find you.'

'So that's why you wanted to know what car I hired and the registration number? So your so-called colleagues would know it was me.'

'You've got it, Mr Cadbury. And now I've got this' — Cultured Voice flicked a hand at the photo — 'I know what you look like, and where you live. Of course, I met the delectable Mrs Merrydrew a few years ago, although she didn't see my face. A pity I haven't got a photograph of her, but there's still time.'

'Leave her out of this,' Quentin snapped. 'I'm the one who foiled your previous plans, not her.'

His captor's voice was scathing when he replied. 'You mean she's not as good a detective as you? So why did you make her a partner in your pathetic little business? A detective agency! How droll.'

He leaned forward, his expression impassive. 'I'm not in the habit of hurting attractive ladies, not unless there's absolutely no alternative. You really should take a leaf out of my book. I've had my share of attractive ladies, but when you lead a life like mine, you don't want to be putting down roots. You never know when they'll trip you up. It's far better to be a lone wolf than to be tied down with a family, having to explain your every move. No, Mr Cadbury, no one is ever truly free all the time they depend on other people.'

Quentin swallowed. He wanted to be off this boat, away from this man, beneath whose cultured voice lay murderous undertones. He feared the end of this conversation, dreaded what Cultured Voice had in store for him, especially if he learned that Quentin had bested two of his employees and taken their camera. And if he knew the police were involved...

'You depend on other people all the time,' Quentin ventured. 'The girl who took this for a start, and the people on this yacht.'

'In a professional capacity only. That's different from getting emotionally involved. My contacts are useful to me, but they can all be replaced. It may take a little time, but there's always someone who'll do anything for money. In fact most people like working for me because I'm so generous. Mind you, I expect a good job. I don't tolerate incompetence, which makes me wonder if you're really up to the task I'm asking of you. Perhaps I should dispense with you now and be done with it.'

Quentin wondered whether he was expected to grovel, to say he was willing and competent enough to transport anything rather than be killed. Damned if he was going to grovel to this cold-hearted man, master criminal or not. Pressing his lips together, he said nothing. One thing gave him hope. If Cultured Voice was talking about him carrying out more jobs, then he wasn't planning on killing him. Not yet at least. Whatever was demanded of him, he would have to pretend to go along with it. He stood far more chance of staying alive on dry land than he did on this yacht.

The cultured voice interrupted his thoughts. 'Where is she, by the way? Don't look as though you don't know what I'm talking about. Where is Mrs Merrydrew?'

'How do I know? The last time I saw her was when I left my hotel after your call this morning. I persuaded her to wait there for me.'

Cultured Voice gazed at him with hooded eyes.

'Really? And she always does what you tell her, does she? I think the delectable Mrs Merrydrew has a will of her own. I've yet to fathom what she sees in a boy who thinks he's a modern-day Sherlock Holmes. Still, I'll say one thing for you – you're not afraid of a challenge, which is why I've decided not to kill you, not until you've done another little job for me anyway. If you prove useful and loyal, I could be persuaded not to kill you at all.'

'Very kind of you, I'm sure.' Quentin's sarcasm had a bitter ring to it. 'What do you want me to do?'

Cultured Voice leaned back in his chair, a triumphant smile on his face. 'There now, that wasn't so hard, was it? I knew you'd see reason. It's nothing difficult – just more of the same, only this time I want a package taken to London. Very convenient for you, wouldn't you say? I'd tell you not to involve Mrs Merrydrew, but I suspect she can be as persuasive as she is stubborn. It makes no difference. If anything goes wrong I'll hold you both responsible, and I know you don't want anything happening to her. I'm guessing you've grown very fond of her over the last few years.'

Quentin glared at him, his anger bubbling up again. 'I wouldn't put her at risk,' he blurted. 'Let's leave her out of it.'

'We could have done, Mr Cadbury, if you hadn't brought her along. If anything untoward does happen to her you'll have the pleasure of knowing it's your fault.'

Sucking in a deep breath, Quentin looked away, his heart contracting. The arrogant man opposite him was right. Refusing to rise to the bait, he said nothing.

Cultured Voice rose. 'Wait here, and don't even think about trying to leave. My friends are at the top of the hatchway with orders to stop you by any means they see fit. Believe me when I say their idea of stopping someone is far less genteel than mine.'

He turned, went to a door and disappeared into what Quentin assumed were the sleeping quarters. Seeking escape, Quentin looked desperately round the cabin, but it was useless. He knew he'd have no trouble beating the older man in a physical fight, but the two thugs on deck were a different matter. Frustration swamped him, leaving him feeling helpless.

The door opened and his captor reappeared with a package, about half the size of the one Quentin had driven around Cornwall.

'What is it?' he mumbled as it was slapped down on the table in front of him.

'Come now, Mr Cadbury, even you're not that naïve. You know what it is. Why else would you tell me that people die from this stuff?'

'So you want me to help more people die, is that the idea?'

'I'm sorry if my trade offends your sensitive nature, Mr Cadbury, but if you hadn't helped ruin my previous sources of income I wouldn't be forced to turn to more distasteful methods of making money. There are a lot of weak people in the world, as I'm sure you know. It's not my fault if they can't live without their daily fix. I'm just fulfilling a need. Supply and demand, you could say.'

An urge to lash out and sweep the new package off the table flooded Quentin, and he sat on his hands to stop himself.

'Enough of this shilly-shallying,' Cultured Voice snapped, his voice hardening. 'This is business. Take the package and guard it with your life, and I do mean your life. That's all for now. Jim will take you back to shore. And no fooling about on the way. We wouldn't want our precious cargo to get wet, would we?'

He made to stand up then sat down again. 'One more thing before you go. Show me your phone.'

'What for?'

'Just hand it over.'

Heat prickled Quentin's neck. Which pocket was his everyday mobile in? He didn't want to pull out the wrong one. It was a 50/50 chance, and he held his breath as he reached into his left-hand pocket, gripped a phone and took it out. He breathed again when, as he handed the phone over, he saw he'd made the right choice.

'I see you've had a call from Australia,' Cultured Voice commented, scrolling through the recent calls, 'and quite a few from this number withheld. Convenient, that facility. What about this other number?'

'Just a friend,' Quentin said, peering at Colin's number as Cultured Voice pointed to it with a gloved hand.

'Mrs Merrydrew?'

'No,' Quentin said at once, glad that Wanda hadn't had occasion to call him in the last few days. 'We don't ring each other much.'

Cultured Voice's finger hovered over Colin's number. For a moment Quentin thought he was going to call it. He felt a beat of panic as he imagined Colin saying something that would reveal he was in on the situation. Quentin held his breath.

'Well,' said Cultured Voice eventually, 'I suppose there's no need as you're together most of the time. Very cosy. Not exactly a popular person though, are you? Not many calls in the last week or so. Still, I expect you have a landline for your little detective agency.' He placed the phone down on the table.

'Yeah,' Quentin agreed, snatching up the phone.

'Do you have the photo you took, by the way? The one at Polly Joke?'

Quentin found the photo and held the phone up for Cultured Voice to see.

'Amazing, isn't it, technology today?' Cultured Voice said, glancing at the photo. 'I think we're done for today.'

Cultured Voice stood up, walked to the hatchway and gave two raps on the wall. The hatch opened and he called, 'Mr Cadbury is coming up now, Jim.'

After picking up his phone and the package and slipping them into his pocket, Quentin pushed past his captor and climbed the steps. Seeing the deck from this angle, Quentin noticed something he hadn't seen before – a second, smaller dinghy, its tarpaulin cover partially blown off by the wind. It seemed the man who had this yacht at his disposal had ensured there was more than one means of escape.

Cultured Voice came up behind him. 'A successful meeting all round, don't you think, Mr Cadbury?'

'If you say so,' Quentin answered, hating himself for acquiescing.

'I do say so, and so should you. After all, you're still alive. If you want to stay that way, I suggest you follow my orders to the letter. I have eyes everywhere, Mr Cadbury. I can track you down even from this boat. And needless to say, keep our little tête-à-tête between us. There are rather a lot of policemen looking for me, so I'm trusting you to be discreet. Goodbye, Mr Cadbury. I've enjoyed our little chat. You can leave for London as soon as you like. I'll be in touch to let you know where to deliver the goods.'

Five minutes later, Quentin was back in the dinghy with the meaty Jim. He watched as the yacht grew smaller and smaller, until he could no longer read its name, until he could no longer see the figure standing on the deck staring after him.

Quentin could hardly believe what had happened. It already seemed like a dream. The most wanted man in Europe had summoned him, brought him aboard his hideout, revealed himself to him. Why?

'What the hell does it matter why,' he muttered to himself on the beach when the dinghy was on the way back to the yacht. Cultured Voice, he realized, had been right about one thing. He was alive. And he definitely wanted to stay that way.

# Chapter Twenty-six

'Did you get any leads from my phone?' Quentin blurted as soon as Philmore answered his call. He shifted uncomfortably in the Honda, which he'd found just as he'd left it.

'Good thinking, but the signal pinged out as soon as we turned off the main road. To be honest we couldn't hear much anyway with that wind. We found your car and followed the path right up to the end, to the top of the bay. We went down to the beach there but there was no sign of you, just some dog walkers and some kids in rock pools.'

Realizing the cove where he'd been wasn't visible from the path, Quentin asked, 'Did you see a yacht anchored offshore from where you were?'

There was a pause, as though Philmore was trying to conjure up the image of the bay. 'Yes, I think there was one there.'

'Well, that's where I was. With him.'

Philmore's sharp intake of breath sounded in Quentin's ear. 'Him? You mean Whitelaw? You actually came face to face with him? Are you sure it was him?'

'Of course I'm sure. I've seen a photo of him now, and that voice is etched into my brain. It was him all right.'

'Why the hell didn't you say straight away—' Philmore began. 'We're wasting time. I need to go and check out this yacht if we're going to catch the bastard.'

'It's called *The Blue Albatross*,' Quentin told him. 'He's got two minders with him, and there's two dinghies.'

'Thanks.'

'Yes, I'm fine, thanks for asking,' Quentin muttered as the line went silent. A sense of hopelessness filled him. He knew time was of the essence, but Philmore had cut him off without a thought of including him in whatever action he decided to take. He consoled himself with the thought that there might not be any action. If he knew one thing about the man on the yacht, it was that he wouldn't wait around to be found. *The Blue Albatross* was probably already under way, and who's to say if Cultured Voice was still aboard? The meaty Jim could have put him ashore further along the coast as soon as he'd returned to the yacht, or Cultured Voice could have taken the second dinghy and gone ashore on his own. Whatever happened, Quentin was convinced of one thing. The man he knew as Cultured Voice would get away again.

* * *

'Where are you, Quentin?'

The warmth of Wanda's sultry tones calmed Quentin somewhat. 'I'm not sure exactly. On a coastal path somewhere near Porthcurno. I could do with a stiff drink.'

'All right. We brought everything from the hotel, and we found one in Penzance on the way here. We'll meet you there and you can tell us about it.'

After noting down the details, Quentin made a five-point turn and drove back along the track to the main road out of the area. Dear Wanda, he thought as he drove. She hadn't even asked what had happened. She had judged from his voice that whatever he had to say could wait.

Exhaustion swept over Quentin. It seemed an age since he'd started out this morning. By the time he'd found the hotel it was nearly five o'clock. The first thing he saw after leaving the car was Colin's white Honda, the back window slightly open. An excited bark emanated from it as he neared it.

'Mozart,' he croaked, peering bleary-eyed through the window.

In the yellow light from the car park lamp he could see the little dog, his paws up on the inside of the window.

'Hello, boy. What's up, aren't you allowed inside? Don't worry, we won't forget about you.'

'Thank goodness you're all right,' Wanda said when he almost fell in the door of the room she'd booked. 'I've poured you a drink.'

Quentin sank onto the bed, taking the glass she proffered with trembling hands and putting it to his lips.

'What have you done to your hands?' Wanda asked. 'And your nose. You've been bleeding.'

When he'd taken a deep gulp of whisky, he gave her a weak grin. 'I had to do a bit of rock climbing, and I had an argument with a boat.'

He shook his head, reliving the events of the afternoon in his mind. He'd been certain Cultured Voice meant to kill him. Now that he realized what a narrow escape he'd had, he couldn't stop shivering.

'It was him, Wanda. On a boat. It was him.'

Wanda stared at him and gasped. 'You– you met him?' Recovering, she went on, 'Let's get those cuts washed, I'll get Colin to go out and get some antiseptic cream. Come on.'

She took hold of his arms and he stood up, letting her guide him to the bathroom, where she filled the sink with hot water, squirted liquid soap into her palms and gently washed the dirt and blood from Quentin's hands and face. She tenderly ran her fingertips over his bruised skin, letting them caress his cheek and linger on his lips.

'Thank goodness I didn't know you were going to meet him,' she whispered huskily. 'I'd have been out of my mind with worry.'

Quentin gazed at her, feeling a shift in the dynamic between them. Before he had time to react, she moved away.

'Get in the shower,' she said, her normal tone resuming. 'I'll get you some clean clothes.'

Too tired to argue, Quentin stripped and stood under the shower, reviving slightly under its warm cascade. Through the doorway, he could hear Wanda talking on her mobile; to Colin, he presumed. Then she reappeared, grasped a huge white towel and held it out for him as he stepped out of the shower. She wrapped it round him and led him back to the bed. He'd never wanted her so much.

Despite his exhaustion, he pulled her to him, kissed her, made love to her with frenzied passion as though it was the last time he'd be able to. Afterwards, she pushed him down and he lay back, his eyes closing. Bloody hell, he thought groggily, Wanda's face distorting into the cruel one he'd been so close to only hours before. So close yet so far. So close…

\* \* \*

The sound of voices woke him. He started and sat up.

'Hello sleepyhead,' Wanda said. 'Colin's got the cream. Let's have those hands.'

Quentin winced as the cream stung the cut on his finger.

'Been in the wars again, eh, Quentin?'

'Something like that,' Quentin said, eyeing Colin and wishing he wasn't here. He just wanted to curl up with Wanda and put the events of the day behind him. But, he realized, he'd kept Wanda waiting long enough, and as he sipped the coffee she'd made, he felt his strength and determination returning. He began relating what happened, although he omitted to mention what the original package had contained.

'So you've got another package to deliver?' Colin asked. 'Drugs?'

Quentin nodded. 'That's what he hinted at, but it could be full of sugar for all I know. I daren't open it. He reckons he'll know if I do, and he'll kill me, I've got no doubt about that. Unless Philmore's managed to get him. It could all be over and we don't know about it.'

'Some nerve this guy's got, I'll say that for him,' Colin said, taking off his glasses and polishing them with the hem of his shirt. 'I expect Philmore will call as soon as he's got anything to tell you.'

'He will,' Wanda said brightly. 'Come on. Let's go down and get some food.'

* * *

It was eight-thirty before they heard from Philmore. They were in the bar after dinner when Quentin's second mobile rang. His muscles tensing, he pulled it from his pocket and walked to reception to cut out the background noise.

'Steve?'

'No good.' Philmore's voice had a defeated edge to it. 'We got to the boat but he wasn't on it. We searched it but there was nothing to find, no drugs or stolen goods. No fingerprints either, except the skipper's, a bloke called Peter Pentewan, and not many of his. He could have wiped it.'

'Yeah, he could,' Quentin said, an image suddenly coming to him. 'And Whitelaw handled my phone, but he's smart. He wore gloves all the time I was there – he doesn't leave a trace.'

'Well,' Philmore went on, 'the skipper denied Whitelaw or anyone else had been on the yacht and denied seeing you. He swore he'd been alone since leaving St Peter Port in Guernsey. That's where he picked the boat up. He said he was hired to take the boat out to check everything was in good working order before it was advertised for sale. He gave the name of the man who hired him, but we can't trace him. We're trying to trace where the boat was registered. Anyway, we impounded the yacht and arrested the skipper, but we haven't got any more out of him.'

'What about what I saw? Doesn't that count for anything?'

'It's your word against his, and anyway all that would do is waste time. It's Whitelaw we're after. Even if the skipper knows where he went, by the time we get it out of him he'll be long gone.'

'Right,' Quentin said, knowing this was true.

'You said there were dinghies–' Philmore began.

'Yes, two,' Quentin interrupted. 'The one I was in and another one on deck.'

'So,' Philmore continued, 'Whitelaw could have taken the second dinghy and been away from the boat as soon as you and Jim were out of sight.'

'Yeah,' Quentin said. 'He wouldn't want to hang around. Any news on the girl and her father?'

'No. We've checked on them and they've handed in the keys to the caravan.'

'Right, well, Whitelaw didn't know anything about our altercation with them. I'm guessing they won't own up to it. They're more likely to say the camera was stolen in a random mugging or something. I don't think they'll want to admit to losing it to me – it would make them look incompetent, and they wouldn't get paid.'

'You might be right,' Philmore agreed.

'So,' Quentin said despondently, 'our friend's gone AWOL again. What about Jim, the guy who jumped me and took me out to the yacht?'

'Looks like he's gone AWOL too. We'll be on the lookout for him, but like I said, it's Whitelaw we want.' Philmore sighed before carrying on. 'Tell me everything that happened to you.'

Quentin related his story in full. 'Listen,' he added, 'I think he'll be watching me from now on, so we need to be careful. He knows Wanda's here, but he doesn't know about you or Colin. At least that's the impression I got. He's given me something a bit more valuable than the last package. Feels like it could be drugs this time.'

'This time? What was it last time then?'

A hot flush crept up Quentin's neck and suffused his face. 'I don't know,' he lied. 'It wasn't drugs, though. He told me it was just a trial run to see if I behaved myself and did as I was told.'

'But the dogs smelled drugs on the package.'

'Yeah.' Quentin recalled sniffer dogs being used for the first package. 'Maybe it was stored next to drugs somewhere along the line.'

'Hmm. So where have you got to deliver this new package?'

'London, but I won't know where till he calls me again. We'll go in the morning. If he thinks I'm driving over two hundred miles after the day I've had, he's wrong.'

'Right. Where are you now?'

When Quentin had relayed the name and location of the hotel, Philmore went on, 'Better get some rest then, and let me know when you're leaving in the morning.'

Quentin ended the call and pocketed the phone. He didn't know what to feel. Angry, more than anything, that he'd been so close to an infamous criminal but unable to stop him escaping. He also felt a sense of impotence, a foreboding that whatever he did, Cultured Voice would always be there, defying the law, lurking in the shadows — and playing on his mind.

* * *

'He got away,' Wanda said as soon as he got back to the bar. 'I can tell from your face.'

'Yep,' Quentin said. 'He's done it again.'

Wanda leaned forward and took his hand. 'It's not over though, Quentin. We've got another package so we've got another chance. He'll want to be sure you don't mislay his precious goods.'

'You mean he's waiting for me to make a mistake or go against him to give him an excuse to kill me? He doesn't need an excuse. It's all a game to him.'

'Why has he given you another package?' Colin asked. 'I can't see the point of risking capture just for the pleasure of stringing you along.'

'It's like the police profiler told Philmore,' Wanda said. 'Quentin is a challenge to him. He wants to show he can outwit him. He's been outwitting the police for years. I think he'll want to go on doing that. He wants to prove how clever he is.'

'I think he's proved that beyond doubt,' Quentin said. 'And if what you say is true, Wanda, then we'll never know when he'll pop up and disrupt our lives. We need to get him, and the only way to do that is to play along with him, for the moment at least.'

He saw the look on Colin's face. 'What? You think I'm reckless? You think I should walk away, leave it to the police? I would if I could, Colin, but I can't.'

'Bit selfish if you ask me. What about Wanda? You're putting her in danger,' Colin snapped.

Quentin pressed his lips together, resisting the urge to blurt out that it was because of Wanda that he had to go along with whatever Cultured Voice demanded.

'Anyway, Wanda love, I could take you away somewhere,' Colin said. 'Just till this is over.'

'Oh, you'd love that, wouldn't you?' Quentin said bitterly. 'Have her to yourself without me cramping your style—'

Wanda banged her glass down on the table. 'Stop it, you two. I'll make my own decisions. I know you're only thinking of my safety, Colin, but—'

'I am,' Colin interrupted. 'Cultured Voice doesn't know anything about me, so you'd be safe with me.'

Wanda pursed her lips. 'Thanks for the offer, but you took us in last year. And I think the same as Quentin. He could come back to haunt us at any time. I can't keep running away.'

Quentin's spirits rose a little, and he beat back the inclination to snap at Colin again. Petty jealousies had no place in their present predicament.

'Of course I'd let Wanda go with you if it kept her safe, and if she'd go,' he admitted. 'But she's right, we can't keep running away, and I can't see any way out of this except to go along with what he says. Which makes me sick,' he added, a note of dejection in his voice.

'Oh well, we'll all feel better after a good night's sleep,' Wanda said, standing up. 'I'll get us another drink then we'll say goodnight.'

Fingering the mole by his ear, Quentin echoed her last word. 'Goodnight. Night it may be, but as far as I can see there's nothing good about it.'

Colin raised his eyebrows. 'You're right,' he said sardonically. 'If there was, you wouldn't be here.'

Quentin caught his eye and felt a bubble of laughter rising in him. 'I suppose I asked for that. A right couple of clowns we are.'

Colin nodded. 'Yeah. Still, the good thing about clowns is no matter how many custard pies they have thrown at them and how many times they fall over, they always get up again.'

Not for the first time since Colin's arrival, Quentin was glad he was there. A look of understanding passed between them, broken by Wanda returning with the drinks. Leaning in close to them, she whispered, 'You two carry on here. I'm going to smuggle Mozart into our room.'

\* \* \*

An hour later, Mozart was duly installed in the hotel room, having been fed, watered and fussed over. Quentin lay in bed, his head sinking into the soft white pillow, gazing up at the ceiling with its subtle mood-enhancing lighting. This hotel, he acknowledged, was several notches above the others they'd stayed at in Cornwall. But then, Quentin realized, Colin had made this booking.

Thinking of Colin made him reflect on their earlier conversation. Was Colin right? Was he being reckless, even selfish, continuing with this quest? But he dared not stop now. He had no doubt that Cultured Voice would carry out his threat to kill him if he did, but what bothered him most was the tiny tinge of relief he'd felt when he'd learned that his enemy hadn't been caught. Because, if Quentin was being really honest, he wanted to be in on that particular party. Perhaps it was because he'd met the man and put a face to the cultured voice. If Cultured Voice had been captured on the yacht, Quentin would have been the reason for his downfall. But that wasn't enough now. He wanted to have a part in the man's capture. And, if he was truthful, as much as he hated Cultured Voice, abhorred everything he stood for, he couldn't help a smidgen of admiration for the way he operated.

'A penny for your thoughts,' Wanda said, breaking into Quentin's musing. 'No, don't tell me. You need to stop thinking about him who must be obeyed, about everything for a bit, and I know just the thing to take your mind off your worries.'

'Really? And what would that be?'

'Come closer and I'll show you.'

Quentin turned to face her, seeing the sensuous lines of her body under the satin nightdress as he pushed the duvet back. In a magical moment, he'd forgotten the cultured voice and its threats of retribution. What the hell, he thought as Wanda's lips closed on his. What the bloody hell.

# Chapter Twenty-seven

After breakfast the following morning they packed up their things ready to leave.

'Perhaps you should travel with me, Wanda,' Colin suggested.

'I will for part of the way, to keep you company,' Wanda said. 'It doesn't matter if I'm with Quentin though. Our friend knows I'm here.'

Quentin nodded. 'He calls you the delectable Mrs Merrydrew. That's his pet name for you.'

'Well, we know he's got good taste,' Wanda teased. 'One of his finer points, I'd say. What did you say his pet name for you was?'

'Never mind,' Quentin said darkly. As far as he was concerned, "a jumped-up little nobody" didn't fit his image.

He called Philmore to tell him they were leaving, then he turned to Wanda. 'We'd better get going. Shame I couldn't see more of Cornwall. I'd like to come back when it's warmer and when I've got time to enjoy it.'

'Well then, we will. Where's the package?'

'Still in my pocket. It's not very big. I suppose he didn't want to trust me with too much. I don't want it on me all the way to London though. I'll put it in my bag.'

When they were ready, they went out to their respective cars.

'I'll go with Quentin now,' Wanda said to Colin. 'I'll come with you after we've stopped somewhere.'

Quentin had just slid into the driver's seat when his mobile rang. 'Number withheld,' he said to Wanda as she climbed in beside him.

Wanda raised an eyebrow and Quentin pressed the green button.

'Yes?'

'Good morning, Mr Cadbury. I trust you got back safely from your unexpected sea trip yesterday. Where are you?'

'Just leaving Penzance.'

'Excellent. The package is expected in London by six o'clock this evening. That's almost nine hours, Mr Cadbury. If it's not there by then, I shall begin to think you've changed your mind about working for me. I'd be really disappointed if that were the case, but then, as you know, all my colleagues and employees can be removed and replaced at any time. Is Mrs Merrydrew with you?'

'Yes,' Quentin said, not seeing any advantage in denying it.

'With that tiresome dog I suppose. It never fails to amaze me how intelligent people can get so attached to an animal. Ties, Mr Cadbury. Dependants. Not conducive to freedom, as I pointed out to you yesterday.'

'Not everyone wants to be as free as you,' Quentin snapped. 'Get to the point.'

'The point, Mr Cadbury, is that I didn't kill you when I had you there in the palm of my hand. A little gratitude wouldn't go amiss. I'll be in touch to check on your progress. Drive carefully and look after my package.'

As the call ended, a feeling of déjà vu came over Quentin. *Look after my package.* He could have been back at the start of this crazy escapade. Would it ever end?

'Bloody hell!' he groaned, and dropped the phone into the well by the gearstick before backing out of the parking space and driving away.

* * *

'I haven't seen Colin for ages,' Wanda said when they pulled in to use the facilities just outside Honiton. 'Perhaps I'll phone and see where he is.'

'Don't bother. He can't answer when he's driving.'

'I thought I saw Philmore and Debbie behind us a while back, so they're still following our signal,' Wanda went on. 'No Colin though.'

'Stop worrying, Wanda. He'll turn up. He always does. Don't know why they're bothering to follow the signal. Nothing's going to happen till we get to London.'

'We don't know that, Quentin. Better safe than sorry.'

After coffee and a snack bought from a van, Wanda took Mozart for a walk on the green area past the picnic tables. Philmore wasn't in sight but Quentin guessed he was on the far side of the parking area, hidden behind the line of lorries.

As Wanda was lifting Mozart back into the car, Quentin felt his phone vibrate against his hip. His usual mobile, he realized as his fingers closed round it. He took it out and checked the display. Colin.

'Hi, Colin. Where are you?' he asked, slipping back into the driver's seat.

He knew something was wrong when Colin answered, 'Newquay police station.'

'What? Why?'

Colin's tone was somewhere between anger and frustration when he replied.

'They said they had a tip-off about a white Honda leaving Penzance and heading out of Cornwall on the A30 with a cache of drugs.'

Quentin gasped, feeling a mixture of guilt and disbelief. Someone had tipped off the police? Meant him to be caught with the drugs? The cultured voice as he'd heard it on the yacht came back to him. *It would be very inconvenient, wouldn't it, having to explain it all? Even a DCI in the Metropolitan Police can't work miracles overnight.*

'They've wrecked my car,' Colin was saying. 'Had sniffer dogs all over it, taken the hub caps and side panels off, but found nothing, which they wouldn't as there was nothing to find. They still seem reluctant to let me go so I've had to tell them what's been going on. I don't think they believe me. I need Philmore to get me off the hook, but I haven't got his number.'

'God, Colin, I'm sorry. I'm guessing they were meant to stop me.'

'Yeah. Just give me his number or I'll be here all day.'

Quentin hesitated, wondering if he should give Colin the number or get Philmore to ring him.

'Come on, man!' Colin snapped impatiently.

'Sorry, Colin. Here we go.' Quentin relayed the number. 'Let us know when you're on the road again.'

No answer. Colin had rung off.

The thought of his rival for Wanda's affections being stopped by the police would usually have made Quentin smile. Now though, the situation wasn't funny; not even remotely amusing. He told Wanda what had happened.

Wanda seemed stumped for words. At last she said, 'But if they had a tip-off, surely they would have stopped all white Hondas? Why didn't they stop us?'

Quentin shrugged. 'Just lucky, I guess, or perhaps when they stopped Colin they thought they had the right car and didn't look for another one.'

'But who— you think it was him? Cultured Voice?'

'Who else could it be? He must be pretty desperate to get me arrested.'

'Why on earth would he want you arrested if he wants the stuff delivered to London? It doesn't make sense.'

'Just to land me in the dirt, Wanda. I'm guessing that's why the package he gave me is so small. He wouldn't want a large amount ending up with the police instead of on the black market.'

Wanda looked baffled. 'But you said he wants you to work for him. How can you do that if you're banged up?'

'You still don't get it, do you? He wants to cause as much trouble for me as possible. He knows I won't get banged up – Philmore would see to that – but it would cause hassle for me, and that's what he wants. It would be worth him losing a small amount of drugs just to upset me. They won't be traced to him. You can bet your life he hasn't handled them without gloves.'

His mobile trilled again, this time with a number he didn't recognize. 'Hello?' he said tentatively.

'Quentin, it's Debbie. The boss says to stay where you are for a bit. He's on the phone to the Cornwall constabulary about your friend, Colin.'

'Yeah, Colin rang me. What do you reckon, Debbie? Is Whitelaw trying to set me up or just wasting police time?'

'Both probably. He'll be fuming when he realizes his little trick didn't work. If he mentions it, don't say anything about Colin. We'll keep him out of it. Just say you weren't stopped.'

'OK,' Quentin said, seeing the sense in this. If Cultured Voice was in the dark about Colin, then not only would Colin not be in danger, he could be useful in the future. 'Let us know when to get going, Debbie.'

He'd no sooner ended the call than another came through. Number withheld. Quentin looked meaningfully at Wanda.

'It's him.' Pressing the answer button, he said, 'Yes?'

There was silence, and then a slight intake of breath. Very short, very quiet, but Quentin heard it. For the first time ever, the cultured voice sounded uncertain. 'Mr Cadbury?'

'Yes.'

'Where are you?'

'Devon,' Quentin said, trying to keep his voice level, 'just outside Honiton.'

'I see.' The cultured voice resumed its usual confident smoothness. 'Is my package still safe?'

'Yes.'

'I'm pleased to hear it.'

Was he? Quentin thought. Wouldn't he be more pleased if Quentin had told him he'd been arrested?

'Carry on,' Cultured Voice said. 'I'll call you again in a couple of hours. You should be almost on the outskirts of London by then.'

'Well?' Wanda demanded when Quentin lowered the phone.

'He was surprised I picked up, and annoyed, I think, but he covered it up pretty well.'

Wanda nodded. 'Maybe it was one of his minions who tipped the police off. Perhaps they gave the wrong registration number. He'll either be blaming them or thinking the police are incompetent.'

'I don't care what he thinks. He's still caused hassle, even if he doesn't know it. Poor old Colin. They'll have to check Philmore's legit and put Colin's car back together before they let him go.'

'Poor old Colin?' Wanda queried, a look of amusement on her face. 'That's a first. Things are looking up.'

Quentin's mouth stretched into a reluctant grin. 'I must be going soft,' he said. 'It's not his fault if he always gets cast as the fall guy.'

'No, it's not, and it's not the first time he's taken a knock for you, so don't you forget it.'

Quentin's second mobile rang. 'Steve?' he said, anxious to find out what had happened. 'Did you sort Colin out?'

'Yes, eventually. Have you heard from our friend?'

'Yep. He sounded surprised that I was still on the move but he's calling again in two hours. Presumably he'll tell me where to go then.'

'Right. Well, I dare say he's got a contingency plan in place in case his ruse with getting you arrested didn't work.'

Quentin couldn't disagree with that. Cultured Voice always seemed to have a back-up plan. 'All right to get going now then, Steve?'

'Yes, but don't go speeding. I don't want to have to unravel another incident.'

'OK, Steve.' He turned to Wanda and grimaced. 'Here we go again.'

# Chapter Twenty-eight

They didn't hear from Colin for another hour. When they did, it was on Wanda's phone.

'Colin. How are you? Everything all right now?'

Quentin guessed that Colin was disgruntled and upset about what had happened. Who wouldn't be?

Wanda was making sympathetic noises into the phone. 'Really? God, that's awful … No, of course it won't go on record. Philmore will see to that … I expect you are. Why don't you go straight home? … Oh all right, we'll let you know what's happening when we know. Bye, Colin.'

'I suppose he's peed off,' Quentin said.

'You could say that.'

'You should have told him he's done us a favour. At least we didn't get held up.'

He felt Wanda's look as it flashed at him from beneath her lashes. 'I don't think that's what he wants to hear just now,' she said.

Deciding that silence was the best strategy, Quentin didn't answer. He sat, concentrating on the traffic and trying not to think about what might happen when they got to London. Where would he have to make the drop-off? Another locker? Idly he wondered how many lockers there were in London. Millions, probably. Railway stations, bus stations, leisure centres, hotels, gyms, police stations... how ironical would that be? Yet Quentin knew a police station was just the kind of place Cultured Voice would delight in using to hide drugs. One in the eye for the police, the Metropolitan Police in particular.

'I wonder where he went when he got off the yacht,' he mused aloud.

'If we knew that, we wouldn't be here now.' Wanda sounded gloomy. 'And what about the bloke who jumped you on the beach? He wasn't on the yacht either, Philmore said.'

Quentin shrugged. 'Who knows? If his only job was to get me to and from the boat, why would he hang around?'

'Yes,' Wanda replied. 'Shame it was too dark for Philmore to arrange an aerial search yesterday. Pointless doing it today. Cultured Voice won't be showing himself. I'm surprised he's come ashore though. Watch out!'

'Sorry,' Quentin said, steering the Honda back into the right lane. 'I lost concentration for a minute. It's what you said.'

'What did I say?'

'You're surprised he came ashore. How do we know he came ashore? He might have been transferred to another boat. Call Philmore, see if he's thought of that.'

'I'm sure he has. I'm not asking him that. It'll look like we think he's an idiot.'

'I expect you're right. Philmore won't like it if he's caught at sea and he's not in on it.'

'Nor will you, will you?'

'No,' Quentin admitted. 'I'd like to be in on it, but if it means it'll get him off our backs then I couldn't say much. I'd be disappointed, but grateful all the same.'

'Well, I don't care who catches him,' Wanda said with a toss of her head. 'I'm beginning to feel like a criminal myself, having to look over my shoulder all the time, frightened to do anything.'

Quentin gave her a sideways glance. Was she wishing she hadn't insisted on coming with him? Worse, was she wishing she hadn't got involved with him in the first place? Was she, as the girl, Sam, had suggested, dangling him on a string? Even now, after everything they'd been through together? Had he misconstrued her tender reaction when he'd returned from the yacht? Silence lingered, until the question that was uppermost in his mind found a voice.

'Do you ever regret it?' he blurted.

'Regret what?'

'Regret sticking with me instead of taking Colin's offer of marriage. I mean, you could be living a nice, comfortable life now.'

'What's brought this on?'

'Well, you know...'

'No I don't. If I wanted nice and comfortable I could have had it under my own steam without relying on Colin or anyone else, thank you very much.'

'I just meant...'

'Anyway,' Wanda went on, 'I had nice and comfortable with Gerry, and look where that got me.'

Quentin nodded. 'I know. It's just... you haven't exactly had an easy time of it since you met me, have you?'

Wanda's voice softened. 'Easy? If you mean do I relish having to dash all over the place at a moment's notice, having to rescue you from sticky situations, you going off and not knowing if or when you'll come back, then no. After all, a woman likes to know if she's got time to have a shower and wash her hair.'

She was making light of things, Quentin realized, but it was her way of telling him she was content with her choice to stay with him. At the moment, anyway. Quentin dreaded the day when she might tell him it was over. After all, how many times had she told him to look for someone his own age? And he still didn't know much about her early life, before she'd married Gerry. She'd promised to tell him when she thought the time was right, and Quentin hadn't pressed it.

He sighed. String or no string, Wanda was the best thing that had happened to him, and she was here, with him, because she wanted to be.

And, for now at least, that's all he needed to know.

# Chapter Twenty-nine

Just before they got to Stonehenge, they pulled in for Wanda to take over the driving. They were almost at Basingstoke when Quentin's mobile rang. Number withheld.

Giving his standard salutation, Quentin said, 'Yes?'

'How are you doing, Mr Cadbury?'

'As well as can be expected under the circumstances.'

'Flippancy doesn't suit you. Where are you?'

'Basingstoke.'

Rustling sounds, like paper being turned over, filled the next few seconds.

'Not too far from London then. Unfortunately all my operatives are tied up for the rest of the day, so you'll have to hold on to my goods overnight, possibly a bit longer. I expect you'd like to go home now. I'm sure Mrs Merrydrew would welcome a chance to sleep in her own bed, though I expect you'd rather she slept in yours. This doesn't change anything though. I'll know if you try any of your pathetic tricks, and if anything happens to my package, you'll be sorry. Go back to your charming little abode and wait there till you hear from me again.'

'He's not got anyone following us,' Quentin said to Philmore when he relayed the call. 'He asked where we were, and it sounded like he was looking at a map when I told him. No news of his whereabouts I suppose, Steve?'

'No.' Philmore's frustration was evident. 'Two boats in the vicinity of *The Blue Albatross* were searched as well but that didn't get us anywhere. We've alerted all the ports and airports but I'm guessing he'll lie low till he thinks it's safe for him to move. At least we know he's in the UK now.'

Or was, Quentin thought. He could have had a private plane hidden away somewhere for all we know.

'I hope he is, anyway,' Philmore continued, as if reading Quentin's mind.

'So do I,' Quentin agreed, but as much as he wanted the chance to catch his enemy personally, he didn't like the idea of coming face to face with him again. Unless, of course, he was in handcuffs or in jail. That was probably the only time he wouldn't be able to make Quentin feel inferior.

'We can go home then?' Wanda asked when Quentin lowered the phone. 'Do you think–'

'Do I think what?'

'Well, if he was hoping we'd be stopped and thought the drugs would be confiscated, has he really arranged for them to be dropped off or is he up to his tricks again? It hardly seems worth his while for the small amount he's given you, but I suppose it's worth quite a bit.'

'Are you kidding? I bet you'd pay more for that than the equivalent weight in gold. At least we know it's definitely drugs now – he won't have palmed me off with a substitute if he wanted me charged with drug dealing, even if it is a charge he knows won't stick.'

'Yes. What if…' Wanda's voice trailed off. 'I mean, his plan failed in Cornwall, but he could be on the phone right now, telling the Metropolitan Police that a white Honda carrying two passengers and a quantity of class A drugs will soon be entering their jurisdiction.'

'No,' said Quentin emphatically. 'He's too clever for that. He'll know there are thousands more white Hondas in London than there are in Cornwall, and anyway, Devon and Cornwall Police will have alerted the Met. He'll know that too.'

'Oh well,' Wanda said after a long silence. 'He's got to arrange a drop-off at some point, so we've still got a chance to nab him.'

Quentin snorted. 'You don't honestly think he's going to come to collect the paltry amount of drugs we've got, do you? If anyone turns up, it'll be one of his henchmen, but we're more likely to be told to leave the stuff somewhere, like we were before.'

'Oh!' Wanda's mouth fell open, as though she'd had an idea and was trying to reconcile it in her mind. The Eureka moment seemed to pass.

'No,' she said, 'that's impossible.'

Quentin waited. 'Well come on, what's impossible?' he said when she didn't elaborate.

'I was just thinking about what he said to you on the yacht. They used your bag to transport goods when they took the Volvo. I thought perhaps he'd done the same thing again, you know, hidden something in the car we've got now. I know the police dog had a go at it, but as Philmore said they're not always accurate. If the police had stopped you back in Cornwall they would have turned the car over like they did Colin's.'

Quentin considered this. 'You mean there could be more drugs tucked away somewhere else? When could they have put anything in this car?'

'I don't know,' Wanda said, shrugging. 'That's why I think it's unlikely. But who knows? At Mousehole? In the hotel car park last night? He always seems to be one step ahead. Unless it's been in here all the time. It could have been put in here before it was left for us.'

'Hmm, I suppose it could. Except that's too risky. We could have got rid of the car at any time, decided to ditch it, had an accident, had it nicked, anything. No, I don't think that's logical. If we were carrying a lot of gear and it was found he'd lose the lot, and he knows Philmore would bail us out.'

'Would he?' Wanda said quietly. 'I mean, would he be able to? I'm not questioning Philmore's integrity – I know he'd do his upmost – but in the light of the evidence, how easy would it be for him to convince others? You weren't wearing a wire aboard that boat. He's only got your word for what went on. How does he know you haven't fallen prey to the promise of wealth and power? All I'm saying is, a kilo of coke stashed in this car would inconvenience you far more than the few hours it inconvenienced Colin.'

'Over my dead body would I get involved with anything to do with drugs!' Quentin almost yelled. 'It's already killing me that we've inadvertently helped him transport some. Philmore must know I'd never have anything to do with that world. What the bloody hell am I doing here if he doesn't believe me about that?' Quentin's voice ratcheted up several decibels. 'I know the damage drugs can do – people dying while slime like that bastard–'

'Stop!' Wanda laid a sympathetic hand on his knee. 'I know that, anyone who knows you knows that, including Philmore. He's on our side. I'm just saying it wouldn't be an easy thing to walk away from if you, if either of us, was caught with drugs, that's all. It wouldn't be Philmore's fault and it's not yours, neither was what happened to Nathan. The world's full of lowlifes. If it wasn't Cultured Voice, it would be someone else supplying the drug market with the stuff.'

Quentin nodded, knowing she was right. None of this was his fault, but if he met all the lowlifes in the world he was sure he'd never find one as callous as the man he'd faced on the yacht. He turned away from Wanda, trying to hide the tears of frustration that had formed in his eyes.

'Call Philmore,' Wanda said gently. 'Tell him we're stopping at the next services. I'm parched.'

* * *

At Winchester services they found Philmore and Francis outside drinking coffee in take-away cups. In her free hand, Francis held a half-smoked cigarette, which she swiftly dropped and ground beneath her shoe.

'I'll be glad to get home,' Quentin confessed. 'Nothing's going on at the moment and we've had a right week of it.'

'So have we,' Francis remarked, looking pointedly at Quentin.

'Quentin's right, Debbie.' Philmore sounded weary. 'The chances of him showing himself now are virtually nil. But that's not the point. The point is he's threatened to kill Quentin if he doesn't do as he's told. I did think we had a chance of nabbing him when we started out, but it looks like that was pie in the sky. Perhaps the most we can hope for is nabbing another one of his gang, and hoping they'll talk. That's if they know where he is.'

'They won't,' Quentin said. 'They won't even know *who* he is.'

'The skipper on the boat and the one who took Quentin to it have seen him,' Wanda pointed out, 'but I bet they don't know who he really is. They probably just take his money, no questions asked.'

'Exactly,' Quentin agreed, 'so maybe we should force his hand.'

Philmore looked at Quentin, suspicion clouding his intelligent brown eyes. 'What are you getting at?'

'Well, we've been playing cat and mouse from one side of the country to the other. Maybe it's time to change that. Maybe I need to pee him off again, since that seems to make him crawl out of the woodwork.'

Feeling the need for support, Quentin cast a surreptitious glance at Wanda.

'I think what Quentin means,' Wanda said slowly, catching the look, 'is that we draw the guy out by deliberately disobeying his orders. Make him come to us instead of us running around after him.'

Philmore's inscrutable expression changed in an instant. 'Don't even think about it,' he snapped. 'The idea of going along with his plan was to save you from getting killed, not increase the odds.'

'Was it, Steve?' Wanda looked at the DCI, her seductive voice low. 'I thought it was so we could catch a criminal who's been making fools of us all for years.'

Bloody hell, Quentin thought, that was near the mark. He saw Philmore's face turn crimson.

'Anyway,' Quentin said hastily into the uncomfortable pause, 'what's the difference if we get him when he's after me or not, as long as we get him. I thought going along with him was the only way too, Steve, but now I'm not so sure. I was inches from him. He was there, right in front of me, and we still didn't get him. If I'd had the tracker on me instead of the car, you might have got to the yacht. We might have got him then.'

'We might have,' Philmore said through stiff lips, 'but you might have been killed in the process.'

'Yes,' Francis said hotly, as if trying to defend her boss's decisions. 'It's our job to protect the public, and that's what we're trying to do.'

'Of course you are,' Wanda said smoothly, seemingly unperturbed by the effect her previous comment had made. 'If you get this guy, you'll be protecting all the innocent people who'll be harmed by the racket he's running.'

She let this settle before continuing, 'So what do you think, Steve? Carry on or rattle him? If he's rattled enough, he might come after us, but rattled people make mistakes.'

'That's true,' Quentin said. 'Whitelaw's made at least one mistake. He managed to get arrested in the Netherlands, so he's not infallible. We'll just have to hope he'll make another one soon.'

The chances of that were about a thousand to one, he knew. If Quentin thwarted him again, Cultured Voice would be angry. He'd want to take his revenge, but he'd be more likely to bide his time until it was safe to do so. He'd already shown that he was a patient man. Which rather put paid to Quentin's suggestion of drawing the man out.

Philmore obviously thought so too because he said, 'He won't do anything in a hurry. He knows he's a wanted man. Being seen in British waters is one thing. Being seen on land is another.'

'Not necessarily,' Wanda countered. 'With the resources at his disposal he's probably safe enough on land. He's good at blending in, practically invisible. And if Quentin goes against him, he'll have another score to settle. You said you think he'll want to settle it personally, so he could be tempted to try something on.'

'Yes,' Quentin said. 'Calling his bluff might make more sense than doing his dirty work for him.'

'His work will get a whole lot dirtier if you cross him,' Philmore reasoned.

'It's dirty enough already,' Quentin said. 'Didn't you say someone was killed in the Netherlands?'

Philmore nodded. 'Yes, but there's no proof he did that himself.'

Well, of course there wasn't, Quentin thought. He's far too careful for that.

'So what do you reckon the chances are of him giving himself away by coming after me?'

'I can't tell you what to do,' Philmore said tiredly. 'It's up to you. But don't forget it could be your life on the line if you upset him.'

And not just mine, Quentin thought, looking at Wanda. Had he made a mistake, suggesting they defied Cultured Voice and deliberately irked him?

'Look,' Wanda said, 'we're all tired and on edge. Let's get home and think about it again tomorrow.'

Looking as if he was about to oppose this, Philmore exchanged a look with Francis. Then, with a defeated sigh, he nodded in agreement.

\* \* \*

Two hours later, Quentin and Wanda stepped gratefully over the thresholds of their respective houses. Quentin almost fell through his front door, pushing it shut behind him, dropping his bag on the floor and calling for Magpie. No answering mew greeted him, so he assumed the cat had gone out. The automatic feeder was half full, and Quentin made a mental note to thank his neighbour for refilling it.

'Home at last,' he muttered to himself, grabbing the kettle and filling it. Opening the door, he called, 'Magpie! Here boy, I'm home!'

The kettle was hissing its way to boiling before Magpie slunk in and sat staring at him in obvious disdain.

'I'm in the doghouse, am I?' Quentin said, bending to stroke the silky black and white fur. 'Let's see what we've got for you.'

He rummaged in the cupboard and found a pouch of chicken pieces in aspic, a favourite of Magpie's. When he'd opened the pouch, he squeezed the contents onto a clean saucer and placed it on the floor. Magpie sniffed at it, then lifted his tail and stalked imperiously out of the room.

'No need to get on your high horse, boy,' Quentin said, knowing this was Magpie's way of showing his displeasure at his absence. 'Some of us have to work for a living.'

As though on autopilot, Quentin made tea and wondered if driving all over Cornwall counted as work.


# Chapter Thirty


'Have you heard from Colin?' Quentin asked Wanda the following day after a mid-morning brunch.

'Yes, he got home late last night. He rang on the way to ask if he should come here first, but I said no. We all needed a quiet night to recharge our batteries. I take it you haven't heard from our friend?'

'If you mean our enemy, no. Either he's got something more important to do or he's waiting to see what I'll do. Another one of his ploys probably.'

'Why don't you go into the office and pick up the messages,' Wanda suggested. 'It'll take your mind off him. I'll stay here with the package. Let me know if you hear anything, but otherwise I'm going to have a relaxing day wrapping Christmas presents. I'll bring that small tree in for you as well. It'll look nice on that table in the corner.'

Quentin decided to take up her suggestion and walked to the rented room on the main road they used as an office. Trying to forget the threats delivered by the cultured voice, he spent an ineffective day gathering information on a woman who'd apparently disappeared, only to be contacted by her husband to say she'd come back safe and well. A Crufts prize-winning dog, allegedly stolen from its owner's garden, had been found wandering around Greenwich Park and returned. A man who'd wanted Quentin to find the perpetrator of graffiti on his property withdrew the case after discovering the culprit was his own son.

'If we don't get some proper paying cases soon, we may as well close down,' he complained to Wanda when he got home that evening.

'Things will pick up after Christmas,' she replied. 'Anyway, we don't really want a big case until we've got rid of this drug business. I've had a good day, though, as you can see.' She indicated the artificial tree, now decorated and with presents arranged around its base.

'Looks great. Where's the package?' Quentin asked.

'Over there by the tree. I had a brainwave and wrapped it in Christmas paper. It's the blue one. Don't look at me like that! After all, you've been burgled once, so it makes sense to disguise it. Imagine having to tell Cultured Voice his precious goods have been stolen! And there's another reason—'

The shrill of a phone stopped her, putting Quentin on edge. He was relieved when he realized it wasn't his but Wanda's mobile.

'Hello, Colin,' she said when she answered it. 'Tonight? Yes, I'd love to. No, I'll meet you there. Bye for now.'

Quentin sent her an enquiring look.

'He'd forgotten he's got tickets for the theatre tonight,' she explained. 'He was going with Emma but she's got a migraine so he wants me to go instead. I should have said no, really, in case you-know-who calls.'

'You go. You've been stuck in all day. If he does call I'll ring Philmore, though I'm guessing I'll be left to stew a bit longer.'

'OK. I'll put my phone on silent but I'll keep checking it, so text if you've got to go anywhere.'

Wanda picked up her handbag and made to leave. 'By the time I get ready and get the tube into town it'll be time to meet Colin. See you later, Quentin.' She dropped a kiss on his head and whirled away.

Quentin stared after her. Only Wanda would think of wrapping a cache of drugs in Christmas paper. He sighed, feeling mentally exhausted. As much as he wished Wanda lived here with him, tonight he was pleased to have some time to himself.

After he'd eaten and showered, he poured himself a whisky, flicked the TV on low and settled into his Aunt Josie's old winged chair. The whisky and the warmth of the central heating made him sleepy. His eyelids drooped, then opened as Magpie jumped up and curled himself onto his lap.

'I'm forgiven then, am I?' he said fondly. 'Shame not everyone's as forgiving as you, eh boy? It's good to be home.'

Ten minutes later, Magpie was purring in harmony with Quentin's soft snores.

* * *

Quentin awoke with a start and a crick in his neck, Magpie still on his lap. Something had woken him, something more than the flicker and low murmur of the TV. What was it? Suddenly Magpie leapt from his lap, his tail high and his fur standing on end like a hedgehog's bristles. He hissed angrily, staring at something behind Quentin's chair. The cat spat, then darted out of the room. Before Quentin had a chance to wonder what was wrong, an arm came from behind and snaked around his neck, and for the second time in a few days he was gripped in a vice-like hold.

Fighting for breath, he clawed at the brawny arm, trying in vain to free himself. He felt the blood thunder in his ears, heard the rasp of his own desperate gasps as he tried to breathe. The muscles in his stomach, still sore from his run-in with Jack at the tin mine, protested as he writhed. A hand came around the other side of his head and covered his mouth. In a last-ditch attempt to shake his attacker off, he bit down hard on the hand, keeping his teeth clamped onto the meaty flesh. He heard a yelp, then a curse as the grip on his neck slackened and the hand fell away from his mouth. Yanking at the arm, Quentin wrenched himself out of its grasp and sprang up, whirling round to see his assailant.

'You,' he croaked, noticing the sausage-like fingers on the hand he had bitten.

'Shut up!' the meaty Jim commanded, wiping blood from his hand on his opposite sleeve. He came out from behind the chair and advanced on Quentin. 'Keep quiet and you won't get hurt.'

'Bit late for that now,' Quentin croaked, fingering his throat where the other man had almost strangled him. Still bruised from his fall in the dinghy, his nose throbbed. 'How did you get in?'

'Back door.'

That's what comes of falling asleep during the evening, Quentin thought.

'What do you want?' he asked between painful coughs.

Jim shook his head as if in disbelief. 'What do you think I want?' he growled.

'How the hell do I know? Look, Jim, or whatever your name is, I've done everything your boss told me to. I've still got his package because he hasn't told me what to do with it.'

'That's what I'm here for.'

Quentin gave a sardonic half-laugh. 'So,' he said, his mind in turmoil, 'he's sent you to do his dirty work for him. Why hasn't he rung to tell me, like he normally does?'

'Shut up and give me the stuff,' Jim snapped.

'What if I won't?'

Quentin saw the meaty fingers ball into fists.

'How did he know I'd be here?' he asked.

Stupid question, he realized. Cultured Voice was like the all-seeing eye.

'None of your business,' Jim said. 'Give me the package.'

Quentin hung there, his arms dangling, desperately trying to think of the best thing to do. Hand over the package and be done with it was the sensible thing. But suppose the meaty Jim had instructions to kill him after he had the package? No. As Philmore had pointed out, this was personal for Cultured Voice, and if he wanted him dead, Quentin wouldn't be here now. So should he hand over the package?

'No,' he said, butterflies beating a tattoo on the walls of his stomach.

'What?'

'No. I won't give you the package. I won't help a drug runner destroy lives. Tell him to come and get it himself.'

It was Jim's turn to gasp. 'You'd better give it to me,' he snarled, 'or I'll take this place apart.'

'Go ahead,' Quentin taunted. 'It's been done before.'

Jim glared at him as if uncertain of what to do. All brawn and no brain, Quentin thought. Used to following orders but no initiative.

'Listen,' Quentin said, more confident alone with this man on his home ground than he'd been in the dinghy with his hands tied, 'he won't shoot the messenger. Just go and tell him what I've said. You've done your bit. He'll have to pay you for what you've already done.'

The other man's top lip curled. 'Pah!' he snorted.

'Just take the money you're owed and get out,' Quentin advised, 'before you do something that'll put you behind bars for years.'

'I'm not going without the stuff,' Jim growled.

Quentin stood his ground. 'Well, you'll have to, because it's not here.'

Jim sprang forward and pushed Quentin into the wall, one huge hand on his shoulder, the other around his neck, his face so close that Quentin could feel his breath on his cheek. Quentin felt himself being pulled forward before being shoved back. His head cracked against plaster, the vibration knocking the clock from its hook and sending it crashing to the laminate floor.

'It had better be here,' Jim hissed. 'Or has your lady friend got it?'

'No!' Quentin's mind raced. He'd have to hand the package over or Wanda might pay the price. He searched for something to say that wouldn't endanger Wanda, but nothing came.

'All right, I'll get it,' he spluttered.

Jim released him and he slid down the wall to the floor. Winded, his gaze darted left and right, seeking escape from the situation. Jim's large frame barred his way to the back door, and Quentin knew by the time he got to his feet and ran to the front, Jim would be on him. Reluctantly, he went to the table and gazed at the presents laid round the tree. Blue paper, Wanda had said. There was red, green, multi-coloured, turquoise. No blue that he could see. Bloody hell, he thought in alarm. Which one is it?

As he dithered, Jim leapt at him. Once again, Quentin was pushed against the wall, a meaty hand encircling his neck.

'Stop playing games,' Jim snarled. 'Where is it?'

'It's there,' Quentin choked. 'I swear it is.'

Grabbing his shoulder with his free hand, Jim yanked Quentin forward and then rammed him back against the wall. Stars floated in front of Quentin's eyes as he slid to the floor for the second time and a vicious foot kicked out at him. Through the mist that blurred his vision and muffled his hearing, another voice came to him. 'Stop!' it said. Then there were scuffling noises, a high-pitched cry and the sound of a door banging. Slowly, the noises faded and he could hear nothing. His eyes closed, he slumped sideways and blessed oblivion engulfed him.

# Chapter Thirty-one

'Quentin.'

Quentin heard the voice as though through cotton wool. A nice voice. One he knew.

'Quentin!' The seductive voice was urgent. 'Come on, Quentin, talk to me.'

Slowly, Wanda's face came into focus. Wincing at the pain in his head, Quentin blinked against the brightness of the light. Allowing Wanda to help him to his feet, he stumbled to the sofa and plumped down.

Wanda's tone was concerned but demanding. 'Where do you hurt? Do you need to go to A&E?'

'I don't think so,' Quentin mumbled, rubbing the back of his head. 'The guy who took me to the boat, he wanted–'

'I know. I gave it to him. I got home late and heard a crash in here. I guessed something was up so I used my keys and came in. The front door wasn't bolted. I could see he had you up against the wall. Next thing, you were on the floor and he kicked you. I didn't know what to do. I had to stop him so I picked up that umbrella you keep by the front door and ran at him.'

Quentin groaned. 'You should have run and called the police.'

'There's gratitude for you,' Wanda said wryly. 'You might have been dead by the time they got here.'

'He didn't hurt you?' Quentin's gaze travelled over her anxiously. There were no obvious bruises or scratches.

Wanda shook her head. 'The package saved me, saved both of us. I told him I'd give it to him if he didn't hurt you anymore. If I'd have brought the gun, I could have kept him here and called the police, but I didn't think of it. I just wanted to get in quickly and see what was going on.'

'So the drugs are gone?' Quentin asked groggily. 'I didn't want to hand them over. Seems strange that he sent someone to collect them when he's spent a week making me drive all over the place to deliver them. Jim was on the boat – why didn't he just give them to him to deliver?'

Ignoring his question, Wanda said, 'Quentin, where's the phone, the one you use to call Philmore?'

'On the bureau but we might as well wait till morning. They'll never catch up with Jim – he'll be long gone.'

A small smile lit Wanda's face, giving it an air of mystery. 'Oh I don't know,' she said, locating the phone and holding it up. Then, the smile faded and concern took its place. 'Quentin, are you sure you're all right?'

'Yeah. I brought it on myself really. Before he took a swing at me I said I wouldn't give him the package. I told him to tell Cultured Voice to come and get it himself, you know, draw him out like we said. After…' Quentin paused. He didn't want to mention Jim's veiled threat about

Wanda. 'After he hit me, I was going to give it to him but... I didn't know which present it was. You said blue.'

'It was blue. Well, turquoise, same thing.'

'No it's not. It doesn't matter now. Anyway, I didn't want to give it to him. I just saw red. It was like the straw that broke the camel's back, that thug coming here after all we've been through.'

'Oh, Quentin, I'm really sorry.'

'What for? It's not your fault Cultured Voice sent a thug to duff me up.'

Wanda looked away, and Quentin saw something in her expression he'd never seen before. Guilt.

She cleared her throat. 'Not that he sent him, no, but it's my fault he roughed you up. If I'd have thought for one minute – well, I told you I had a brainwave yesterday – if I'd finished telling you, you'd just have given him the drugs and he'd have left you alone.'

Quentin was baffled. 'Told me what?'

Wanda looked directly at him now. 'That I took the tracker off the car and put it in with the drugs.'

# Chapter Thirty-two

'The tracker's in the drugs? The drugs can be tracked?' Quentin stuttered, stunned by her revelation.

'As long as it's not found, yes. That's one of the reasons I wrapped it up. I had to open the paper a bit to show him the drugs were in there, but he was convinced enough to take them. I told him we'd been burgled before and that disguising them as a present was a good cover.'

'Wanda, you're a genius! Ring Philmore now and tell him. He can get someone on it.'

From Wanda's side of the conversation, Quentin could only guess at Philmore's reaction. Despite his aching body, he straightened at Wanda's final words.

'There is a proviso, Steve. I think it's only fair that after all we've done, we're involved in any action that could lead us to whoever the drugs end up with, or at least that Quentin is. He's the one who's taken all the risks.'

Quentin's heart swelled at this, and his love for Wanda deepened. 'Thanks, Wanda,' he said when the call had ended.

'He's going to get the tracker followed straight away. Let's hope they can reach it before the drugs are handed over. He'll let us know when there's anything going on. Now I'm going to get you a brandy and you're going to bed.'

'Bed! You don't seriously think I could sleep now, do you? I won't say no to the brandy though.'

'I don't suppose he'll deliver the drugs tonight,' Wanda said when she'd poured them both a generous measure.

'He might,' Quentin countered. 'I shouldn't think Cultured Voice will want him holding on to them for long.'

'He let you hold on to them,' Wanda pointed out. 'Still, like you said, he was probably testing you. Looks like he's suddenly got impatient.'

'Well, I don't care how impatient he is. I just want him caught, or at least to leave us alone.'

'So do I, but there's nothing we can do now except wait, so we might as well be comfortable. Sleep on the sofa if you don't want to go to bed. I'm going back to mine. Mozart's been on his own all evening. Ring if you hear anything. From the state of you, I'll have to drive anyway.'

And as he watched her go, Quentin had to admit that she was probably right.

\* \* \*

Even though he'd slept for part of the evening, and irrespective of his sore head, Quentin managed to sleep for a few restless hours before his mobile woke him. Hoping it might be Philmore with some news, he scrabbled around on the throw that he'd used as a blanket, only to realize it was his other phone.

'Hello,' he said breathlessly, managing to press the green button before the ringing stopped.

'Good morning, Mr Cadbury. I apologise for the delay in getting back to you. I was unavoidably detained. I trust you've slept well?'

The cultured tones irritated Quentin. 'I might have done if you hadn't sent your roughneck to break into my house and duff me up,' he snapped. 'It beats me why you're bothering with such a small amount of drugs. I know its street value is high but it can't be anything to you. I'm sure you can get plenty more where that came from.'

Silence. Quentin waited for the tirade. When it didn't come, he thought Cultured Voice had rung off. 'Are you there?' he asked, suspecting his words had sent his enemy into a silent, seething rage.

When the cultured voice replied, it was the quietest Quentin had heard it. 'Are you telling me that one of my men came into your house and attacked you?'

'Don't play the innocent with me,' Quentin said. 'You know very well he did.'

'Actually, Mr Cadbury, I know no such thing. Was this man Jim, the one who brought you to the boat?'

Quentin was thrown. It wasn't in Cultured Voice's nature not to take credit for things he'd organised. 'Er, yes,' he admitted.

Another silence. Then, 'I see. Did he tell you I sent him to hurt you?'

'No, I just assumed—'

'So what did he say?'

'He wanted the package, the one you gave me.'

'Did he indeed.' The pause that followed left Quentin in no doubt that now his adversary really was in a silent, seething rage. One of his gang had disobeyed him.

'He wasn't acting on your orders then?'

'No, he was not. Did you give him the package?'

'I didn't, no. That's why he roughed me up.'

'Well, Mr Cadbury, I'm pleased to see that your backbone is as strong as your principles.'

Quentin gulped. He'd have to own up. 'He has got it now, though. My partner intervened and handed it over to stop him bashing my head in.'

'Ah. The intrepid Mrs Merrydrew. Perhaps I was a bit hasty when I said you shouldn't depend on people. Mrs Merrydrew, it seems, is very dependable. Well, I'm sorry you've been inconvenienced, Mr Cadbury. Believe me when I say that when I want you to be inconvenienced, you'll know about it. I need to go now. That doesn't mean I've finished with you, far from it, but for now I've got another, rather unpleasant, matter to attend to. Goodbye, Mr Cadbury. Have a nice day.'

Quentin lowered the phone from his ear. Bloody hell, he thought. His head was swimming, and not just from where he'd cracked it against the wall.

# Chapter Thirty-three

'What?' Wanda sounded incredulous over the phone. 'You mean the guy who broke in wasn't acting on orders?'

'Apparently not. I didn't think our cultured friend would go to all that trouble for so small an amount of drugs. Something felt off about it. I'll tell you one thing though, Wanda, I wouldn't like to be in Jim's shoes. Me and Cultured Voice, that's a different bowl of fish, but Jim…'

'But why did he do it?' Wanda asked.

'I don't know,' Quentin said slowly. 'I've got a feeling he was going to take off with the stuff, sell it and make off with the proceeds. I'm sure that's what Cultured Voice thought. He was fuming.'

'Hmm,' Wanda said. 'So what's our next move?'

'I'll ring Philmore and find out if anything's happened with the tracker. If nothing's going on, why don't you come in for breakfast?'

'You come here,' Wanda suggested. 'I'm sure you don't feel like cooking after the night you've had.'

'Lovely. Thanks, Wanda. I'll just ring Philmore and I'll be in. All right, boy,' he added as Magpie stalked in and turned green eyes on him. 'I won't forget your breakfast.'

\* \* \*

'So what did Philmore say?' Wanda asked as she put a plate of bacon and eggs in front of Quentin.

'They traced the tracker to Jim's address in Tower Hamlets, so the drugs must be there,' Quentin told her. 'Nothing since then, so it looks like the package is still intact. He'll have to get a move on though if he wants to escape Cultured Voice's wrath.'

'What about us escaping Cultured Voice's wrath? We didn't deliver his package for him, did we?'

Quentin shrugged, then wished he hadn't. Every movement pulled on his tortured muscles. 'He can hardly blame us for that, can he?'

'Well,' Wanda said, 'we've disrupted his plans – again. Maybe he'll have to do something he hasn't planned and make a mistake.'

'Or maybe he'll make mincemeat of us both,' Quentin answered.

'I don't think so, Quentin. Like Philmore keeps saying, if he wanted us dead, he'd have done it by now. After all, he could have killed me that first time, but he didn't. He only threatens me to get you to do what he wants.'

Quentin pursed his lips. 'I still think you should get away, Wanda,' he said. 'Philmore said he'd find you a safe house but you can go to Colin's for now.'

Wanda sent him a cool look over the rim of her coffee cup. 'So I swan off while you're in danger here? I don't think so. We're in this together.'

Quentin nodded. He'd known she would say this. 'Look, Wanda, I didn't say anything before but... when I was on the yacht, he said if anything went wrong he'd hold us both responsible. That means you're in as much danger as I am.'

Wanda sent him a disbelieving look. 'And you've only just decided to tell me?'

'I... I didn't want to alarm you, or Colin.'

'Quentin, you can't keep hiding things like that from me. I know you're trying to protect me, but we're supposed to be a team and I need to know everything that's going on. I'm a mature woman, not a china doll.'

'I know, you've proved that enough times. I'm sorry. It's just...' He tailed off, unable to find the right words.

'Look,' Wanda went on, 'if he's just trying to get back at you — at *us*,' she added pointedly, 'he can do that any time. It's no good running away. We'll turn into zombies if we have to hide away. We need to work and I enjoy the detective agency. I don't see why we should be forced to live a different life.'

'Neither do I, but he's threatened to end it. Wouldn't you rather be alive somewhere else than dead here?'

'Don't be so dramatic. If you want the truth, I think he quite admires you.'

Quentin snorted. 'He calls me a jumped-up little nobody!' he said, forgetting his pledge not to reveal this.

Wanda's face was deadpan. 'Maybe, and yes, you're not exactly Sherlock Holmes or Inspector Morse and you make mistakes and sometimes things go wrong, but you've put an end to his criminal rings more than once. He may think you're a pain but, at the end of the day, he's got to respect that you stick to your principles and keep at things until they're finished. He knows you won't give up any more than he will.'

Quentin's heart swelled. He looked across at Wanda, this sophisticated, beautiful, sexy woman who had stuck by his often-inept attempts to solve crimes, and thanked God she had come into his life.

'I wish you'd marry me,' he blurted, astounded at his own words.

Wanda blinked. 'Let's not beat about the bush then,' she said with a hint of amusement. 'What happened to "why don't you move in with me?"'

'Well, why don't you? I'm not being sentimental, Wanda. If anything happens to me, what will happen to all my worldly goods? I suppose I should make a will, leaving everything to you.'

'Your worldly goods?' Wanda shook her head. 'You mean your detective books, your running machine, and your Aunt Josie's china? Oh, and Magpie, of course.'

As if sensing Quentin's hurt, she leaned forward and took his hand.

'That's a sweet thought, Quentin, but nothing's going to happen to you. If you make a will in my favour, you'll only have to change it again when you've met a nice girl and settled down.'

Quentin didn't answer. He sat, staring down at his empty plate. He couldn't see himself with anyone but Wanda.

'No one else can give me what you've given me,' he muttered, fingering the lump on his head.

Wanda gazed at him, opened her mouth as if to say something but apparently changed her mind. Looking away, she said softly, 'They could give you children.'

'You could still have children,' Quentin said at once. 'Lots of people have a baby later in life these days.'

Wanda stood up, snatched up the plates and began walking away.

'We don't have to have children. It's not that important to me,' Quentin said quickly, realizing he'd touched a nerve.

He himself hadn't even thought about having children. But if Wanda wanted children, why hadn't she had some with Gerry? Gerry had been nearly twenty years older than her. Perhaps that had made a difference. And she was nearly fifteen years older than him. Is that what was holding her back?

He picked up the cups and went out to the kitchen where she was loading the dishwasher. He slipped his arms round her waist and kissed the back of her neck.

'I'm saying no more about it,' he whispered into her ear, 'except we're a team, Wanda, and I never want to be without you – not today, not tomorrow, not ever.'

He straightened up. 'Why don't we take Mozart for a walk to blow the cobwebs away?'

'Good idea,' Wanda said, sounding more like herself. 'How's your head?'

'I'll live,' he said. 'I mean, I couldn't run a marathon, but a gentle stroll will be all right.'

'OK. I'll just stick this lot in and then we'll go.'

Relieved that things seemed to be back on a normal footing, Quentin retrieved his phones and keys and went home to get his coat.

# Chapter Thirty-four

Except for the evergreens, the trees were bare in Greenwich Park. People ambled along the paths, hats pulled low and scarves wound tightly against the December cold. Pulling the collar of his waterproof tighter, Quentin watched Mozart as he trotted along beside

Wanda, stopping for long moments to sniff at things that caught his interest. Mozart, Quentin was sure, possessed Jekyll and Hyde qualities; he was the best-tempered Westie he'd ever known – he didn't even fight with Magpie. Yet if he was on the scene when he or Wanda were in danger, he turned from sweet-natured pet to aggressive protector in an instant.

They were only halfway through their walk when Wanda's phone rang.

'Hello, Colin,' she said when she answered it.

Quentin listened as she told Colin what had happened last night, struggling to catch the words before the wind whipped them away.

'He wanted to know what the other guy was like when you'd finished with him,' she told him as she put the phone away.

'Huh,' Quentin huffed. 'I didn't get a look in. If things go on like this I think I'll take up martial arts instead of running.'

'Running comes in very handy when you need to get away quickly,' she reminded him. 'Come on, I'm freezing. Let's get back now. I need to get some housework done.'

* * *

As Quentin let himself into his own house, Magpie rubbed against his legs and mewed.

'What's up, boy?' Quentin glanced around, making sure there was no one about to creep up on him. 'You tried to warn me last night, didn't you? All right, so I was a dork, falling asleep and leaving the door unlocked. Don't look at me like that. It's all right for you with your nine lives.'

Quentin went out to the kitchen and checked that the back door was locked and bolted, wondering how the term "dumb animals" had come about. True, animals couldn't speak, but sometimes they had an uncanny way of letting you know what they wanted to say.

Feeling restless, Quentin called his mother in Australia. He felt the need to touch base, speak to someone with his own blood in their veins. He hung up hastily when he realized it was late over there and that his parents would be in bed.

Unable to settle to anything, his mind returned to Cultured Voice and his racketeering. Drugs. Cocaine, heroin and every other addictive substance on the planet. Destroyers of lives. Killers. Nathan, he murmured involuntarily. Cocaine had killed his friend and there had been enough of it stashed in the package Jim had taken to kill someone three times over. Why hadn't they destroyed it, flushed it down the loo, anything but pass it on? And was the meaty Jim still sitting on it?

Impatient for news, he rang Philmore.

'Sorry to disappoint you, Quentin,' the DCI said. 'The bloke hasn't moved today.'

'What if he finds the tracker?' Quentin asked.

'Well, we're watching him so we'll just have to follow him without it. As far as we can trace, he's not a dealer himself, so there's a good chance he won't find it and just pass the whole lot on to whoever distributes the stuff. We need to keep him under surveillance until we know who that is, and hopefully we'll nab the whole gang.'

'Let's hope so, Steve. I don't fancy his chances going against Whitelaw. Whitelaw was more concerned about him disobeying his orders than what happened to his precious package.'

'Well, he would be,' Philmore reasoned. 'I shouldn't think he'd take kindly to anyone stealing from him, and he certainly won't trust Jim not to talk if he's caught. As far as we know, he's one of the few people who have met him face to face, so he can identify him. Still, that won't stop Whitelaw. He's proved he can disguise himself and get away with it several times.'

'Yes, you're right. Have you got anything on this Jim?'

'Full name James Butler, only been at the Tower Hamlets address a few months, arrested for theft seven years ago and for grievous bodily harm five years ago, served two and a half years of a five-year sentence. That's about it.'

'OK, Steve. Let me know when he's on the move.'

After he'd rung off, Quentin sat for half an hour, Magpie on his lap, wondering what to do before his gaze fell on the half-full bottle of whisky on top of the bureau. He stood up to go to it. Pain stabbed at him and he changed direction. In the kitchen, he swallowed two painkillers and washed them down with a glass of water.

* * *

At eight-thirty, Quentin looked across Wanda's dining table at Colin, whom Wanda had asked to stay for dinner when he'd visited her unexpectedly that afternoon. He'd hoped Colin would leave early so that he and Wanda could have a quiet evening together, but evidently Colin had other ideas. They'd just decided to watch a film when Quentin's second mobile rang.

Seizing it from where it rested on the nearby cabinet, Quentin barked, 'Steve?'

'He's on the move, just got into a car with the drugs. The surveillance team will be able to follow the tracker and we'll catch them up.'

'We're on our way,' Quentin said, standing up. 'Let me know which way he's headed.'

He pocketed both his phones and picked up his keys. 'We'll have to take your car, Wanda, or the one we had in Cornwall. Mine's in the lock-up.'

'We'll go in mine,' Colin told him. 'No arguments. I know the roads better than you.'

With no time to argue, Quentin nodded and shrugged on his jacket while Wanda grabbed her handbag and coat. They were in Colin's Honda before the phone rang again.

Quentin switched to loudspeaker so that Wanda and Colin could hear.

'Looks like he's making for the A12 north. I'll get back to you.' Philmore sounded agitated.

Quentin imagined him sitting beside the driver – possibly DS Francis – gritting his teeth and hoping against hope that they weren't on another fruitless chase.

After several more calls, they found themselves emerging from the Blackwall Tunnel and onto the A12 northbound, where the traffic was mercifully light. It was nearly forty minutes before the phone rang again.

'We're at Waltham Abbey – off the A121, skirting Epping Forest. He's pulled into an industrial estate, next to a boarded-up garage on the left just past the signpost. When you get here, stop inside the gates and turn your engine and lights off. Keep out of sight and don't ring in case–'

The line went dead.

'Keep your eyes peeled,' Colin said. 'I don't want to miss the place.'

After what seemed like an hour but was actually only ten minutes, the disused garage came into view. The entrance to the industrial estate lay just beyond. Using the sidelights only, Colin nosed the Honda through the gates, then switched them off when he'd eased the car round so that it faced the exit.

'What now?' he asked, cutting the engine. 'Not much point coming all this way just to sit here in the dark.'

'We walk,' Quentin said decisively. 'Though lord knows which way. This place looks pretty big.'

'We should split up,' Wanda reasoned. 'Then at least one of us might see something.'

At that moment, a beam of light flickered above the single-storey units ahead of them.

'There's the answer,' Quentin said, excitement rising in his stomach. 'Bring the torch, Wanda, but don't use it unless we have to, and don't make a sound. Turn your phones off. We don't want to mess things up. Colin–'

'I'll stay here in case I have to stop someone getting away,' Colin said solemnly. 'I've done it before, though I didn't get any credit for it.'

Ignoring his snide remark, Quentin nodded agreement, secretly glad that Colin wasn't coming with them. He slid out from the car and, together with Wanda, ran towards the nearest unit, creeping along its prefabricated wall.

They'd just rounded a second corner when they heard a kerfuffle; shouts of 'Police, stay where you are!' filled the air while light flared in the adjacent alleyway. Quentin felt as though he'd been dropped onto the set of a TV police drama. He hurried towards the noise, followed by Wanda. As they drew close to where the alley met the passageway that traversed each row of units, a figure flew past.

Quentin heard Philmore's voice boom, 'Get that man!', and immediately he slipped into running mode and went after the figure. Vaguely aware of running feet some way behind him, he increased his pace, every step pulling at his still-bruised muscles. Coming to the end of the first alley, his quarry broke cover and ran onto the concourse towards the gates.

Before Quentin could reach him, he saw Colin jerk the Honda forward to block the exit. The fleeing man – Jim, Quentin realized – reached the car and wrenched open the driver's door, grabbing Colin by the neck and yanking so hard that Colin was pulled out like a snail from its shell. Colin hit the concrete with a thud and rolled sideways, his feet and ankles landing between the front and back wheels of the Honda.

Quentin got to the car just as Jim jumped into it. With the engine still running, Quentin had seconds to decide whether to tackle Jim or to pull Colin clear. Groaning audibly as pain shot through him, he bent, caught hold of Colin's arm and heaved. The back wheel grazed Colin's shoe as the vehicle shot forward and, with a roar of an engine and a smell of rubber, the Honda sped through the gates into the night.

The sound of pounding feet brought with it two uniformed policemen, one already talking into his radio. From somewhere outside the fence, an engine was revved into life and a police car hurtled by.

'What happened?' Colin croaked, sitting up and putting one hand on the opposite shoulder. His glasses had fallen off, and in the beam of a policeman's torch, Quentin retrieved them from where they lay.

'He got away, didn't he?' Colin remembered. 'My car — he's got my car.'

'Never mind, sir,' the taller of the two police officers said. 'At least you've still got your legs, thanks to this man.'

Colin, evidently still somewhat dazed, tried to get to his feet. 'Stay put for a bit,' Quentin advised. 'I'm going to find Wanda.'

Pretending not to hear the officer's order not to intrude on a crime scene, Quentin retraced his steps and homed in on the unit from which activity emanated. As it came into sight, he saw Wanda standing unobtrusively by the wall of the opposite unit. He slowed and walked up to where she was, following her gaze to the knot of people gathered in the pool of light spilling from the open door.

Three men, each handcuffed and looking defeated, were being guarded by uniformed officers. A fourth, also handcuffed but with a defiant expression on his hard face, stumbled out from the building followed by two more uniformed officers. He halted in front of someone who stepped forward to speak to him. Philmore. Quentin couldn't quite hear what was said, but the answer didn't need to be heard. The man simply stared at Philmore and spat directly into his face.

Wanda gasped, and in a flash she'd drawn a wodge of tissues from her pocket. As Philmore drew back, she moved forward swiftly, proffering the tissues. Philmore took them and wiped his face.

'Take him away, Sergeant,' he said calmly.

The man who had spat glared at Philmore in obvious contempt, then almost swaggered towards the car he was being guided to. This man, Quentin guessed, held more sway than the other three, one of whom looked no more than a boy.

When they'd been driven away, Philmore turned to Quentin and Wanda, drawing them out of the hearing of the uniformed officers.

'That was a good night's work,' he said, still rubbing his face as though he could erase the very memory of the saliva on his skin. 'There's enough stuff in there to supply London's habit for a year, with a street value to match. The drugs squad will be pleased.'

'Sorry, Steve,' Quentin said sheepishly, 'Jim got away. I almost got to him, and Colin tried to stop him, but he got the better of Colin and drove off in his car. One of your cars chased him though, so they might get him.'

'Great,' Philmore said, stiff-lipped. 'You supplied the getaway car. That'll go down well with the super.'

Quentin pursed his lips. He wanted to protest, but he understood Philmore's frustration.

'Don't worry,' said a female voice behind Quentin.

Quentin turned to see DS Francis. He had no idea how long she'd been standing there.

'If he's in Colin's car, it'll be easy to find him,' she went on. 'We can alert the ANPR unit.'

'I suppose so,' Philmore agreed reluctantly. 'We'll put out an APB on this Jim. If he's got any sense, he'll ditch the car and either lie low or disappear altogether.'

'How did he get away from you when the others didn't?' Quentin asked.

It was Philmore's turn to look sheepish. 'If we'd have had time to arrange a proper stakeout, he wouldn't have. Jim was right by the door when we went in, I guess ready to leave after delivering the drugs, and managed to get past us. He runs fast for a big man. The others were more towards the back of the building.'

'What I can't understand,' Wanda interrupted, 'is why such a small amount of the stuff was brought here. Surely the package he took from Quentin's could be handed over on a street corner?'

'Yes, that's what surprised us, and that's why, when we saw where he was going, we took a chance, assuming there would be more than one dealer inside, and we were lucky. That guy, the cocky one' – Philmore touched his cheek where he'd been spat on – 'I'm sure I've seen a mugshot of him. If I'm right, the drugs squad have been after him for ages.'

'Won't they mind you muscling in on their territory?' Wanda asked.

'Probably. They've been alerted, just didn't get here in time. Anyway, it doesn't matter who catches these scum as long as they're caught. Right, Debbie, we're done here.'

Without another word, the DCI turned and strode away, leaving Quentin feeling exasperated at being left with so many unanswered questions.

'Well, thanks, Quentin, thanks, Wanda, for leading us to a unit full of drugs,' Quentin muttered.

'Perhaps he's frustrated at not getting Cultured Voice,' Wanda speculated. 'Maybe he was clinging on to a wild hope that he would be here himself.'

'*He's* frustrated!' Quentin exploded. 'How does he think *I* feel?'

'You should feel pretty good. After all, we've led the police to a cache of drugs and caught some of the dealers, and they'll get Jim too, I'm sure they will. Come on, let's find Colin and go home.'

'And that's another thing,' Quentin grumbled. 'How are we going to get home without Colin's car?'

# Chapter Thirty-five

It was the next day when they discovered that the meaty Jim, according to the youngest of the men arrested at the industrial estate, had a connection to one of the gang and had learned where to take the stolen drugs.

'Well,' Wanda said, 'I bet our friend Cultured Voice won't like that much.'

'No,' Quentin agreed. 'He's kind of hot on loyalty. Still, at least Colin's recovered from his attack, and he's got his car back.'

Colin's Honda had been found abandoned in Canning Town with no permanent damage. It spent the morning being forensically examined but yielded nothing except Jim's fingerprints and DNA, which could have been gathered from his home anyway. No sign of Jim himself had been found.

'He's still in the country,' Philmore informed them. 'They found his passport in his flat. And you'll be pleased to know that one of the people we arrested last night told us enough to trace the hierarchy quite a long way up, maybe all the way up, so that particular drugs route could be shut down. Not the devil we were after – he's not involved with that particular gang – but a good result all the same. Oh, and by the way, *The Blue Albatross* was traced to a shell company, so we'll have a hell of a job trying to find the owner. Still, if we can get this duplicitous Jim, perhaps he can help us find Whitelaw.'

Quentin doubted that. He suspected that the man who had sent him on a pointless chase to Cornwall was too careful to be caught a second time. Nevertheless, he allowed himself to bask in the knowledge that he, Wanda and, yes, Colin too, had played an important part in bringing down a gang of criminals and the confiscation of a cache of illegal drugs.

After having dinner at Wanda's that evening, he went home to sleep in his own bed. They were both tired after the previous late night and felt the need to catch up on some rest. Rest, however, was denied to him when he was woken by the ringing of a phone.

Realizing it was his second mobile, he scrabbled for it and snatched it up, glancing at the luminous hands of his bedside clock. 2 a.m. Steve Philmore's voice sounded in his ear.

'Quentin, I thought you'd like to know about your mate Jim, the one who got away last night.'

'What?' Quentin said, rubbing his eyes. 'Have you got him?'

'You could say that. They've just pulled his body out of the river.'


## Chapter Thirty-six


All thoughts of sleep were driven from Quentin's mind and a shiver ran through him. The man who'd taken him to the yacht, who'd attacked him in his own home and led them to the industrial unit – dead.

'Are you sure it's him?' he asked, his voice tremulous.

'Well, he matches the description we've got on file, and he had a driving licence giving his name as James Butler. We'll be checking the other details we hold for him, but can you come in earlyish tomorrow? We'll show you his photo and you can confirm he's the bloke who took you to the boat and broke into your house.'

'Yeah, course,' Quentin said. 'Ten o'clock?'

'Ten's fine.'

'Will you be on this case?' Quentin asked.

'It hasn't been assigned yet but probably not. I'll ask for it though. They might let me have it as it's connected to Whitelaw. They only rang me about it because of the APB, and I asked to be notified if he or anyone connected with Whitelaw was found.'

'Right. And was he killed? It wasn't an accident?'

Philmore gave a mirthless laugh. 'Not unless he stabbed himself before he hit the Thames.'

Stabbed. 'Bloody hell,' Quentin said. 'Who found him?'

'A couple coming home from a party saw him in the water. The river police pulled him out and alerted us. Looks like our yachting friend has been busy.'

Chaotic thoughts chased themselves around Quentin's head. 'You think he's behind it? You think he had him killed?'

'Well, that's the obvious answer, unless you know differently?'

'What? No, I just thought, you know, because Jim led you to the unit full of drugs, maybe that gang was involved.'

'That's a possibility, but Whitelaw's still high on our suspect list.'

'Right.' Quentin couldn't think of anything else to say. 'OK, Steve,' he said eventually. 'Thanks for letting me know. See you tomorrow.'

Despite his previous involvement with crimes and criminals, Quentin had never been involved with a murder. Wanda was right. He was no Sherlock Holmes or Inspector Morse. They seemed to take murder and dead bodies in their stride. But they weren't solving crimes in the real world. He was. And he had to admit, at least to himself, that he was scared. If Cultured Voice had been prepared to have Jim killed for double-crossing him, what could he do to Quentin – or Wanda?

* * *

'We don't know for sure that Cultured Voice had him killed,' Wanda pointed out over breakfast the next morning. 'It could have been a random attack, or if he's been involved with this other gang they may have wanted him out of the way.'

'That's what I told Philmore,' Quentin conceded, 'but I'm not sure he thinks so. He said someone was killed just before Whitelaw was arrested in the Netherlands. He probably arranged that too. His dealings have stepped up a notch since we first came across him.'

'Well,' Wanda said after a moment's thought, 'there is one way to find out if Cultured Voice is responsible. Ask him.'

'Ha! As if he'd admit that on an open telephone line.'

'Why wouldn't he? He threatened you on an open telephone line.'

'Threatened, yes, not admitted to murder. I can't ask him unless he contacts me, and what would I say? Are you a murderer as well as a thief and a drug dealer?'

Wanda didn't answer, she just sipped her tea. It was several minutes before she voiced what they were both thinking.

'So what are we going to do about it?'

They looked at each other for what seemed like an age.

'Well,' Quentin said eventually, 'I'm going in to confirm that the guy they pulled out of the river last night is the one who broke in here, but Philmore's pretty sure it's Jim, so it's just a formality really. Listen, Wanda, now we know what he's capable of, are you sure you want to stay here?'

'Are *you*?'

Am I? Quentin thought. 'Yes, I'm staying,' he said at last, 'but that doesn't mean you have to.'

'We either both stay or we both go. After all, we've been on his blacklist for nearly three years and we're still here.'

'Well then,' Quentin said, 'we'll just have to wait it out. I'd better go. I said I'd be there at ten.'

Wanda stood up. 'I'll come with you. I need to be there or Philmore will talk you into sending us away, or sending me anyway. Come on then. Let's get it over with.'

\* \* \*

It was ten-thirty before they were in Philmore's office and Quentin had confirmed from a photo of the man they'd pulled out of the Thames that it was the same man who'd taken him to *The Blue Albatross* and broken into his house. DS Francis brought them coffee and sat by Philmore's desk. She looked tired, as though she hadn't slept, and sat rotating her thumbs.

Despite his interrupted night, Philmore seemed alert. His brown eyes had crinkles at the corners and furrows bracketed his mouth, but otherwise he looked the same as when Quentin had first met him.

'We've had a tip-off today,' Philmore said. 'One of our DIs has a snout in the drugs business. Apparently Jim approached someone he knew in the gang we arrested and said he could get his hands on some cocaine; he wanted to know what price he could get for it.'

Quentin and Wanda exchanged glances.

'So Jim wasn't working for this gang? Only for Whitelaw?' Wanda asked. 'But he was planning his own little deal, to make some money off his own bat? How did he think he'd get away with that?'

'He probably thought he could make a swift deal and disappear before Whitelaw found out,' Philmore said. 'He can't have known Whitelaw long or he'd have known better.'

Shivers ran down Quentin's back as another possibility came to him. 'He could have blamed me,' he blurted. 'He could have told Whitelaw I'd lost the drugs or got rid of them or sold them myself. If Cultured Voice, Whitelaw, hadn't rung me when he did, he might have believed him. It would have been me in the river then.'

Sensing Quentin's distress, Wanda felt for his hand. 'Do you really think it was Whitelaw who had him killed?' she asked Philmore.

'Yes. Not that we'll ever be able to prove it. He's not likely to have done it himself, and even if we find the killer, they won't know who ordered it. If Whitelaw's got any sense, he'll lie low.'

'Yeah,' Quentin agreed. 'He'll bide his time and pop up when he's good and ready.'

As if noticing the low mood, Francis changed the direction of the conversation. 'Have you seen Colin since his tumble the other night?'

'Not yet,' Wanda told her.

'This isn't the first time he's come a cropper while he's been involved with you two,' Philmore said, looking from Quentin to Wanda.

Quentin gave a rueful grin. 'Yeah, he always draws the short straw.'

Philmore's gaze lingered on Wanda, as if he knew she was the reason Colin was prepared to act the patsy.

'Well,' he said, 'I suppose there's nothing more to be done until Whitelaw rears his ugly head again. Thanks for what you've done, both of you.'

'As far as he's concerned, we haven't done anything except let him make idiots of us,' Quentin complained.

'That's not your fault, not his time.' As if realizing this sounded as though he blamed Quentin for Whitelaw's previous escapes, Philmore hurried on. 'I mean you tried, and that's all any of us could do. He'll make a mistake one day, and when he does—'

Quentin's thoughts were going in a different direction. Cultured Voice had been three steps ahead the entire time, and now he might get away with murder. By the time he was caught, Philmore would be retired and he and Wanda would be old and grey. If they were lucky.

'What, you think that's it?' Wanda asked. 'It can't be. We disrupted his plan, and he won't let that go.'

'You didn't disrupt his plan this time,' Francis said. 'Jim did, and it looks like he's already dealt with that. All right, so you didn't get pulled in for suspected drug dealing, but that's nothing compared to what Jim did. So, yes, Wanda, that's it for now.'

'Is there anything about him that might help us identify him in the future, Quentin?' Philmore said. 'Anything you noticed when you were with him?'

'No,' Quentin said, thinking back. 'Apart from his voice, he's completely nondescript. I already told you he smoked cigars and…' Quentin visualised the man by the companionway as he took long, leisurely puffs on his cigar, then tossed it overboard before pulling on the latex gloves.

'Yes,' he said. 'He had a signet ring – a big one, gold.'

Francis noted this down.

'Well, there's nothing else we can do now,' Philmore continued. 'I'll let you know if there's any developments. Take care, you two.'

They were being dismissed, Quentin realized. He looked at Francis and she shrugged. Wanda stood up and he joined her.

'Bye then,' he said.

As they left the building, Quentin had a strange feeling of incompleteness. When he'd encountered the man he knew as Cultured Voice previously, his criminal ring had been broken up and his activities stopped. As well as what Philmore had said, some sixth sense told Quentin that this man wasn't behind the operation conducted from the industrial unit in Epping Forest. Cultured Voice had his own agenda and Quentin didn't doubt that his drug smuggling operation would continue to function.

'That's it then,' he muttered. 'What a bloody farce.'

'That can't be it,' Wanda decided, 'or he wouldn't have wanted to meet you face to face. Why would he go to all the trouble of getting you to the yacht if that's all there was to it?'

Quentin shook his head. 'No idea. He said he wanted to know what I looked like, though he had that photo of me at the ice rink. Perhaps he just wanted to meet the person who'd put a spanner in his mucky works. Or maybe he wanted to see me before he added me to his hit list.'

'Don't let's think about that. I vote we ring Colin and see if he wants to come into town and we'll take him to lunch. We owe him that. There's that nice Italian place we went to before. Then we'll walk along the embankment, if you're up to it.'

Quentin grunted reluctant acceptance, not relishing having to make conversation with Colin or walking. But then what would he do otherwise? Go home, sit around thinking how disappointingly this case had turn out?

'Oh what the hell,' he said, trying to sound cheerful. 'I could do with drowning my sorrows, and I quite fancy Italian.'

'There you are then.' Wanda smiled, and reached for her phone.


# Chapter Thirty-seven


By the time they were on their second bottle of Valpolicella, Quentin was feeling better. They'd brought Colin up to speed with events and he was as shocked as they had been. After twenty minutes of discussing everything that had happened, they agreed not to talk about it for the rest of the day and concentrate on pleasanter things. The restaurant was busy and the service consequently slow, but Quentin didn't mind. The wine and ambiance of the place relaxed him and for the first time in almost two weeks, he enjoyed a meal without wondering where he would be the next day.

Wanda had just gone to retrieve her coat when Quentin felt his mobile vibrate against his hip. He fished it out and checked the display. Number withheld. Jumping up, he yelped with pain, then lumbered slowly outside, away from the background noise of the restaurant, pressing the answer button as he went.

'Yes?' he said, covering his other ear until he found a quiet doorway.

'Having a day out, Mr Cadbury?'

'Just lunch,' Quentin replied tersely, imagining the face he'd seen only inches from his on *The Blue Albatross*.

'How civilised. In my opinion, lunch is greatly underrated. I rang because I've got some good news for you.'

'Really?' Quentin said, emboldened by the wine. 'What, you're not going to kill me like you did Jim?'

'Ah, the unfortunate Jim. I assure you I had nothing to do with his untimely demise. I don't trouble myself with inconsequential matters if I can help it. I didn't need to kill Jim. He got himself killed. I simply let someone in the right quarters know that he wasn't trustworthy. After all, if he double-crossed me, he might have double-crossed them. No one likes a rat, Mr Cadbury. I advise you to take note of that.'

'Honour among thieves, you mean. Did you ring me just to boast about your criminal achievements?' Quentin asked, his head beginning to pound from the wine.

'You disappoint me, Mr Cadbury. I thought after our little chat on the yacht you'd be more amenable. And you sound as though you've enjoyed your lunch rather too much. I'll get back to you when you're in a better frame of mind.'

'Now hang on a minute—'

Realizing he was talking to himself, Quentin lowered the phone and stood staring into the street, not seeing the steady stream of people passing by. A motor scooter roared past, jolting him back to the moment. He started towards the restaurant, stopping when he saw Wanda and Colin coming out.

'Well?' Wanda demanded, evidently guessing who the caller had been.

Quentin spread his hands in exasperation. 'Lord knows. He said he had good news for me but he didn't say what.'

Wanda looked troubled and Colin suggested they walk along the embankment as planned.

'We need to clear our heads,' he said, and for once Quentin agreed with him.

The stroll along the south bank of the Thames was bracing. From Westminster Bridge they weaved their way through the winter crowds, past people queuing for the London Eye and through those milling around outside the Southbank Centre, the Tate Modern and all the attractions that visitors travelled hundreds of miles to see. They walked for well over an hour, Wanda taking a special interest in the Globe Theatre, recreated in its original Tudor style and where many of Shakespeare's plays were performed. Then they headed to Waterloo station, where Colin left them to go home.

'Call me as soon as you hear anything else from him,' he said. 'I don't know why I bother saying that. You never do.'

'I will, Colin,' Wanda promised.

* * *

'I was enjoying myself until Cultured Voice spoiled it,' Quentin grumbled when they were back at Wanda's. The effects of the wine had dissipated and his head was clearer.

'It was nice while it lasted,' Wanda agreed.

She made tea while Quentin lit the log burner, then they sat in front of the fire watching the flames leap and flicker. Dusk was falling and Wanda closed the curtains against the encroaching night. The log burner was the one thing in Wanda's house that Quentin envied. She didn't use it very much but when she did, it made the room cosy.

Wanda snuggled up against him on the chaise longue, Mozart at her feet.

'I could go to sleep now,' she admitted.

'So could I, if I didn't think *he* would ring.'

'Well then,' Wanda said, walking her fingers down his chest, 'what we need is something to distract us. You'll sleep well enough then.'

'Think so?'

Wanda pouted. 'You always do,' she whispered, turning her face to his.

'It'll be cold in the bedroom.'

'Who needs a bed?' Wanda taunted. 'The floor was good enough the first time, and the fire wasn't even alight then.'

'I hadn't had my ribs kicked then either.'

'Well, I know how to treat a man gently.'

So you do, Quentin thought, recalling her treatment of him after he'd returned from the yacht. She'd acted and spoken as though she truly loved him. She had said she loved him before, but was that the same as being *in* love with him? Would she ever agree to move in with him, or would the issue of children always be between them? Why couldn't he ask her, beg her to reveal her true feelings? Because, he realized, he was afraid she would give the same answer she'd given for the last three years.

He sighed, then nibbled her ear. 'You're very persuasive, Mrs Merrydrew.'

'Yes,' she said, turning her face to his. 'And you're very talkative, Mr Cadbury.'

# Chapter Thirty-eight

'So you've done it again.' Colin looked at Quentin from across the table in the Cutty Sark, the pub on the Thames where he had joined Quentin and Wanda for dinner. It was a day later, and they were still no wiser as to why Cultured Voice had contacted Quentin out of the blue two weeks ago and what good news he had now to impart.

'I know you haven't done what you set out to do, Quentin, but you've done pretty well,' Colin continued, removing his black-framed glasses and polishing them with the hem of his shirt.

'*We've* done pretty well,' Wanda interrupted. 'That includes you, Colin.'

Quentin didn't disagree, and Colin looked gratified. 'So,' he went on, 'why the long face?'

'It's just – being so close to an infamous criminal and not getting him,' Quentin said with a heavy sigh. 'Still, I suppose I should be used to it by now.'

'What about the couple who stole your car?' Colin asked. 'You promised to keep me updated.'

Wanda relayed what Philmore had told them – that they'd traced Sam and her father, matched a thumbprint to the Volvo and charged them with car theft. Apart from the pictures of Quentin, the photos on the camera showed nothing of interest.

While she was talking, Quentin recalled the dressing-down they'd had from Philmore about the gun. Even when he'd been shown it, recognized it from a previous encounter and knew it wasn't real, they'd suffered a lengthy lecture about carrying an offensive weapon. Oddly though, after they'd promised not to use it again, he hadn't confiscated it.

'Anyway,' Wanda was saying, 'all in all, even though we haven't caught our cultured friend, we've got a bunch of dirty dealers arrested, and that's a victory in itself.'

'Yes,' Quentin began, then stopped as his mobile rang, his heart racing. He let out a sigh of relief when he heard his mother's voice.

'Mum! Everything all right?'

'Yes dear. I just rang to see if you've finished with that case you were on. You didn't answer your home phone, so I thought maybe you were still away.'

'No, I'm home, Mum, but I'm out at the moment. Can I call you tomorrow and we'll have a nice long chat?'

'That'll be lovely. Bye for now then, Quentin. Love to Wanda.'

'Bye, Mum,' Quentin said. His spirits had lifted at the sound of her voice.

They came crashing down when his phone rang again. Number withheld. Quentin's blood chilled. He stiffened as the familiar voice said, 'Mr Cadbury.'

'Yes,' he said, looking at Wanda and Colin with a frown and holding his free hand over his other ear.

'I hope you're feeling more amenable now. Out again, are you? Let me guess – the Cutty Sark, that quaint little pub on the Thames that you like so much. Am I right?'

'Yes, but how–'

'Because you're so predictable, Mr Cadbury, no other reason. And it seems you've interfered with my business again. Not content with turning down the honour of working for me, you've deprived me of a number of my operatives. Jack was quite compliant until his daughter got involved, and Samantha was careless enough to lose her camera. She hasn't admitted it, but I wouldn't be surprised if you had something to do with that. Really, what am I going to do with you?'

Stumped for an answer, Quentin shrugged and spread his hands as though the caller could see him.

'It's very exasperating, Mr Cadbury, and so inconvenient,' the cultured voice went on. 'I'm going to have to recruit more people, and that will take time. But the good news is that, despite all the trouble you've caused me, I've got to thank you.'

'Wh-what?' Quentin almost choked on the word.

'Oh yes, Mr Cadbury, I believe in giving credit where it's due. You've been an excellent decoy.'

'Decoy?'

'Yes, decoy. You didn't really think I would trust you to handle my valuable goods, did you?'

Confusion swamped Quentin. What was this man going on about now?

'But you said I had to do a job for you,' he began.

'And you did, Mr Cadbury, you did. It's true you were sent to Bradford Bridge and the Eden Project to be photographed and to have your car replaced but, you see, while you were running all over Cornwall, tying up much of its diminutive police force, my longest-trusted operatives were transporting large consignments of drugs from Cornish seaports to other parts of the country. For example, while you were having your tête-à-tête with Samantha at St Michael's Mount, a large consignment was being unloaded from Newlyn, and while you were busy putting a toilet roll in a locker in St Austell, I was in Padstow overseeing another successful transaction. This is a new venture for me, so I wanted to be there to make sure it was a worthy enterprise. Except for when we met on the boat, a risk I took for the pleasure of meeting you, I was nowhere near the places you were sent.'

Dizzy with disbelief and anger, Quentin couldn't speak.

'I see that's surprised you, Mr Cadbury. There's something else I'm grateful for. I don't know how you managed to find the place where my rival's goods were stored, nor do I care. All I know is that my rival in this unsavoury business will be going to prison for a long time, so I'll be free to take over his routes. In short, I've doubled my income overnight. So thank you, Mr Cadbury. Thank you very much.'

When Quentin, still at a loss for words, didn't answer, Cultured Voice carried on.

'Are you sure you won't work for me? I could double your income overnight too.'

Quentin gasped, unable to believe what he was hearing. Before he had time to reply, the cultured voice continued.

'I can see you're a man of your word. I was hoping you'd see sense and cooperate with me, but apparently that's not to be. Still, there's plenty of time. You're young, Mr Cadbury. Perhaps in a few years' time, when Mrs Merrydrew has left you for someone more suited to her maturity and refinement, and you've had a taste of how many cruel things this world can throw at you, you'll think again. I'll check in from time to time to see if you've changed your mind. Meanwhile, don't try to track me down. You know that's impossible. You're safe for now, Quentin, but not completely off the hook. Remember that. Goodbye, and give my regards to your policeman friend, not to mention the delectable Mrs Merrydrew.'

Quentin's mouth fell open in astonishment. He lowered the phone and stared at it as if he might see the caller's face on the screen.

'Was it him?' Wanda asked uncertainly.

'Yes.'

'Well? What did he say?'

Quentin shook his head. 'I've been had. He never wanted me to deliver drugs. He used me as a decoy.'

Colin and Wanda exchanged curious glances as Quentin gave them the gist of the conversation.

'He knew where I was,' Quentin added. 'He must have a crystal ball – it was like he could see me. And he wasn't like the last time, when he was absolutely furious and went on and on about how he'd take revenge.'

'So does that mean he's not going to kill you after all?' Colin asked.

Quentin shrugged. 'I think he was saying that, in a roundabout way. And… he called me Quentin.'

'Is that it?' Colin said looking puzzled. 'He's changed his tune, hasn't he? Is he going soft or something?'

'Well,' Wanda said, 'I think I'm right. He sees something in you, Quentin. Perhaps you remind him of himself at your age. Or maybe he just enjoys an ongoing challenge.'

'I'm nothing like him, Wanda,' Quentin said.

'Of course you're not, but who knows how his mind works?'

'And who cares?' Colin's voice brought Quentin back to the moment. 'Anyway, Quentin, you've got something to celebrate. You've helped bring down a drug smuggling racket, you've met a notorious criminal face to face and survived, and you're no longer in imminent danger. I think the champagne should be on you.'

Taken aback by Colin's words, Quentin stared at him. Colin had actually given him credit for what he'd done, actually admitted that he'd played a part in at least one consignment of drugs being discovered. The fight against illegal substances and their devastating effects was far from over, and the ongoing attempts to capture the man he knew as Cultured Voice would continue, Quentin knew. Nevertheless, he felt his spirits lift, his heart lighten.

'I haven't heard the last of him, he made that clear enough,' he told them.

'I don't suppose you have,' Wanda agreed. 'But at the moment, we're safe in our beds again. I think you're right, Colin. Champagne.'

Quentin gazed at the woman he loved who, he allowed himself to think, might even love him. Then he turned his gaze to Colin, reluctantly acknowledging that he was a good friend.

'Champagne? Good idea,' he said brightly. He felt warm under Wanda's lingering look and Colin's genial one, then had a moment of panic when he realized his bank balance might not cover the cost of the champagne. As if on cue, a barman appeared at the table with a bottle of champagne in an ice bucket. Dom Pérignon.

'Mr Cadbury?' the barman asked, looking at Quentin for confirmation. When Quentin nodded, he said, 'This was just ordered for you by a gentleman at the bar.'

Stunned, Quentin looked across the busy room towards the bar.

'He left,' the barman said. 'He said to give you this too.'

Quentin took the envelope, tore it open and read the message on the single sheet of paper.

*Life's too short for cheap champagne, Mr Cadbury.*
*Enjoy it while you can.*

Quentin read the message again, unable to believe his eyes. Then he looked at the champagne. A man at the bar. Could it have been?

Five minutes later, when champagne bubbles fizzed in their glasses, he held his high.

'Here's to respite from a wanted criminal, to the Cadbury and Merrydrew detective agency, and...' He paused, slipping an arm round Wanda and chinking his glass with Colin's. 'To friendship.'

Fingering the note he'd slipped into his pocket, he thought of the final line of the message, unseen by Wanda and Colin.

*Goodbye for now, Quentin. Until the next time.*

## THE END

If you enjoyed this book, please let others know by leaving a quick review on Amazon. Also, if you spot anything untoward in the paperback, get in touch. We strive for the best quality and appreciate reader feedback.

editor@thebookfolks.com

www.thebookfolks.com

# More fiction by the author

## THE MYSTERY OF THE HIDDEN FORTUNE

*Book #1 in the Quentin Cadbury Investigations*

Quentin Cadbury, a useless twenty-something, is left to look after his late aunt's London house when his parents head to Australia. But burglars seem determined to break in, and not even the stray cat he befriends can help him. As the thieves are after something pretty valuable, and illegal, he must grow up pretty fast to get out of a sticky situation.

## THE MYSTERY OF THE LUCKY CAT

*Book #2 in the Quentin Cadbury Investigations*

Private detective Quentin Cadbury has his neighbour's
recently demised cat in a holdall. Quite why, will be
explained. But when he tackles a mugger, his bag gets
mixed up with another. This has different contents – some
very suspicious goods. Seeing an opportunity to catch a
criminal, he blunders into a dangerous situation.


## THE MYSTERY DOWN UNDER

*Book #3 in the Quentin Cadbury Investigations*

Evading a London gangster with a bone to pick, private
investigator Quentin Cadbury and his sidekick Wanda
Merrydrew decide to visit Australia to catch up with
Quentin's family. Yet when they discover a burglar is
causing upset in their quiet Sydney suburb, they can't help
but get involved. Can Quentin catch a thief and prove his
mettle to his ever-disappointed father?


*All FREE with Kindle Unlimited and available in paperback
and hardback from Amazon.*

# Other titles of interest

**MURDER ON OXFORD LANE**
by Tony Bassett

A budding chorister doesn't return home from practice but his wife doesn't appear concerned. DS Sunita Roy becomes convinced he has been murdered but she has her own problems in the form of an ex-boyfriend who won't take no for an answer. Will she keep her eye on the ball when all expect her to fail?

*FREE with Kindle Unlimited and available in paperback!*

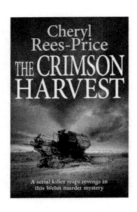

## THE CRIMSON HARVEST
### by Cheryl Rees-Price

Unflappable cop DI Winter Meadows has his wedding plans interrupted when bodies begin to turn up on his patch. The Welsh police have a serial killer on their hands and no stone is left unturned in the hunt. But only a detective who truly understands the community will be able to catch a killer in their midst.

*FREE with Kindle Unlimited and available in paperback!*

**TO CATCH A LIE**
**by John Dean**

DCI Jack Harris's day off is interrupted when a man's body is found. The detective suspects the murder is connected with animal rights activists' attacks on local anglers but it seems he's fishing with rotten bait. The investigation takes him to Scotland, and out on a limb with regards to the opinions of his team.

*FREE with Kindle Unlimited and available in paperback!*

*Sign up to our mailing list to find out about new releases and special offers!*

www.thebookfolks.com

Printed in Great Britain
by Amazon